She was going insane.

Joel kissed her with an intensity that made Katy tremble. The human body wasn't meant to be wound up like an old-fashioned clock, but she wanted this to go on forever.

Every kiss, every touch seemed to be for her arousal only. She was on the roller coaster of love, the peaks and valleys coming in such quick succession she could hear herself shrieking.

"Wow."

"I'll take that as a compliment." Joel nuzzled her ear with wet little kisses. He was sweet and gentle, and she cuddled against him, sighing in contentment.

Was this the way sex was supposed to be? She felt limp, languid and terribly seductive. She didn't want this magical time to end.

"Joel?" Katy's voice was a tentative whisper.

"Um?"

"Is it just in books that men can, you know, perform beyond expectations?"

He roared with mirth and rolled to his back, pulling her on top of him.

"Let's see what happens in the next chapter, little librarian."

For more, turn to page 9

"That's exactly your problem, Mace," Zoe explained.

"What do you mean?"

"You go into things with a preconceived notion. You thought I'd have an Aunt Bea-ish house. I didn't. You thought there couldn't be a story here in Hiho. There is. And you thought...I don't know *what* you thought about kissing me."

"Zoe, kissing you is all I've been able to think of for quite some time. Last night, when you were with that lawyer, I was crazy with thinking you might kiss him."

"Kiss Rob? Ew."

Robert Pawley was the vanilla pudding of mankind.

Now, there was nothing wrong with vanilla pudding, if a person liked that sort of thing. But Zoe was pretty sure she preferred...what would she call Mace? No, he wasn't a dessert at all.

He was barbecued wings.

Not just plain old barbecued wings, either. He was definitely the killer variety that only some restaurants served. Hot, spicy and, in this particular case, just a bit dangerous to the brave women who gave them a try!

For more, turn to page 197

HARLEQUIN DUETS

ISBN 0-373-44166-5

Copyright in the collection:
Copyright © 2003 by Harlequin Books S.A.

The publisher acknowledges the copyright holders of the individual works as follows:

YOU'LL BE MINE IN 99
Copyright © 2003 by Pamela Hanson and Barbara Andrews

THE 100-YEAR ITCH
Copyright © 2003 by Holly Fuhrmann

This edition published by arrangement with Harlequin Books S.A.

® and TM are trademarks of the publisher. Trademarks indicated with ® are registered in the United States Patent and Trademark Office, the Canadian Trade Marks Office and in other countries.

Visit us at www.eHarlequin.com

Printed in U.S.A.

You'll Be Mine in 99

Jennifer Drew

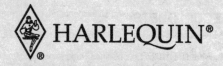

HARLEQUIN®

TORONTO • NEW YORK • LONDON
AMSTERDAM • PARIS • SYDNEY • HAMBURG
STOCKHOLM • ATHENS • TOKYO • MILAN • MADRID
PRAGUE • WARSAW • BUDAPEST • AUCKLAND

Dear Reader,

When our editor asked us (Jennifer Drew is the pseudonym for the mother-daughter writing team of Barbara Andrews and Pam Hanson) to write this special Duets novel, we were thrilled. When she told us we'd be partnered with our good friend Holly Jacobs, we were delighted.

Our clever editors told us they wanted the story of a town with a "birthday crisis" and a makeover or two thrown in, and Hiho, Ohio, was born.

The only question was when?

The citizens of Hiho think they're celebrating the town's centennial, only our hero's great-great-grandmother got confused when filing the incorporation papers.

The town is going all out for the centennial celebration, not realizing it's only 99. Hunky Joel Carter is invited to the festivities because the town was founded by his ancestors. The only thing that interests him in the backwater burg is the luscious librarian, Katy Sloane.

Toss in a bizarre beauty contest, an ugly SUV and small-town cloak-and-dagger doings, and you have the recipe for one unusual birthday celebration!

So blow out the candles and dive in!

Jennifer Drew

Books by Jennifer Drew

HARLEQUIN DUETS

*Bad Boy Grooms

To Andrew, who's relentless, and Erik,
who's relaxing, with love from Grandma and Mom

1

THE BEAUTY PAGEANT contestant with rusty auburn hair dropped her baton for the third time. As she snatched it up from the basketball court's hardwood floor, the seat of her hot pink Capri pants seemed in imminent danger of splitting.

"Grandma, you have to concentrate," her pint-size coach with bright-red braids said. "It's even harder when it's flaming."

"Do you think the kid will be in the contest, too?" Joel Carter asked his boss, who was sitting beside him on the fold-out bleachers of the Hiho High School gym.

Herbert Edson, known throughout the automobile industry as Big Bert, glanced at the well-endowed but over-the-hill contestant practicing in a space in front of them and shrugged off Joel's less-than-serious question.

"According to the rules," Bert said in a voice that seemed too soft for his impressive height and muscular build, "all they have to be is eighteen and currently single. I guess Granny must qualify."

"So does half the town," Joel responded gloomily, more to himself than to the CEO of Vision Motors.

Joel loved his job as marketing director for the small but aggressive auto company. He'd started work for Vision when he graduated from Ohio State, and it still amazed him that, at age twenty-eight, he'd been promoted to head of his department in the Cleveland-based corporation.

Even if he hated Big Bert's idea of using a small-town beauty contest winner to promote the company's new line, he couldn't afford the luxury of losing his job over it. He was helping his younger brother, Jon, through dental school since their father's estate had only been adequate enough to let their mother live comfortably with her sister in Florida. Jon had two years to go, and Joel was determined he start his practice without college debts hanging over his head.

Unfortunately, he didn't think Big Bert's idea was a good plan. A professional model made a lot more sense even though the Incline, a car-truck hybrid, was being marketed to middle America buyers who would enjoy seeing one of their own in an ad campaign.

When his boss heard that Joel, a descendent of Hiho's founder, was the guest of honor at the town's one-hundredth anniversary celebration, he decided to offer a modeling job to the new Miss Hiho as a prize. The company was building a new assembly plant in nearby Mayville and capitalizing on the publicity the town's centennial was garnering from large statewide media outlets could only help the launch of the new sport-utility vehicle. So a local spokesperson made some sense if they could feature her as a beauty contest queen to add glamour to the promotion. It would also be an excuse to have the model in a bathing suit. In theory, Bert's idea could work, but Joel had serious doubts. Using an amateur could also be a lot of trouble.

"The blonde jumping around on the stage is a possibility," Bert said optimistically.

Joel had already dismissed the fledgling ballerina practicing on the empty stage at the end of the gym. She was cute, but her mother had been micromanaging everything since the pair came into the gym. If the girl couldn't put on her dancing shoes without Mom hovering over her, she'd drive any good photographer nuts.

He wished, not for the first time, that his great-great-grandparents, Hiram and Hortense Hump, had stayed in Erie, Pennsylvania, instead of starting a new town in Ohio. The couple had owned a general store, the Wal-Mart of their day, but they'd sold out and moved their business to a rich farming area in southeast Ohio. Hortense became the first postmistress and the first county clerk, and Hump's General Store in Hiho had prospered.

Joel understood that kind of restlessness but didn't share it. He was happy in the metropolitan area of Cleveland and had no desire to move. His father had been a city manager who'd changed jobs every few years in search of new challenges.

Growing up, Joel had lived in more "population 10,000 or less" places than he wanted to remember.

Hiho reminded him of all the dreary little towns he'd hated as a child, but his mother would have been terribly disappointed if he'd refused the honor of being in Hiho for the centennial. She wanted to come herself, but was recovering from dental surgery that would, most likely, keep her away.

"All we need is a girl who's sort of Midwestern-cute,'' Bert said, still scanning the mostly female crowd scattered around the gym for possibilities. ''You know, sweet and genuine. If she can deliver a few words in the TV spots, all the better. If not, we'll work around it.''

''It would be easier to use a professional actress or model,'' Joel pointed out, knowing he'd be ignored. When Big Bert got an idea, he was unstoppable. No wonder he'd successfully launched a new company in the cutthroat auto industry.

''It's only a cattle call today,'' Bert said, more to himself than to Joel. ''The beauty contest's a week from Sunday. That gives the girls a couple more days to sign up. Wait a minute! There's a possibility.'' He wagged his thick finger in the direction of the doorway, where a tall woman with a bobbing black ponytail was leaning over the sign-in table where a gray-haired woman presided.

''Look at that sweet behind,'' Bert whistled between his big square teeth.

He ran his hand through thinning gray-blond hair and fidgeted with his navy-and-silver striped tie.

Joel looked. He figured the gray suits they were wearing made them as conspicuous as FBI agents at a Hell's Angels beer blast, so he wasn't surprised when the woman straightened and glanced directly at them. She couldn't have heard Bert's comment, but Joel felt like fidgeting under her gaze.

''That's what we need—a pretty girl who looks down-home and wholesome,'' Bert said. ''Men will be hot for her, and women will love that she's a regular woman who made good as a beauty queen. It will feed into their fantasies and make them take a long, hard look at the Incline when they're ready to buy a new car.''

''She doesn't look like beauty-contestant material to me,'' Joel said.

''Forget the wire-frame glasses and the hair,'' Bert said. ''She has the body. Look at those long legs. Put her in a bikini and do a little makeover magic, that girl will be our Incline model.''

Could Bert be right? Joel wondered. Worn blue jeans and an oversize red Hiho Hornets sweatshirt didn't disguise her dynamite body, but she was far from glamorous in round glasses that were perched on her nose and the kind of ponytail elementary schoolkids liked to yank.

''I know two things—cars and women,'' Big Bert said. ''There's our winner. Your job will be to make sure she gets a good makeover, then sign her up as soon as she wins.''

''The blond ballerina has a better chance, I think.'' Big Bert knew cars, but Joel wasn't so sure about women. His boss was married to wife number three, a wannabe Marilyn Monroe clone, who shattered her glamorous image every time she opened her mouth, which was often.

''I'm heading back to Cleveland now,'' the big man said. ''You'll be gone how long?''

''Two weeks.'' Two weeks of unwanted vacation, not that he didn't have months accumulated. ''But I have my laptop with me. I'll be able to work….''

''Never mind about the office stuff,'' Bert said. ''Damn, I'd rather sit on a sawhorse than these narrow boards they call bleachers. My butt is numb.''

Joel stood, flexed his buttocks and agreed the seats were a pain, but he was bothered more by the odor of stale sweat and janitor's cleaning supplies that permeated the old combination gym and auditorium. It reminded him of all the crummy small-town schools he'd attended. Besides being the new kid more times than he liked to remember, he'd usually been the shortest and the smartest boy in his classes, not a formula for popularity. Fortunately, in high school he'd had a late growth spurt that brought his height to six foot two and, with some athletic ability, had won a college scholarship.

Now he lived in Cleveland with a job he liked. He loved sailing on Lake Erie and dating women who wouldn't have given him the time of day in his runty years. He'd left small-town life behind, but on the first day of his sojourn in Hiho he was vividly reminded of the small Midwestern towns where he'd grown up.

"Your job here is to make sure that girl gets a makeover and is crowned Miss Hiho Centennial. Then sign her up to promote the Incline." When Big Bert repeated an order, it was futile to argue.

"I'll do my best," Joel said with feigned enthusiasm.

"All right, ladies." A raspy, hollow-sounding voice came from the loudspeaker as Big Bert hurried out the door, heading back to civilization. "Everyone who's already registered, line up in front of the stage. Our librarian, Katy Sloane, is going to hand out the rule sheets. She has some extras if you have friends who haven't signed up yet."

Joel stood on the polished honey-tan hardwood gym floor beside the bleachers as the dark-haired woman he and Bert had been discussing carried a stack of papers to the group slowly assembling in front of the raised stage.

"Katy will have extra copies at the library, too. If you have any questions, you go see her in the children's department," the unseen male announcer said.

The disembodied voice had a slight drawl made tinny by the speaker system, but the contestants milling around at the front under a drooping basketball net listened intently.

Joel had a bad feeling. Katy was efficiently handing out the rule sheets, but there was no reason to believe she was a contestant herself. He moved closer for a better look at Big Bert's choice for the Incline spokesperson.

She had assets all right, taut thighs that strained against the material of her worn jeans, breasts that swelled against the hornet logo on her bulky sweatshirt, a pleasing oval face with great cheekbones and sapphire-blue eyes that radiated good humor. Yep, Katy Sloane had potential, but she was also a genius at hiding it. Her round glasses, which seemed to constantly slip down her nose, were better suited for an octogenarian. Her hair was black and thick, carelessly held back by a yellow rubber band. He couldn't see a trace of makeup.

She reached the end of the line of contestants—at least twenty hopefuls—then glanced up and met his gaze.

He'd gotten a shock once trying to fix a faulty toaster. Looking directly into her eyes gave him the same jolt without being painful or scary. Her shimmering eyes mesmerized him. They were easily the deepest and richest blue he'd ever seen, even with the distraction of too-thick, shaggy eyebrows.

He shook his head, tried for a casual smile, and discovered his mouth was hanging open like a slobbering basset hound's.

"Would you like one?" she asked in a voice as smooth as satin.

He realized she was holding out one of the rule sheets.

"Oh, no thanks. Well, maybe I will look at one. If you have enough, that is."

"Is your girlfriend thinking of entering?"

"Girlfriend?"

He dated women and sometimes slept with women, but he hadn't called anyone a "girlfriend" since he'd reached six foot two and finally scrounged a few dates in high school.

"Oh, no, I was just curious. I'm here for the centennial." Two long weeks of the preparations and events, he remembered without enthusiasm.

"Do you have relatives in town?" she asked.

In Cleveland he'd write her off as nosy, but here in Hiho she probably thought she was being friendly—and she was. With a smile like hers, she could ask him anything, and he'd probably be happy to answer.

"Not exactly." He grinned because he was suddenly enjoying himself. "My great-great-grandfather had something to do with founding the town."

"Are you Hiram Hump's descendent?" She looked and sounded delighted.

"Guilty."

He couldn't imagine why she seemed so enthusiastic until he remembered how little happened in small towns.

"Mr. Hump, I'm so happy to meet you."

She reached out to shake his hand, but all her remaining rule sheets fluttered to the gym floor. They both bent to retrieve them at exactly the same instant, and their heads collided with a resounding thump.

He didn't actually see stars, but he was knocked on his backside. He probably looked as silly as he felt, and it didn't help his dignity any when she started pulling on one of his hands with both of hers to help him up.

"Oh, Mr. Hump, I'm so sorry!"

"Please, I'm Joel Carter. The Hump name died out when my grandparents had daughters but no son."

He managed to scramble up with all the dignity of a baboon in a tutu.

"I always did have a hard head. Are you sure you're all right? I can get you a cold cloth," she offered.

"No, I'm fine."

To demonstrate, he bent over and tried to gather up the fallen papers. He scooped up most of them, but felt disturbingly light-headed. When he straightened, the yellowish-white cement-block walls of the gym seemed to be swirling.

She was quick to notice him wobble. She took his hand and led him to the nearest bleacher, then insisted he sit and hang his head between his legs.

"So you don't faint," she said, keeping her soft, cool hand on the back of his neck. "I can't tell you how sorry I am."

They'd attracted a crowd, but she shooed them back.

"Give him some air. This is Hiram Hump's descendent, our guest of honor,'' she announced to everyone within hailing distance.

He had a flashback to the third grade when Ben Juke had smeared a peanut butter sandwich all over his face while half the school watched and laughed. Even when she released her viselike grip on his neck and let him sit up, he felt like an idiot.

Several women clucked at him sympathetically, but kindness didn't help. The centennial guest of honor had given the town something to talk about.

KATY APOLOGIZED AGAIN—and again. She knew she was babbling, but she was furious at herself. All this gorgeous, sexy man had wanted was the beauty-pageant rules. Her job as a pageant volunteer was to hand them out, which she would have done as soon as the contestants started arriving except she'd run out of paper halfway through printing them off at home. She'd hustled over to her friend Judy's place to borrow some and found her in a crisis over her boyfriend taking Nadine Jameson to Twin Forks for a movie last weekend. Of course, everyone in town—except Judy—already knew about it.

How complicated was it to hand a man a sheet of paper? Katy should have paid attention to the job and not quizzed him on his personal life, namely whether he was getting the rules for a girlfriend. But wasn't it great that someone who looked like him didn't have one?

Bad enough she'd dropped the papers. Why, why, why hadn't she let him be chivalrous and pick them up for her? No, she had to dive for them herself and knock him on his butt with her armor-plated head. No wonder her social life was so lukewarm.

Not that she didn't have one. She'd been dating Rob Pawley, lawyer and elusive bachelor, a couple of times a month for almost forever. She was becoming a stereotype of the small-town spinster-librarian. Good thing she loved her job and Hiho. Except for an occasional halfhearted and unsuccessful attempt to bed her, Rob exhibited about as much passion as the bronze statue of Hiram Hump in the town square. To her credit, she was chairperson of the committee to put a statute of Hortense beside her husband, a project that was going nowhere in spite of the centennial fervor that had perked up the town.

The guest of honor was holding his head in his hands and staring at the floor. No, his beautiful chocolate-brown eyes were focused on her feet, her big, broad, decidedly unfeminine feet. Worse, she was wearing her scuffed white-and-black running shoes, half a size too large so she could wear heavy socks to jog.

"Are you sure I can't get you something, Mr. Hump? A drink or a cold cloth?"

Oh, no! He wasn't Mr. Hump. He'd explained that clearly enough. He probably thought her brain cells were made of Silly Putty. Worse, she was so rattled, she couldn't remember his real name.

"Call me Joel," he said with an ironic little smile that at least assured her he was fully conscious. "It's Carter, not Hump."

"I'm so sorry! Of course, you told me that. I'm just a little flustered. It's not every day I knock a centennial guest of honor on his…"

Oops! Just what he wanted to hear, a replay. The crowd she'd tried to disperse was still hovering within hearing distance taking in her every goof.

"Keel." He helpfully supplied a nautical term which, she assumed, meant bottom.

She heard muted giggles behind her and knew what the town would be buzzing about tomorrow. Her cheeks felt hot, and she probably had her infamous beet-red blush.

"I was going to say head," she lied.

"What's your talent?" he asked, rising to his feet with a reassuring degree of steadiness.

He topped her by at least three or four inches. It was really nice to look up at a man instead of being eyeball to eyeball as she was with Rob.

"I'm the children's librarian at the library south of the town square."

"I didn't mean your occupation. Your talent for the beauty contest," he said, looking at her with a peculiar expression.

Did he think she was entering the contest? Yeah, right! Put her in a pair of three-inch heels, and her talent would be not falling on her face.

"I'm not a contestant. I'm only a volunteer. My job is printing up the rules, passing them out, stuff like that."

"You'd be a shoo-in to win."

"Me? No, I don't think so."

Hadn't he seen Brandi Rankin? Her mother, Melinda, had been grooming her since she was toilet-trained for a big opportunity like Miss Hiho Centennial. She was blond, cute and petite. Not only that, she had a real talent, and she'd been in dozens of kids' beauty contests. She'd even won a few.

"Have you always lived in Hiho?" Joel not-Hump-but-Carter asked.

She wanted to hear more about why he thought

she was beauty-contest material, but he linked his arm in hers and steered her toward the gym's main exit.

"Yes, I'm a native. I grew up here and went to Cloverleaf College. The only time I've been away was to get my master's in library science at..."

He interrupted her. "Sounds like you'd be an ideal person to represent the town as Miss Hiho. It could lead to other things."

Why was this gorgeous hunk talking about her as a contestant? When they reached the door, he put his hand on her back just above her waist and guided her out to the semidark corridor outside the gym. The hall lights reflected dimly on rows of old green lockers, the same ones her class had used years ago.

"What other things?" she asked.

He kept his hand on her back, and she imagined the warmth of it even through her Hornet's sweatshirt, which was thick enough to be a pot holder.

"I haven't had dinner," he said, looking at the illuminated face of the old clock above the exit that led outside. "As a volunteer, would you consider pointing out a nice restaurant and joining me there?"

"You want me to have dinner with you?"

Maybe she'd banged his head even harder than she thought.

"Please."

The way he said it made it sound teasingly seductive.

"Friday night the kids pretty much take over the town, especially in May."

"Why May?"

"No football or basketball, and it's still too early to hang out by the lake or go to stock car races over in Hasting. So they pretty much occupy the town, sitting on their cars on Main Street or hanging out in food places.''

''Not much to do in small towns.'' He sounded critical.

''Sure there is. Friends get together. Sometimes I baby-sit for my sister and brother-in-law. They have twin girls, Haley and Ari. I adore them.''

''Your whole family lives here?''

''No, my folks retired to Florida. Dad owned an insurance agency and Mom was secretary to the superintendent of schools. Now they play golf and use their metal detectors on the beaches.''

''My mother's in Florida, too. She's a widow now. Lives with her sister.''

''I guess a lot of older people get tired of Ohio winters.''

''Do you?''

''No, I love cross-country skiing and ice skating.''

''Can you dance on roller skates? That would be a good talent for the beauty contest.'' He took his hand away from her back and opened the heavy door to the outside.

After her demonstration of poise and grace passing out papers, did he seriously think she could give a dancing exhibition on skates without falling over her own feet?

''No way,'' she said with what she hoped was finality. ''If you're interested, Fat's Tavern has a Friday night fish fry.''

Where else could she go in jeans and sweats with a man whose silky dove-gray suit fit like a second skin? His shirt was gleaming white under the parking lot lights. A tie with a pearl-gray and soft blue swirly pattern hung against his chest, and she had the strangest urge to lay her cheek against it.

"Is your car here?" he asked.

"No, it was a nice night, so I walked."

Also the gas gauge was so far below empty she'd cruised home from work on fumes. Since she was already late getting to the sign-up session, walking had been quicker than going to the service station. The advantage of living in a small town was there was always someone she could ask for a ride home.

"Ride with me then," he said.

Should she worry about getting into a car with a stranger? It wasn't a sensible thing to do, not even in Hiho, Ohio, but this was Hiram Hump's great-great-grandson, the founder's descendent. She was a centennial volunteer. It was probably her duty to see that he found a good dinner.

Walking beside him made her feel dainty and petite, two decidedly unusual sensations. She had to wonder why he was being so attentive after she'd knocked him on his butt, but it was better not to dwell on it. She had too much imagination, and she couldn't help wonder if his abused part was as sensational as the rest of him—the broad shoulders, slim waist and hips, dreamy eyes, strong chin, seductive lips...

"Here's my car," he said, interrupting her pleasurable cataloging of his assets.

She'd expected something sporty, a Jag or a Corvette, a car as sleek and desirable as its owner. Instead he opened the door of a boxy vehicle, the color of watered-down mud. If cars had parents, it would have been the offspring of a minivan and a station wagon with fat bumpers and a spare tire mounted on the rear.

"What is it?" she asked.

"A prototype of the Incline, Vision Motor's new sport-utility vehicle. What do you think of it?"

"It's a little dark here." Not too dark to see a better name for the clunky heap would have been the Decline.

"Actually, it's the other reason I'm here," he said.

If he wanted to explain this car, he'd have to do it without any encouragement from her. She loved racing and knew cars better than most men, but she also knew ugly when she was standing next to it.

"I'm head of marketing for Vision Motors," he said. "My boss was here with me for a while. He'd like to hire the winner of the centennial beauty pageant to model in some TV and print ads for the Incline."

"Why?"

"He wants a good, wholesome, middle-American beauty. The centennial tie-in makes for good press."

This wasn't adding up at all. Why ask her if she was a contestant? Why suggest she could dance on skates as a talent? Did they want a winner who would match this homely, ungainly, boxy car? Would it be one of those advertising campaigns that featured the least likely spokesperson, an old woman complaining about her burger, a total nerd slurping foamy beer?

She didn't feel flattered by his dinner invitation anymore.

"The best place to eat is the Keystone Inn," she said in the same voice she used when library patrons made a fuss about fines for late books. "Turn right out of the parking lot, go past two traffic lights and turn left at the third. You'll see a sign, and that will direct you to the restaurant.''

''I thought you might join me....''

How could she make dinner conversation about a car she hated at first sight without being impolite to the town's honored guest. ''It's nice of you to ask me, but I think I'll pass.''

''A ride home?''

''No, thanks. I like walking.''

She turned away and headed briskly toward home. Vision Motors probably wanted a bimbo to do a really silly, demeaning commercial. Well, Joel Hump-Carter's head was softer than vanilla pudding if he thought she'd ever be a beauty pageant contestant.

2

WHAT DID HE DO WRONG?

Joel watched the long-legged librarian race out of the parking lot. The early-evening shadows made pockets of darkness under the massive maples lining the streets, but whenever she passed through a sunny patch he could imagine how she'd look spotlighted on the high school stage with other beauty contestants.

Maybe Big Bert was right. Katy Sloane did have potential. She walked with the grace of a Thoroughbred, head held high and shoulders squared. He felt a little light-headed watching the faded denim stretched over her sleekly rounded behind—or maybe he was still reeling from the sledgehammer blow when their heads bumped. Why didn't the collision bother her, and how was he going to convince her to wear a thong in the swimsuit competition?

Whoa, he told himself. Before she could become Miss Hiho, she had to want it. It was easy for Big Bert to point her out as the woman he wanted as the model, and Joel had to agree with his choice. But his boss was dead-set on having the beauty queen tie-in, which meant Joel couldn't offer her the job unless she won the contest.

When she was out of sight, he got into the new Incline on loan from the company for his two weeks in Hiho. Did she turn down his dinner invitation because she didn't like the vehicle? That made no sense at all. More likely, she just didn't trust him, and why should she? He did have an ulterior motive for seeking her company, as well as a personal one. What *had* happened to him when they locked eyes in the gym?

He hadn't paid much attention to her restaurant directions, so he drove west to Pawley Avenue, the north-south artery of town, and slowly cruised past the aging graystone library, the fifties-era brick courthouse and the town square, where his ancestor's portly presence was preserved in bronze. Some grubby preteen boys were pelting the statue with hard rubber balls, apparently intent on bopping the old boy on the tip of his prominent nose. Joel wasn't at all inclined to protect his great-great-granddad's visage by chasing them away. Considering the mess he was in, he'd like to lob a few himself.

The stoplight was red at the intersection of Pawley and Main Street. He could see a sign for Pete's Eats to the left, but decided to pass on dinner there. If he went straight, he'd get to the town's strip where his motel was tucked behind a small shopping mall. Instead he turned right onto Main Street with a vague idea of catching up with Katy if she lived in the southwestern part of town. Of course, she was probably taking a short cut, and he wasn't about to search all the narrow alleys in town for a woman who wouldn't even share a burger with him.

He was driving cautiously, watching out for the swarms of kids who made the whole town their playground, when he saw a tall, familiar figure walk past the *Hiho Herald* building.

His breath caught in his throat, and he became aware of the vein rapidly pulsing in his sore forehead. He told himself he had a job to do—convince Katy to become a beauty pageant contestant—but work had nothing to do with the peculiar effect she had on him.

She darted down an alley, seemingly oblivious to the Incline not far behind her, and he impulsively made a left turn to follow her.

The alley was a rutted dirt and gravel car path that provided access to small single-car garages with broken or mostly open doors. Most of the residents seemed to use the garages for junk storage, leaving their vehicles parked haphazardly on both sides. He squeezed past a rusty pickup with a roll of wire fencing on the truck bed and narrowly missed clipping the rear of a mud-spattered dirt bike parked at a jaunty lane-blocking angle. Obviously the owner had an attitude and didn't think about his neighbors' safety. He was probably the town bully who'd gotten his kicks in grade school dropping spiders and garter snakes down the girls' shirts and stealing lunch money from little kids.

This alley reminded Joel of everything he hated about small towns. The trash was concealed behind deceptively inviting houses built maybe fifty or seventy-five years ago, monuments to the myth of small-town friendliness. As long as the front yards were clean and tidy, the mess in the alley didn't matter. He loathed the hypocrisy of it.

Even though he had to move through the alley at a crawl to keep from bouncing the car in deep ruts, he came abreast of Katy before he'd figured out what to say.

He lowered the window and said the first thing that came to mind.

"Sure you don't want a ride?"

"Did you follow me?" she asked without stopping.

"No, I just happened to see you."

This was not a promising beginning to a conversation, let alone a sales pitch to get her to enter the contest.

"Hop in. I'll drive you the rest of the way," he said in what he hoped was a beguiling voice.

"No, thanks. I live right there." She pointed at a narrow two-story house with a sharply peaked attic and green shingled roof. "The yellow corner house."

Big snowball bushes were in bloom on either side of the half-dozen or so weathered steps leading to the back door. The melon-size white flowers made the house look more inviting than any of the others backing onto the alley, and someone had spaded a small garden between the house and the closed garage.

He had a vague feeling he should apologize for something, but instead he blurted out what was really bugging him.

"Why don't you like the Incline?"

She stopped walking and stood, hands on hips in a challenging stance, and looked it over from roof to wheels.

"It's not my kind of car."

"That's not an answer."

"It's chunky. Squarish. Even the color is drab."

He'd had his choice of butterscotch or mocha. He sort of liked the caramel-tan, so that's what he was driving.

"You're one of those women who picks a car by its color?"

"Not really."

He'd hit home. Whatever was behind the closed garage door was bright and probably red.

"It's a big house for one person," he said, quickly switching topics for diplomatic reasons.

He wanted to ask if she lived there alone, but reminded himself he was under orders from his boss to woo her for the contest, not for himself.

"I have the bottom floor. There's another apartment upstairs."

He was so intent on her, he was surprised when a horn blasted behind him. Looking over his shoulder, he saw a car full of teenagers inches from his bumper, trying to get through the alley.

"Hey, road hog, you don't need to line up for the parade until next week."

"Move your buggy or we'll move it for you!"

"Garrett Holmes, your mama taught you better than to yell at strangers," Katy called over to the driver. "You can back out the way you came if you can't wait for us to finish a conversation."

"Sorry, Katy," the loutish-looking boy with stringy brown hair said.

Much to Joel's surprise, the kid did as she suggested and backed out the alley.

"Thanks," he said sheepishly, aware he'd been saved from an unpleasant situation—by a girl.

"Your ugly car is blocking the alley," she said.

"It's not supposed to be a sports car or a luxury vehicle, but it drives well," he replied, feeling compelled to defend the Incline. "Get in. I'll give you a demonstration."

"You want me to ruin my reputation by riding in that crate?"

At least she laughed when she said it.

"The rugged look is in. We're marketing it for weekend off-roading or hauling kids, groceries, lumber, paint, whatever."

She raised an eyebrow and looked at him over the little round glasses slipping down her nose. Her sapphire-blue eyes sparkled with skepticism and something more elusive that was partly teasing and partly challenging.

"Ever think of contacts?" he asked absentmindedly, still fascinated by her gaze.

Why did he care what she wore or what she thought about the Incline? As a marketing director, he knew a hundred different people would have a hundred different opinions about any one vehicle. Vision Motors couldn't sell everyone on the economy and practicality of the new SUV. It would be a success if they appealed to their target market. What difference did the opinion of one small-town girl make?

"I have some." She didn't sound defensive even though he knew it was none of his business whether she wore contacts or not.

"Oh, nice," he said lamely, forced to remember the beauty pageant. "Good for special events."

"You're not still thinking about the Miss Hiho contest, are you?" she asked with exasperation.

"Since you brought it up…"

"You want some clown to do commercials about your awful car," she accused him.

"No, absolutely not! Not the clown part anyway. My boss wants a beautiful all-American girl…."

"I'm twenty-five, and I don't think of myself as a 'girl.'"

"A beautiful woman," he corrected himself, beginning to understand her resistance to the idea. "The last thing Vision Motors intends is to exploit anyone in a negative way."

"I bet," she said, still skeptical.

"You'd be the perfect spokesperson for the Incline."

"You want someone who looks like they belong in your butt-ugly, car-truck hybrid."

He was disgusted with himself for hurting her feelings and felt compelled to try one more time, if only to make her feel better.

"Honestly, we're not looking for an unattractive woman. We need someone who will make the car look better."

Score one more against him. He'd met more than one habitual liar who began every other sentence with *honestly*.

"Mission impossible," she said, but at least she didn't sound angry.

"Do me a favor. Come get a bite to eat with me. You're on the centennial committee. Consider it an act of hospitality."

"I'm only a pageant helper."

"Do it for Hiram and Hortense," he said, unable to hold back a grin.

"Well, when you put it that way…"

She grinned, too, and walked around to the passenger side of the car.

"Tell me where to go." Oops, not exactly the way he should have phrased it.

"Considering you're the guest of honor, I'd rather not."

She fastened the seat belt, giving him a few seconds to admire thighs too shapely to conceal under drab denim.

"It's your call on food," he said. "Anyplace you say."

Now that he had a dinner companion, he was hoping for a restaurant where the service was slow and the atmosphere intimate. Katy the librarian made him believe in Big Bert's girl-spotting talent.

"I've been hungry for a chili dog, but I'll have to go in the house for my purse. I didn't bother taking it to the high school."

Most of the women he knew wouldn't take out the garbage without purses slung on their shoulders. No wonder Katy's walk seemed smooth. She didn't have a lopsided gait from carrying a twenty-pound bag of girlie stuff.

"No need, it's my treat," he assured her. "Where do you keep your key?"

He visualized a couple of warm secretive hiding spots, but she quickly dashed his hopes.

"This is Hiho, Ohio. I don't have to lock up my apartment like a fortress every time I leave for a little while."

He should've guessed. In small-town mythology, nothing bad ever happened.

"So where are we going?" he asked.

"The Dairy Delite. People come from all over the county for their chili dogs. They start slow-cooking the wieners in spicy hot sauce first thing in the morning. By now they should be at their peak. Then they load them in a homemade bun and pile on finely chopped onions.''

''Heartburn heaven,'' he murmured under his breath, but he had to be here for two interminable weeks. He might as well go native and risk the local ''gourmet'' food.

''Turn right,'' she said, pointing at the street beyond the alley. ''Take a left onto Main Street, then a right at the Shear So Dear. That's the beauty parlor on Bigelow Street.''

Across Main Street from the older residential area where Katy lived were newer homes and the elementary school. The high school and baseball fields were north of the Main Street business district and east of Pawley. The town square, public buildings and Cloverleaf College were west of Pawley. The football stadium was behind the classrooms and administration building and was shared by the college and high school. It would be the focal point of the Centennial Celebration, his Waterloo, so to speak.

He supposed the town was pretty, lots of red brick and massive maples, and they'd certainly done some cleaning and planting for the event. Swaying tulips in dozens of colors and yellow daffodils were all over the place, but he was missing some good sailing weather on Lake Erie. His idea of beauty was the shimmering surface of a great inland lake rippled by gentle waves.

''That's the old Hiller House,'' she said with enthusiasm. ''Legend has it that President Taft had supper there when he was drumming up support for his campaign.''

Joel glanced at a monstrous Victorian house the

owners had repainted in periwinkle blue with pink trim.

"It's an antiques shop now," Katy said as though he couldn't see the four-foot-high sign on the manicured front lawn.

At least he had to give her credit for trying to show him the town's highlights, what few there were.

"Are you sure I can't buy you a nice dinner, maybe a steak or a seafood platter?" he asked. "A reward for helping with the pageant."

"No, thanks. Anyway, I should be treating you after knocking you over. Is your head okay now?"

She sounded so darn contrite he wanted to comfort her.

"I'd forgotten all about it," he lied.

He tried to brush hair over the lump on his forehead with his fingers, but winced when he touched it.

"Oh, you do have a bump," she said with distress.

She ran her fingers lightly over the bruise. Surprisingly, it didn't hurt when she touched it. In fact, her gentle exploration made the back of his neck tingle pleasurably.

"I'll never forgive myself!" She brushed away the hair he'd tried to use to conceal it. "I feel just awful about it. What a way to welcome the centennial guest of honor! A bump like that must hurt horribly."

Okay, maybe she was overdoing the sympathy, but there were worse things than having a beautiful woman do a drama-queen bit for his benefit. And oddly enough, she sounded totally sincere.

What surprised him even more was how beautiful she really was. Up close he could see her skin was flawless, lightly touched by the sun for a natural radiance. Her eyes were vivid blue like the deepest depths of Lake Erie on a sunny day, and no amount of makeup could improve them. He'd crown her Miss Hiho on the basis of eyes alone, but even her ears were pretty, close to her head with cute unadorned lobes. How often had he wanted to kiss a woman's lobes and been thwarted by the hardware punched through them? He wondered if she'd be turned on if he traced the whorls with his tongue. Or better still, he'd like to nuzzle her long, slender neck and sample the lipstick-free fullness of her sensual lower lip.

He was losing his mind!

He couldn't hit on the woman his boss wanted as a wholesome beauty to sell Inclines. Anyway, she was probably a nice girl in the old-fashioned sense of the word. Great-great-Grandma Hortense would probably approve of her.

They reached the Dairy Delite and parked in one of the spaces in front.

"Should we order takeout and go back to your place to eat?" he asked hopefully.

"Nope. There are picnic tables in back."

He followed her into a tiny building painted in a bizarre pattern of somewhat wiggly green-and-white stripes. Three tiny round tables with wire-back ice-cream chairs and a tan linoleum counter with a computerized cash register were in front of a menu that ran the length of the inside wall.

"Do you want one or two dogs?" Katy asked.

He should have been the one to ask her what she wanted, but she did everything so cheerfully and naturally, his macho side didn't bristle.

"One is plenty."

The aroma of raw onions and hot chili made his eyes water.

"And a big lemon-lime soda—make that huge," he told a gum-chewing young girl behind the counter, her green-and-white paper hat worn at a cocky angle on a cascade of honey-blond curls.

"The secret of eating chili dogs is to wash them down with a really big sundae. The milk in the soft ice cream neutralizes the onions and chili powder," Katy said.

"That really works?" He was skeptical.

"Sandy, I'll have a nutty hot fudge swirl sundae, but be sure to leave off the nuts."

"Sure, Katy. I know you're allergic to them," the girl said. "Is this the guy you knocked on his butt in the gym?"

"Just a minor collision," Katy said, blushing. "We bumped heads, and my skull is as hard as concrete." She glanced at him and asked, "Do you want a fudge swirl, too?"

"Sure, with peanuts."

"Give him my peanuts, too," Katy directed the girl.

"Takeout or here?"

"We'll eat outside here if there's a free table."

"No one's eating out there now. Just chase the kids away."

No gourmet chef ever made a bigger production out of a presentation than Sandy did getting their order ready and putting it on two trays. By the time they had their food, Katy had a full update on Sandy's boyfriend's jock itch and his unfortunate habit of never getting anywhere on time.

They carried their meals outside, and Sandy hadn't

been kidding about chasing kids away. A pack of a dozen or so, all preteens and relentlessly noisy, were climbing over three weathered wooden picnic tables with attached seats.

"Let us use this table, okay, guys?" Katy asked, putting her tray on one end.

To Joel's surprise, the rowdy kids gave up the one she'd chosen without protest. Several of the girls, including the one who'd been giving baton lessons to her grandmother, talked to Katy in high-pitched voices. They called her by her first name and gave every sign of adoring her. When she shooed them away, they didn't seem to resent it.

He sat across from her and bit into the big pile of crisp, fresh onions and the chili underneath. One taste converted him from skeptic to glutton. It really was tasty.

"This is great," he said with surprise.

"Um." Her mouth was full, and her tongue flicked out to capture a dab of chili on her upper lip, a lovely match for the lower one he'd been eyeing with speculation.

Before he blew this burg, he had to kiss those gorgeous pink lips, if only to prove they couldn't possibly be as special as he was imagining. A victory kiss after she was crowned Miss Hiho would be very nice, but he didn't know if he could wait that long.

"It's as good as you said," he assured her between bites.

"Are you sure one is enough?" she asked.

"Oh, yeah, one is plenty."

He licked the last bit of chili out of the cardboard bun holder as she giggled approval.

They were dipping plastic spoons into the last of

the sundaes that had been topped with sinfully huge mounds of whipped cream when a ruckus on the other side of the paved picnic area distracted them.

Most of the kids were still hanging around, and a small boy with a wildly curly mop of sandy hair was being tormented by a pair of bigger boys, both with dark-haired buzz cuts and mean faces that marked them as brothers. The smaller boy was protesting and seemed on the verge of tears when one of the bullies called him a stupid sissy-baby. The bigger boy pushed his victim with one hand knocking him against a picnic table.

"That's what I hate about small towns," Joel said with more vehemence that he'd intended. "I'd better break it up."

"Hellooo, as if no one ever gets mugged or hassled in big cities." She grabbed his hand to restrain him. "Wait a minute."

"Hey, a mugging is impersonal. Those kids are being mean for the fun of it. I know. I was the nerdy undersized kid who got picked on in the small towns where we lived."

He pulled his hand away and stood up, then realized the situation had changed.

The baton "teacher" with red braids was charging toward the biggest bully with her arms outstretched like battering rams. She slammed into his chest with the palms of both hands and knocked him flat on his back even though he was half a head taller and twenty pounds heavier.

"Wow, that little girl is tough," Joel said as the bigger boy scrambled away on hands and knees followed by his cohort.

"Kerri Smithson. She's watched the movie *The*

Matrix at least seventeen times. The little guy who was being picked on is her cousin. She's an only child of a single mom, so she's fiercely protective of her relatives.''

"Wow," he said again. "No girl ever came to my defense."

"Too bad you didn't grow up here. I would've knocked down a few bullies for you. I was feisty when I was a kid and tall enough to stick up for myself and my friends."

"That would've been the ultimate humiliation since I'm older than you."

"Not by much, I bet. I'm twenty-five."

"I'm three years older. In elementary school, that's a generation."

"When did you grow so tall?"

He caught her looking him up and down, her lips pursed in what seemed to be approval. She met his eyes and actually blushed.

"Not until high school," he said. "I was a late bloomer."

"I grew early, but I was a klutz, even in high school. I never quite got all my parts working together smoothly."

"That doesn't seem to be a problem now," he said with admiration.

"Thanks, but don't spoil the compliment by suggesting I dance on skates or parade around on a stage in spike heels with body parts hanging out of a teeny, tiny bikini."

He'd forgotten the beauty pageant for a few minutes, but he was convinced more than ever she could win. *If* he could get her to enter. She was going to be a hard sell, but at least it would be fun trying.

Everything about her was adorable, even the way she cleaned her lips with her tongue, then blotted them on a paper napkin.

"The kids were so nice about giving up this table, I should treat them to a cone," he said, nodding at the small cluster still hanging around the picnic area. "Do you think it'd be okay with their parents?"

"Sure, we're not a cyanide-in-the-ice-cream kind of town."

"Can I get you some coffee while I'm in there?" he asked.

"No, thanks."

"Well, I'll be right back. What's the super-heroine's name again? Kerri?"

"Yes."

It was fun playing the Pied Piper, leading the half-dozen remaining kids into the Dairy Delite. Kerri negotiated sundaes for all the kids instead of cones, and Joel gave in willingly. He left them eating their syrupy treats at the tables inside and went outside with his cup of hot coffee.

The picnic area was deserted, and Katy had cleared away their disposable dishes. He hurried to the front, but she wasn't waiting by the Incline. In fact, she was nowhere in sight.

She was gone, and he wasn't happy about it, not happy at all.

3

KATY HAD DUMPED the remains of their dinner in the outdoor trash bin as soon as Joel was out of sight. If she knew Kerri Smithson as well as she thought, he'd be tied up on the cone deal for a fair amount of time, long enough for her to vanish.

Running was cowardly, she told herself, but it was also prudent. He was determined to get her to enter the Miss Hiho contest, and the idea was ludicrous. There was no point in discussing it, especially not with a marketing man who made his living persuading people to buy something as ugly as the "Decline."

She jogged for a couple of blocks, but was forced to slow down when her chili dog declared war on the fudge sundae giving her a sharp pain in the side. She waited a minute until the components of her dinner declared a truce.

It was her lucky night. Benny Koontz rumbled up behind her on the bike he'd assembled from the parts of several junkyard motorcycles. She waved him to a stop.

"Hey, Katy, what's up?"

"I was jogging, but I've got a cramp. Would you mind running me home?"

"Okay, but you'll have to wear my spare helmet."

"Sure, no problem."

Jennifer Drew — 43

She gingerly picked up the bright yellow helmet hanging on the back of the bike, trying not to wonder who'd worn it last. She had a thing about wearing other people's clothing, and wearing the snug-fitting headgear was about as appealing as putting on someone's used underwear. But no way could she run all the way home doubled up with a stomachache. She plopped the helmet on her head and fastened the chin strap.

Benny tried to look like a motorcycle gang biker when he was out riding. Today all he was wearing with his jeans was a wide studded belt, scuffy black boots, a cherry-red helmet and a too-small black leather vest. His massive hairy arms had garish tattoos of dragons and snakes, and his hair hung down his back in a long, greasy brown tail.

In his case, looks were deceiving. He'd been two grades ahead of her in school and had graduated valedictorian of his high school class. Now he taught math at Cloverleaf College and sneaked out for a ride on his bike when his wife let him.

Katy climbed behind him on the seat, and it was a tight squeeze. Benny's massive rump allowed little room for a passenger. In fact, he'd custom built his bike to fit his generous proportions.

To his credit, he drove slowly and safely. He also insisted she hang on to him, and wasn't that a challenge! One hand slipped off the skimpy vest and connected with his hot, hairy belly.

Was she being punished for dragging Joel to the Dairy Delite for volcano dogs, the town's nickname for the less-than-gourmet concoctions of chili, greasy wieners and onions? Why had she done it? She could be eating prime rib at the Keystone Inn instead of listening to her stomach rumble over the roar of Benny's bike.

Truthfully, she was just a tiny bit afraid of Joel. He was so cute—no, that wasn't descriptive enough. He was suave, charming, debonair.

"Debonair." She said the word aloud, deciding it fit.

"What'd you say?" Benny shouted back at her.

"I appreciate the ride!" she yelled.

"No problem. You live on Tetley Street now, right?"

"Yes, in the old Cook place."

In Hiho, houses kept the original owners' names for generations. A later resident had to die in battle or be elected to high office to affect a name change.

"Thanks!" she shouted when Benny stopped in the alley by her entrance. The upstairs apartment got to use the front door.

"Anytime. Be sure you strap the helmet back on the bike so it won't fall off."

She pulled off the hard yellow dome and secured it on the rack beside a black nylon pack, resisting the urge to scratch her head until Benny roared down the alley.

"Home, sweet home."

She went inside and walked through the kitchen with its dated appliances and worn tan-and-brown linoleum to the living room that faced west. The setting sun made her squint and draw the heavy gold drapes furnished by the landlord over the long, narrow windows. Her bedroom was in the former dining room. The landlord had converted it when he had made the house into two apartments. The wide arched opening was still there, and she rarely bothered to put the portable bamboo screen in place to block off a view of her sleeping area.

Her parents had left her ample furniture when they moved to Florida—a couch and recliner upholstered in sturdy forest-green wool, cherry end tables and coffee table, several rockers that had been handed down in the family and her old bed with matching maple dresser.

Someday she intended to buy cheerful patterned slipcovers for the living room furniture and replace the drab drapes, but there was always too much else to do. When she wasn't working, she was a member of a bowling league, a softball league and a pool league. She volunteered at the hospital gift shop and helped with vacation Bible school. Also she liked to get together with friends and go to country auctions and flea markets to indulge her one collecting passion—the tiny glass and ceramic slippers she displayed on built-in shelves beside the fireplace. Call her Cinderella, but she couldn't resist a miniature shoe.

Her apartment looked more like a college dorm room than a permanent dwelling, thanks to the red, blue and yellow plastic milk crates that served as bookcases, magazine holders, shoe boxes and general clutter collectors. She'd tacked up concert and travel posters to serve as art until she got around to finding something better. For now, the place suited her fine. When she had a little spare time, she was more into gardening than decorating. She'd already spaded her vegetable garden beside the garage. She was hoping the raccoons wouldn't get all her peppers again this year.

Riding behind Benny had been like cuddling up to

a hot air balloon, and her dinner was generating enough heat to raise the temperature in the room. She stripped off her sweatshirt as she walked into the bedroom, then unzipped her jeans and stepped out of them, tossing them on the bed with her shirt and bra.

Even bare to the waist, she still felt warm, but she hated to run the small air-conditioning unit set into one of the bedroom's three windows. It rattled the frame and was noisy enough to wake the neighbors across the street. She rarely turned it on, preferring the fresh air that came through the other two windows.

It was too early for bed, so she pulled on ratty gray cotton knit shorts, destined soon to be a dusting rag, and a faded red Cloverleaf College T-shirt. She worked the rubber band out of her hair with a wince and gave her head a good brushing to shake the creepy feeling of wearing Benny's spare helmet. As far as she knew, not even his tiny little wife, Annabelle, ever rode with him on his bike, so maybe the extra headgear was mostly for show.

The chili was giving her a vision of a tall glass of icy water. She was trying to get ice cubes out of a plastic tray when her doorbell rang. She pushed aside the yellow-checked curtain covering the windowed part of the door and felt her heart race into triple time.

''Oh, it's you,'' she said, knowing her visitor could hear her through the flimsy door.

She gaped at Carter through the glass. It hadn't occurred to her that he might remember where she lived and come here.

''You disappeared on me.'' He sounded ticked.

"Sorry." It was the polite thing to say, but she wasn't at all sorry she'd bolted.

"Can I come in?"

"I don't know. You could be an ax murderer."

"I'm betting your door isn't even locked."

He turned the handle and pushed it open a few inches, making her back up instinctively. She didn't know what to do when he slipped through the opening and stepped into the kitchen.

"I didn't invite you in."

"Only vampires need an invitation to enter a house."

He ambled over to the kitchen table and sat on one of the two bright orange ladder-back chairs. Painting the old wooden chairs had been one of her few projects in the three years she'd lived there.

"You might as well sit down," she said with an unusually cross edge in her voice. Really, the man went too far!

"Give me five minutes, and I'll go quietly. I won't even besmirch your reputation by telling anyone you know how you dumped a guy who bought you dinner."

"I only went to show you where it was. We certainly weren't having a date," she said.

"You went to torment me, to haze the new boy in town. Those chili dogs should come with a 'hazardous to your health' warning."

"I ate one," she said with a feeble attempt at indignation.

"You dropped half your onions on the ground when you thought I was distracted by the kids."

She didn't bother to claim she'd done it accidentally because, of course, she hadn't.

"Please sit down," he said, gesturing at the other chair and moving a pile of magazines from the seat to the table.

"I like standing."

She also remembered she was braless under her T-shirt, something he hadn't missed if the focus of his gaze was any indication. She nearly looked down to see if her nipples poked at the cloth too obviously, but checked herself just in time. Maybe sitting with her arms across her chest was a good idea. She plopped down, pushing the chair away from the table to put space between them. When she nervously crossed, then uncrossed, her legs, he noticed that, too.

"I was pretty sure your legs were spectacular, and I was right."

He said it the way a man appraises a racehorse, and she wasn't in the least flattered.

"Well, you have a cute butt," she said, trying to be as obnoxiously chauvinistic as he was. "Of course, I haven't had an opportunity to check it out for hairy moles and other defects."

"If you'd like…" He stood and fiddled with the black leather belt holding up his suit pants.

"In your dreams!"

Okay, so he'd called her bluff, and she'd chickened. It was still her home, and being the centennial guest of honor didn't give him the key to everything in town.

He sat down, put his arms on the table, and gave her a look that hot-wired her nerves.

"I know I have no right to badger you, but you knocked the socks off my boss, Big Bert Edson."

"He hardly saw me! He never said a single word to me."

"He's a decisive guy. Anyone who can launch a new automotive company in today's market has to have good judgment. He wants you as the Incline spokesperson, and I agree you'd be great."

"He has good judgment, and he built the Incline? You just lost that argument."

"Here's the plan," he said, ignoring her skepticism. "Next week I'll work with the chamber of commerce to up the stakes in the beauty contest. The winner gets a chance to represent the Incline in a publicity campaign, and that kind of work pays well, very well."

"So do it," she said. "It has nothing to do with me. I'm not entering the contest."

"You could win it hands down."

"Baloney."

"You were the only woman in the gym tonight who has the class to pull it off."

"Double baloney."

He laughed. "I haven't heard anyone say that since grade school."

"I am not interested in being on display like a carnival freak. It's not my thing. No way. Find someone else. Someone who wants to do it. Anyway, there's no chance I'd win out over Brandi Rankin. She's been in beauty contests since she was five, and she has a real talent—dancing."

"She's cute, but not what Big Bert wants."

"He wants a performer. That's not me. You should look for a person with patience and poise— and good posture. That's not me, either."

"Your posture looks fine to me." He gave her

another long, appraising look, which only made her hunch her shoulders.

"We want a wholesome but sophisticated woman, someone other women will identify with and men will want to, well, you know."

"Men will want to date? You want to use sex to sell that bread box on wheels you're passing off as a car?"

"A sport-utility vehicle, but yeah, something like that." He had the grace to sound sheepish. "But the ad campaign will be done tastefully. You'll never feel exploited or belittled."

"Why me? Lots of women would love the job, but I'm not one of them."

"Because my boss thinks you're perfect, or you will be after…"

"After what?" She stood up, knocking the chair over and forgetting to keep her arms crossed.

"After a little detailing, just enough to show off your best points."

"Detailing! I'm a person, not a car."

"I've noticed."

He said it in a way that made her insides feel soft and mushy.

"At least enter the contest and give it a shot. You'll have fun, and you can make up your mind about signing a contract with Vision Motors when you win the title."

"No."

"Think it over."

"I'm a behind-the-scenes kind of girl. Don't waste your time on me. Look for someone else. There are lots of women prettier than me in Hiho."

"Good idea, except I'd like to keep my job."

"Sorry, but I have to say no. That's final."

"I wish there was some way to make you change your mind."

He stood up and looked at her with those soulful eyes. Was that a practiced gaze, one that stood him in good stead in more personal situations? She was afraid her no would turn to yes if...

All he wanted was her name on a contract, that and her integrity. How could she help promote a vehicle she'd hated on first sight? He made her feel like like a lovesick teenager, but she wasn't going to enter the Miss Hiho contest.

"I won't change my mind," she assured him as he moved slowly toward the door.

"By the way, there is one other thing you could do for me—for the good of the town, that is."

Oh, oh! Had he guessed she wouldn't mind a reason to see more of him? Having him right here in her space was making her decidedly weak-willed about everything but the contest.

"I brought a bunch of old papers from Hiram's estate, things my mother kept because they had family significance and were too historical to throw away. She asked my brother and me to take care of them, and we agreed they should go to the town Hiram founded. Trouble is, they're a mess after years of attic and basement storage. They need to be organized." He glanced at the untidy pile of magazines on the table and the papers cluttering the counter by her phone. "But maybe that's not your kind of job."

"I'm a librarian. I can organize," she said. What did he think librarians did? "I'll be glad to help with the papers."

"Thank you. I'll probably call on you."

She was tailing him to the door, belatedly deciding she was careless about leaving it unlocked. From now on, she'd barricade herself in the apartment and hide when handsome, smooth-talking, sexy strangers came calling.

Or maybe not.

"I'm sorry about running off. Thank you for dinner."

She offered her hand to be shaken, but he pulled his biggest surprise yet. Before she could react, he leaned close and brushed his lips on the corner of her mouth. Stunned but entranced, she closed her eyes and heard the door shut after him.

It hadn't been a real kiss, she thought with disappointment. He'd only touched his lips near hers, more a cheeky tease than a kissy-kiss.

She rubbed her fingers where his lips had made contact and thought of…peanuts!

If he still had peanut oil from the sundae on his lips, she could look forward to hives.

But all she regretted was the brevity of his light little kiss.

JOEL GOT BACK to the Sleepy Time Inn just as the sun was disappearing on the western horizon. From his room he had a better-than-average view of the sunset since his window overlooked the grassy parking area of the Davis County Fairgrounds. The motel was two separate row buildings with parking in between and a small fenced pool at the far end. The dull yellow buildings had all the charm of army barracks, but at least he was in the newer section which, judging by the plumbing and knotty pine paneling, meant that part had been built about fifty years earlier. Rooms in the other row backed onto the Hiho Mall, so he was spared the truck deliveries and traffic of the shopping area.

The downside was he could see where his supposed moment of fame and adulation when he represented the town's founder would happen. Yeah, and all everybody would be talking about was how he'd been knocked on his butt by a girl in the high school gym. Fifty years from now someone would still remember that Hiram Hump's descendent got beaned by the beautiful Katy Sloane. How he hated small towns.

Hiho was certainly going all out for the celebration. The grandstand and exhibition buildings on the fairgrounds were freshly painted, gleaming white and ready for the centennial festivities. He looked around the dark little motel room with pseudo-colonial maple furniture, a flowery green-and-yellow spread on a king-size bed and heavy tan drapes. It was home for two weeks, but he didn't have to like it.

He was the guest of honor, but he wasn't even sure what that entailed. Probably a lot of chicken-and-mashed-potato dinners with local dignitaries besides being grand marshall of the parade. He'd learn more tomorrow when he met with the guy from the chamber of commerce.

The motel was on the access road to Highway 42, not quite an hour away from Mayville where the new Vision Motors factory was being built. Joel itched to be there with Big Bert checking out the construction, but his orders were pretty clear. It was his job to use the centennial to get publicity in the media for the company, then sign Miss Hiho to promote the Incline. Given how much was riding on the success of the new model, he didn't have a choice. But his boss had certainly complicated the assignment by pointing his finger at Katy the librarian.

Was the Incline ugly? Boxy, yes. Utilitarian, certainly. It had been designed to appeal to practical, cost-conscious drivers, not to compete with sporty models. But butt-ugly? He didn't think so.

He also didn't think he had a snowball's chance in hell of convincing Katy to enter the beauty contest even though he had no trouble at all visualizing her onstage, her long gorgeous legs displayed in a skimpy bathing suit and high heels.

He shrugged off his suit jacket and loosened his tie, then turned his attention to the blinking red light on the answering machine. His first message was from his mother, although he hardly recognized her voice. The dental surgery made her sound as if she had a mouthful of marbles.

"Hi, sweehar." She couldn't handle the *T*s yet, but he was used to her endearments. "You're checked in, so I guess you go' har okay. Call me 'morrow. Nigh' is my bridge nigh'."

Every night seemed to be her bridge night, but he was glad she had friends and activities in Florida.

"Oh, Jon go' his grades from den'al school. A's and one B. You can be proud of your lil bro. Bye now."

Joel *was* proud of him, but he would be relieved when Jon became a wage earner instead of a student being educated in a costly program. Joel was willing, even glad, to help out, but subsidizing his brother did add to his job pressure. He didn't have any option but to do things Big Bert's way.

He listened to the second message, pretending he

wasn't disappointed when it was Petey Louden, his contact on the chamber of commerce, who started talking.

Had he really expected Katy to call him at the motel because she'd changed her mind about the contest? He wasn't that stupid.

He should've either kissed her properly or not kissed her at all. What kind of message did a half-hearted little peck send?

Petey's jocularity on the message boded ill for their two-week relationship. Joel met more than his share of hale-and-hearty backslappers in his work. Mostly they wore out his patience by taking ages to say what was on their mind. Petey called him "good buddy" throughout the message even though they'd never met and gushed about how happy everyone was to have Joel there for the colossal Centennial Celebration.

Joel seemed to remember Louden sold cars for a living. He shuffled through the business cards in his wallet while he waited for Petey to get to the gist of his message. Yep, there it was, Louden had enclosed it in his confirmation letter. The city volunteer worked at Fillmore Motors.

"I hate to let you down on breakfast," Petey went on, "but something urgent came up. I hope you don't mind being on your own all day. I'll meet you for dinner at the Keystone Inn tomorrow as planned."

Mind? He was relieved. He had enough work lined up on his laptop to keep him slaving away through two weeks of forty-eight-hour days.

Also, he could think of a more pleasant way to pass a Saturday in Hiho, Ohio. Fortunately he had an excuse to see Katy again. His ancestors' papers were stuffed into an old duffel bag and were every bit as disorganized as he'd claimed. He hefted the bag onto a table littered with takeout menus, motel regulations and tourist pamphlets, but his cell phone rang before he could unzip it.

"Joel Carter," he said, answering it.

"Joel, how are things progressing there?" Big Bert never bothered with the niceties of polite conversation.

"Fine." It was the only answer his boss accepted.

"Good. Well, you have my cell phone number. I'll probably be checking on things here in Mayville over the weekend. Got the electricians working double time, so I'm going to keep on their butts. I'll be back in Cleveland Monday and Tuesday, then on-site at the new plant for the rest of the week, if I can swing it."

The phone went dead. Big Bert didn't waste words on farewells, either.

Joel pulled off his tie and tossed it on the bed, then took off his shoes. He planned to strip to his briefs, do some sit-ups and push-ups, then enjoy a long hot shower, but his curiosity was aroused. Did the old papers need enough organizing to justify several visits with Katy? A trickier question was whether he wanted to see her for business or personal reasons.

The papers were tied into two big bundles by a dirty cord that had cut into the pages. He broke the strings easily, and started spreading out newspapers, documents, letters, receipts, birth and death certificates and other paper paraphernalia that marked his ancestors' passage through life. Many of the edges were ragged and the pages yellowed with age, but most of his family's history was in pretty good condition.

Joel turned on the desk lamp to examine them more closely and found himself interested in spite of his usual indifference to his forebears. He started to separate the personal papers from those relating to the town, then decided to mix them up again. He was going to ask for Katy's help, so he wanted them as disorganized as possible. Still, it was fun handling the old documents.

He found Hiho's official certificate of incorporation in the middle of the second pile. He scanned the document, a printed form with spaces filled by elaborate handwriting in faded brown ink. It took a minute for the incongruity to hit him.

The town charter was dated February 10, 1904. Hiho was celebrating its centennial a year early.

Why did the residents think the town was a hundred years old in 2003?

He kept searching and reading until a letter from the state capitol shed light on the discrepancy. Hortense had filed the papers in May 1903, but she must have been dyslexic or something. She'd made some errors on the form that some bureaucrat insisted be corrected, so she had to file again. The second, and official, recognition didn't come until 1904 although the town's government was fully in place in 1903. So why was the centennial being celebrated this year? He did know about the courthouse fire that had destroyed the official records, so was it possible the townspeople didn't know? He turned to the newspapers to try to solve the riddle.

If an early copy of the *Hiho Herald* was the source for the centennial date, someone should have read further. The Hump family had preserved the edition that had erroneously announced that Hiho was officially recognized as an incorporated town, but a later edition contained news of the glitch and the arrival of the second, and correct, confirmation in February, 1904.

It didn't matter to him when Hiho celebrated its centennial. In fact, he'd hate to be the one to tell Big Bert it was the wrong year when his boss wanted to use the Centennial Celebration queen to kick off the Incline campaign as soon as possible.

Did anyone else in town realize the error? Did Katy? At least he'd have something interesting to talk about to justify spending more time with her.

After all, the first rule of marketing was persistence.

4

JOEL WOKE UP, showered and shaved. His mind was made up on how to spend this sunny Saturday morning.

He put on khaki shorts and a short-sleeved turquoise madras plaid shirt after shaking out the wrinkles. A female friend had once told him he looked good in aqua, but that wasn't the reason why he'd packed three blue-green shirts. He liked the color, and he appreciated not having to wear suits, ties and stiff commercially laundered shirts every day for the next two weeks. It was a small compensation for time lost from work hanging around Hiho.

Of course, his idea of casual didn't run to overalls and T-shirts advertising beer, so he'd still probably stand out. It wouldn't be the first time he'd been the oddball in a small town.

He checked himself in the mirror more from habit than interest, but couldn't help wondering what Katy thought of his looks. They were average, he guessed, but he'd always wanted a more interesting face, maybe a cleft chin, craggy nose and high cheekbones. People tended not to remember him because his features were too regular. Still, women seemed to like him the way he was. They probably thought he looked safe and conventional, the kind of man they could bring home to meet the parents.

He made do with self-serve coffee and bagels available in the motel lounge, then made conversation with a bored desk clerk, who sported a pointed black goatee, about what was going on in town.

"Is the library open on Saturday?" he asked, getting to his main question.

"Just in the morning." The clerk, younger than the facial hair suggested, fiddled with his beard, rolling the tip into a sharper point.

"Can you tell me the hours?"

"Guess I could call. Probably have a recorded message seeing as it's only 8:45."

"Would you, please?"

This was no jolly innkeeper who would brighten Joel's two-week stay in the town's only motel. After more beard-pulling and some gum-chewing, the kid got an answer on the phone.

"Nine-thirty till noon. Closed Sunday. Open nine-thirty to five-thirty every day but Wednesday when they're only open after supper from seven till nine."

It was more information than Joel needed, but he filed the hours away for future reference. If he had one asset, it was a good memory.

He went back to his room and killed time with a newspaper he'd picked up in the lobby, then stuffed the Hump papers back into the duffel a few at a time, making a point to turn some upside down and backside out. He wasn't trying to waste Katy's time, only make the job complicated enough to give him an excuse to see more of her.

When he left the motel, it was still too early to go to the library. He didn't want to be lined up waiting when the door opened. How eager would that look?

So he bought gas for the Incline and ran it through a quickie car wash to get the road dust off.

Even though it felt as if he'd stalled for hours, the library had only been open fifteen minutes when he got there.

Hiho had a Carnegie library, one of many donated by the Scottish-born steel magnate and philanthropist early in the twentieth century. Many towns had probably replaced their late-Victorian buildings with larger, more modern facilities, but Hiho's was still in use. The place had character, Joel had to admit. It was built of massive gray stone blocks with a red tile roof and long narrow windows that were similar to those on a castle. The long, steep steps in front certainly weren't up to code on handicapped access. Joel was able to park in front at one of the metered spots along the street since the courthouse, which shared the block, was closed. Maybe there was an easier entrance off the parking lot in back.

The building rose up two stories with towers on the two front corners rising another five feet or so. It was a lot of library for a little town, but it had been built in an era when public buildings were generous in their space. No doubt the optimistic residents at the time expected the town to grow into someplace impressive.

The inside had a hush-hush atmosphere and a large curved desk to check out and return books. A separate reading room was to the left where he could see a couple of elderly men hunched over newspapers at one of the long golden-oak reading tables. The floor was made of narrow wooden boards faded to a dull grayish-brown and so worn the surface was uneven.

To the right were metal stacks of adult nonfiction

with Dewey decimal signs on the end of each one. There was also a big wooden card catalog, something not often seen in the computer age. Fiction had its own section behind and to the left of the desk where a computer looked as out of place as the flame-haired young woman in a bright yellow sleeveless dress who was in charge of checking out books.

Maybe Katy wasn't working this morning. If not, he would go to her house. But if she wasn't home, there was no way he could track her down.

He stepped up to the desk.

"Can you tell me if Katy Sloane is working today?"

"She sure is."

The redhead looked him over with such undisguised curiosity he nearly checked to see if his fly was zipped.

"Can you point me in her direction?" he was forced to ask since the woman seemed disinclined to volunteer information.

"In the kid's department down the stairs."

She pointed toward the front door which he now saw was surrounded by a wall mural depicting the heroic struggle of the Humps' journey to the site of Hiho. The scene was short on authenticity. He was pretty sure they hadn't encountered any hostile Native Americans or wild bears on the relatively short wagon trip from Erie, Pennsylvania, and he couldn't imagine Hortense with a Bible in one hand and a rifle in the other. Her photo in the family album showed a placid-faced, plump woman in a plumed hat big enough to house a colony of birds. She wore round metal-framed spectacles and carried a big dark umbrella, both accessories absent in the mural.

He thanked the librarian and hurried toward the

stairs. He could feel the redhead's appraising eyes creeping down his spine and checking out his southern regions. He wondered if this was how women felt when they had to walk past a construction gang catcalling and whistling. People in this town didn't have enough to occupy their attention, and he couldn't be more unhappy about his role as boredom-reliever.

If he hadn't been focused on seeing Katy when he came in, he might have noticed the two yellowing signs on the wall to his right. The stairs going up led to offices, meeting rooms and the audio-visual department. The down staircase snaked toward the children's room.

He had a strong feeling he'd been here before, not in this town or this building, but in one much like it on his family's wanderings. It even smelled familiar as though the building itself had absorbed a century of odors from books, heat registers, cleaning supplies, damp clothing, people, dust and old wood. It wasn't unpleasant, just evocative of childhood experiences. Structures made of concrete, tile and metal didn't retain the past the way the old stone-and-wood library had.

He ran down the stairs two at a time, feeling more like a kid than he had in years. The double doors to the children's department were open, and he walked into a whole different world. The big room had been transformed into a fantasyland with murals showing fairy-tale scenes in bright primary colors. Kids could play in a castle of colorful plastic cubes or make pretend journeys in a wooden train. There were round tables with racks of jigsaw puzzles and kid-size chairs. The bookcases were low enough to give the smallest child access.

Katy was sitting cross-legged on the bright orange carpet with a handful of surprisingly attentive little kids. She was holding up a picture book but telling the story without looking at it. She saw him, of course, but continued her story until the protagonist and his pony rode off into the sunset on the last page.

Her hair, ineffectively held back from her face by big daisy clips on either side, wasn't much of an improvement over yesterday's ponytail, but Joel couldn't take his eyes off a stray lock brushing her cheek. He wanted to catch it between his fingers and…

Was he losing his marbles? The last thing he needed was a crush on a small-town girl. He knew her type. She undoubtedly wanted a husband, one who would settle down in good old Hiho for a life sentence. That definitely wasn't him. No more small towns for him—ever.

That didn't mean he couldn't admire the way her bright yellow Capri pants hugged her calves and thighs, exposing bare, slender ankles above brown sandals. Her sleeveless white tank top couldn't have been plainer, but the way it hugged her torso was pretty spectacular.

"Ari, come sit down, and we'll have another story," she called over to a pint-size dynamo who was trying to scale a bookcase using a shelf as a stepping stone.

"My niece," she said, acknowledging his presence for the first time. "And this is my other niece, Haley."

"We're twins," the little one beside Katy solemnly declared. "We're both three."

Katy hugged the angelic little girl as her sister bounded into the center of the cluster of children and made room for herself by shoving a boy almost twice her size.

"Ari, it isn't nice to push. Come sit here by me."

Katy laid down the picture book and put her arms around both nieces, real cuties with light brown curls, big blue eyes and flowery one-piece jumpsuits, one pink and one blue.

"Their mommy is getting her hair cut across the street at Shear So Dear," Katy explained. "Jeffrey's mom is at the supermarket. Tony and Tammy are waiting here while their dad goes to the hardware store. Isn't it great they could come to the library?"

"Great," he said. Great for the parents who got free baby-sitting while they did their errands.

"Shelve some books, Katy!" one of the boys urged. "Make Dr. Seuss go home."

"Not right now, buddy. Look, we have a guest. Joel's great-great-great-great-great-granddaddy was Hiram Hump, and his great-great-great-great-great-granny was Hortense Hump, who really deserves to have her statue in the town square, too. They're the people in the mural by the door upstairs. But he's Mr. Carter, not Mr. Hump. Say hello to our visitor."

A chorus of singsong voices sang out, "Hello, Mr. Carter-Not-Hump."

If she'd been expecting him, he would've accused her of rehearsing them. And she'd greatly exaggerated the number of greats!

"Let's have another story. I'll make one up for

you. Would you like to sit with us, Mr. Carter-Not-Hump?''

He'd like to sit *on* her if she kept calling him Carter-Not-Hump, but he lowered himself to the floor just outside the circle of kids where he could watch the storyteller.

"This is the story of *Penelope the Perplexed Princess.* Do you know what *perplexed* means?''

"She has red spots all over?" Haley asked solemnly. Her twin was busy trying to open the three buckles on each of her dusty blue sandals.

"Leave your shoes on, honey," Katy said.

For some reason, even the hyperenergetic preschooler did what Katy asked. From what little Joel had seen of the three-year-old set, a day in the monkey cage at the zoo would be more relaxing.

"*Perplexed* means puzzled. You know, when Mom asks you to do something, and you don't understand the reason why.''

"My mom makes me watch my dumb sister," Tony complained.

"That's to keep her safe," Katy said with a good-natured patience that made Joel want to hug her. "Now Penelope the perplexed princess didn't want to be a princess. She hated doing princess things like drinking royal tea that tasted like boiled cardboard. She'd rather eat cakes and tarts. She especially hated having to keep her pinky finger out straight while she held the royal teacup.''

Katy wiggled her little finger, and Joel imagined kissing the knuckles and guiding her hand down his torso until neither of them could think of anything but...

"Isn't that right, Mr. Carter?"

"Eh..."

Talk about a guilt flash! She'd caught him absorbed in a naughty fantasy about her in the middle of a kids' story hour.

"Oh, right," Joel agreed, feeling more like a visiting idiot than the town's man of the hour.

"Naturally the princess wanted to play with the other children in the castle even if their parents did have jobs like cooking and cleaning and taking care of the cows and pigs.

"The princess hated her fussy, princessy dresses. She wanted to wear jeans so she could climb trees."

Princessy? Joel raised his eyebrows, and Katy winked at him.

"The princess didn't want her hair made into silly corkscrew curls with a hot iron."

She demonstrated by twisting a lock of her raven-black hair around her finger. It was almost more stimulation than Joel could stand after noticing the way her nipples made tiny bumps under her shirt even though she was obviously wearing a bra.

"Then the princess said, 'No, no, no, not even if you make me live in a stable.'"

If she quizzed him about the story, he'd flunk for sure. While he'd been speculating about her various anatomical treasures, he'd missed part of the narrative.

"And that's what happened. The princess was sent to the stables to teach her a lesson, and she had a wonderful time mucking out the horse stalls with the stable boy."

"What's mucking?" her niece Ari asked.

"Cleaning them, like Mommy cleans your house."

"Did she live happily ever after?" Haley asked.

"Oh, yes, very happily, because she knew what she wanted and wouldn't let other people make her into something she wasn't. Now who would like to do a puzzle?"

The group stampeded to the tables to find their favorites, leaving him as an audience of one for the storyteller.

"I got the message," he said sheepishly.

She smiled broadly revealing perfect pearly-white teeth.

"You'd rather be up to your knees in manure than play princess?"

"It was just a kid's story," she protested, but her grin was mischievous.

"Aunt Katy, show us the funny way you shelve books," the serious twin, Haley, pleaded.

"Maybe in a couple of minutes, sweetheart. Finish your puzzle first."

She stood up, brushed imaginary dust off the seat of her pants—a chore he would gladly have performed for her—and smiled again.

"I didn't come to talk about the beauty pageant."

"Oh?"

"No, I brought the Hump family papers. You did seem willing to have a look at them."

He scrambled to his feet with none of Katy's fluid grace. What was it about her that made him feel gauche? He was the sophisticated city boy now, so why did this small-town girl make him feel like a rube?

"Sure, I'd love to see them. You can leave them with me, and I'll get right to them this afternoon."

"Before I give them to you," he said, thinking

quickly as he saw his chance to be with her vanishing, "there are a couple of things I need to point out."

"Okay. Ari! Don't put puzzle pieces in the drinking fountain. They don't need a bath." She shrugged and turned her attention back to him. "Three-year-olds. I love their energy."

He could say the same about her but didn't. What would her reaction be if she realized he was turned on by her like an adolescent on a testosterone high?

"About the papers…"

"I've sort of got my hands full right now," she said with an apologetic smile.

"Have lunch with me. We can go over a few things then."

"Okay. The library closes at noon, but I'm in charge of locking up. About a quarter after would be good. I'll meet you in back of the building."

She said okay. He'd expected rejection. It took all his self-control not to hoot and holler, which was ludicrous considering their dinner date had been nothing but a prank to her. He had no reason to believe she had the slightest interest in his company.

"We'll go someplace nice," he said emphatically.

"Whatever…" She scooted across the room to lift Ari off a cart loaded with books waiting to be shelved.

He left the library marveling at Katy's energy and enthusiasm.

Who was he kidding? She'd made an impression he couldn't believe was possible. He hadn't been so fascinated by a woman in ages, if ever. She was unsophisticated and anything but eager to become better acquainted with him, so why was he so attracted to her? Was it a diamond-in-the-rough thing? Was his interest triggered by the challenge of making her into a beauty queen?

Naw. He just wanted to spend a few days and nights getting well-acquainted with her, and that wasn't going to happen. Too much was riding on the centennial for the guest of honor to try to seduce the town librarian.

He left the library checking his watch. Twelve-fifteen seemed a long time to wait until he could see her again.

THE KIDS HAD all been collected before the hands on the big round wall clock indicated it was noon and time to close the library, but Katy had to help shoo away the adults upstairs before she could leave. Kerri Smithson's mom, Linda, was working the circulation desk, but she was only a part-time employee. A librarian had to close up.

There was more to it than locking a door. Katy had to check both floors and the basement, including the men's and women's restrooms. Years ago, before she worked there, a couple of juvenile hell-raisers had hidden away at closing and wreaked havoc, unshelving row after row of books along with other vandalism. Now the rules called for a search-and-seizure operation before the staff could lock up.

Old Mr. Anders didn't want to leave until he finished the *Wall Street Journal.* He was well into his eighties and never missed his morning read. She had to photocopy three articles for him to take with him before he'd budge.

By the time she was ready to exit through the staff door in the basement, it was twelve twenty-five.

Had Joel waited? She caught herself biting her lower lip and checking her wristwatch every ten seconds.

Why did it matter? He was only there for the centennial. Even if she did allow herself to be attracted by his warm brown eyes and sexy little grin, nothing could come of it. She hated that he had an ulterior motive for being nice to her. All he wanted was to involve her in that wretched beauty pageant.

She'd never had any enthusiasm for girlie contests. They reminded her of 4-H competitions at the county fair when all the farm kids paraded their livestock. Anyway, she didn't want to make a fool of herself when there was no way she could win. Kerri's grandmother had a better chance if she managed to toss her flaming baton without starting a fire.

What disturbed Katy most was the possibility, however slight, of winning. If she actually won and became Vision Motors' Incline spokesperson, her whole life would change. She liked it just the way it was. Sure, someday she wanted a family of her own, but not yet and not with anyone she knew. There was no hurry. She was only twenty-five, and her life was full, satisfying and pleasurable. She had lots and lots of friends and as much social life as she had time for. Which reminded her, she couldn't spend all day on the Hump papers. She and Rob Pawley were going to dinner and a movie that night, and Saturday was laundry and catch-up day.

She hurried up the recessed steps from the basement exit to the parking area and was flooded with disappointment. The lot was empty. There was no sign of the butt-ugly Incline or Carter.

Well, who needed him? She and Rob weren't exactly involved, but she didn't sit home Saturday nights. They were really good friends, and most people thought he'd be a great catch.

She wasn't so sure, though. Yes, he was a good prospect for someone else, but not necessarily for her. A lawyer and the administrator of the Pawley Family Trust, Rob's ancestors had come to Hiho early on and founded the faucet factory, for many years the town's main industry. Ownership of it had changed hands now, and a good part of the family fortune was locked up in the charitable trust. That's what made the centennial so important. Old George Pawley had wanted the town to survive and prosper in the future, so he'd stipulated that huge grants be given to Cloverleaf College and to the city when the town was a hundred years old. The college had already broken ground for a new building based on the upcoming bonanza, and funds promised to the city would mean a massive renovation of the library and an updating of services. The large gift would also make her job much more secure since the library was always struggling to exist on a skimpy budget.

Rob was definitely a "catch," as her friends sometimes teased, but Katy was pretty sure they'd never be more than friends. He made an occasional half-hearted attempt to lure her to bed, but it was more a macho thing than any burning desire to take their friendship a step further.

"Drat!" she muttered to herself when it was obvious she'd been stood up.

Was Carter getting even for the bump on his head or the fiery chili dogs? Or was he just too impatient to wait ten minutes for her?

She walked around to the front of the library on

the uneven flagstone path to make sure he wasn't waiting there. The instant she rounded the corner of one massive stone tower, a horn startled her so much she clutched her heart.

The boxy tan Incline was passing in front of the library on Pawley Street. He honked again to be sure he had her full attention.

She froze and waited. Should she be mad that he was late? How could she when her heart was pounding with excitement and she felt like shouting with joy.

He parked, got out and walked toward her.

"I was worried you'd ducked out the front door. Thought I'd drive around the block to see if you were waiting there. You know, in case I didn't get the directions right. Or you'd changed your mind."

He smiled, and her knees nearly buckled. This wasn't good, not good at all.

"I had trouble getting rid of a patron," she said, embarrassed because her voice cracked. "Library rule. Don't lock anyone in."

"Come on."

He took her hand and led her to his vehicle. She knew things were bad when the car started looking better to her.

5

"NICE DAY," Joel said as he settled down beside her in the driver's seat.

"For a change," Katy said. "We've had a cold, wet spring."

"It's been cold and wet in Cleveland, too."

Good grief, he must think she was competing for ninny of the year. But how could she dazzle him with sparkling conversation while she was subtly getting a look at his knees? He definitely passed her knee test. They weren't bony and protruding, nor were they plump and pink, a real turn-off in her book. Joel's were neither milky white nor artificially tanned. A thin white scar on the right knee piqued her curiosity, but mostly she thought they were cute.

"You probably didn't notice the cooler in the rear," he said.

"No." Why should she? It wasn't the ugly Incline she was checking out.

"I hope you don't mind a picnic lunch," he said. "I bought a cooler, filled it with ice and had the Keystone Inn package up a lunch from their noon buffet. I thought we could picnic in the park or someplace."

"Won't your papers blow away if we eat outside?"

She loved the idea, but was suspicious of his motive for going to so much trouble.

"We'll leave them in the car and start sorting after we eat. Give us a chance to talk first."

Aha! This wasn't just about old documents. He was going to pressure her about the dumb beauty contest.

"We could take the picnic to my house," she suggested coyly to see what his reaction would be.

"Really?"

See boy light up like Christmas tree. See girl extinguish lights.

"Or even better, we'll picnic in the town square. Won't that be appropriate for a descendent of the town founders?"

"I guess."

Obviously he was lukewarm to that idea, but she was downright hostile to being in a beauty contest.

He parked on Main Street near the town square, commented on how easy it was to find a parking spot in Hiho and got out to unload a sizeable blue-and-white plastic cooler from the rear, at which point she had serious reservations about picnicking in the town square.

"Kids like to skateboard around Hiram's statue," she said as they walked toward it. "Looks like they're out in force today."

"Must be a dozen," he said blandly.

"There are benches but no tables."

"It will be a first for me, lobster salad and champagne on my lap."

"You brought champagne?" she blurted out in surprise.

So much for being blasé and sophisticated. Why

didn't she pretend the bubbly was no big deal to her even though it was a wedding beverage seldom seen in Hiho?

"With plastic goblets. Sorry about that."

He grinned at her. She smiled back. A blur of color streaked between them, and they both instinctively scattered.

"Tom Ferris, you nearly smashed my toes!" she shouted after the reckless skateboarder.

"Sorry, I couldn't stop," he said, circling back.

Her eyes met Joel's, so dark they seemed black. They connected the same way they had yesterday in the gym. She felt a shuddering sensation, a collapse of tension as if she'd cut the strings on a marionette.

"This is crazy," she said, not quite recognizing her own voice because it was so husky.

"Sure is." He didn't look away, and she couldn't.

"We can't picnic here."

"Does seem hazardous."

They weren't talking about lunch, and both knew it. They were strangers with nothing in common. If she had any sense at all, she'd make a dash for home, lock the door and hide under the covers. She didn't believe in love at first sight or psychic connections. Even if she did, things like that didn't happen to a practical, down-to-earth person like her.

"Pigeon droppings, too." She gestured in the direction of the benches randomly lining the walkway.

If that wasn't a mood-stopper, she didn't know what was.

"I'm open to suggestions." The way he'd locked eyes with her, he probably had a few to make himself.

She shivered even though they were standing in the noonday sun on a beautiful May day.

"I know a way to sneak into the football stadium if you're game."

"I'm game."

She led the way back to the Incline and directed him to the stadium with as few words as possible.

The campus of Cloverleaf College was picture-pretty with its stately late-Victorian buildings and tree-lined paths, never mind that it was overcrowded and desperately in need of new classroom facilities. West of the campus the stadium was surrounded by asphalt parking used by students and faculty except on game days when it was full of sports fans. It was deserted today.

"Park anywhere," she said. "No way this car can be inconspicuous."

He took out the cooler, and hefted a black duffel over his shoulder.

"I can carry something," she offered.

"Thanks, but I can get it all. Where do we go?"

"You're sure you don't mind a little breaking and entering?"

"Are you trying to back out?"

His words were challenging, but there was something else in his voice. She didn't dare look directly at him again. Maybe he was a hypnotist or a wizard. He'd certainly laid some kind of whammy on her back at the town square. She still felt shaky and slightly disoriented. Her only hope was that he'd refuse to follow her when he saw the route in.

Football being of no small importance to local fans, the stadium was a good size and well maintained. It was laid out on a large flat field with a fortresslike cement structure on the south side that housed the press box, locker rooms, restrooms, ticket office and refreshment stand. The whole setup was surrounded by a high mesh fence with entrances on either side of the building. These, of course, were padlocked, and scaling the fence was out of the question. It was topped by barbed wire, a wise security measure given the cost of maintaining a pristine playing field.

"You weren't kidding about breaking and entering," he said with more amusement than trepidation.

"Don't worry. They probably wouldn't arrest the centennial guest of honor. Come on."

There were several doors leading into the gray concrete building, including ones to the restrooms. Katy headed straight for the women's room.

"Isn't it locked?"

"Of course. It always is."

She stopped in front of a green door with WOMEN painted on it, reached up to the narrow ledge of the jamb and plucked a key from its hiding place.

"I was a cheerleader," she said. "Not a very good one. I was always on the bottom of the pyramid. But I was loud. This is how we got in for practices, but we had to promise never to tell about the key."

"You're going in through there?"

"We're going in. There's another door that will put us inside."

She unlocked the outer door and held it open. Joel didn't look happy, but he stepped into the musty, deserted restroom.

He kept his eyes forward, looking neither left nor right as they walked past the sinks and stalls.

"Now I know," he said after they emerged on the tarmac that surrounded the playing field.

She giggled because he'd been shy about treading on forbidden territory even when it wasn't in use. Really, he was a nice person even if he did have a rotten job that involved trying to make her enter a beauty contest. She had to keep that firmly in mind and forget making googly eyes at him.

The bleachers on the home side were nestled against the building, and additional tiers were in the end zones and across the field. A small concrete building on the far side served as a locker room for visiting teams. It was a pretty generic football field for a very small college, but it was well maintained with bright green natural turf and fading chalk lines that would be renewed when the season started in the fall.

"Home team or visitors?" she asked.

"Your call."

"Visitors. I see a shady spot where the metal bleachers won't blister our behinds."

She led the way straight across the field avoiding the chalk residue. He lagged behind, but she didn't slow down.

"You have a great walk," he said, catching up as she started to climb to the top row of bleachers.

"Yeah, right, until I put on spike heels and start wobbling like a chicken on stilts."

Flattery will not get me to parade around in a skimpy bathing suit in front of the whole town, she thought, stomping down hard on the seats as she bounded upward.

"Katy."

Something in his voice made her turn to look at him.

"I didn't ask you to have lunch so I could bug you about the pageant."

"You didn't?" She couldn't believe how badly she wanted to believe him.

"Cross my heart."

He made the gesture, calling attention to dark silky hair where the top three buttons of his shirt were open.

"Well...good." She didn't know what else to say.

They settled down on the very top bleacher where the scoreboard made a backrest. Joel laid the duffel aside, put the cooler between them on the seat and opened the hinged top with a flourish.

He even had a corkscrew. She watched while he made a smooth job of popping the cork on the dark, wet bottle of champagne. He poured the golden bubbly into a plastic goblet and handed it to her, his damp fingers brushing hers. When he'd filled a goblet for himself, he raised it to her.

"Cheers."

"To your visit in Hiho. I hope you come to love it as much as I do."

He gave her a crooked little half grin and drank.

The lunch was pretty special, she learned as she watched him unload a liberal sampling of the Keystone's famous weekend luncheon buffet. There were fresh shrimp, celery and carrot sticks, lobster and macaroni salads, cocktail sausages, crunchy garlic rounds and delicate cheese puffs.

"This is spectacular," she said as he filled a red plastic plate for her. "You have gourmet tastes."

"No, I'm trying to impress you."

What could she say to that? *Impress away, I already think you're gorgeous?*

"You've succeeded."

She picked up a celery stick and nibbled while he loaded his plate. He had nice hands, something she especially appreciated on a man. His nails were immaculate on strong, slender fingers, but, of course, she didn't really believe the old wives' tail about long fingers being a sign of generous endowment elsewhere.

"Oh, I forgot to give you an olive. Do you like them?" He held out a ripe black olive.

"Love them." Well, sliced on a pizza they were okay.

Her lips parted.

He slid the olive between her lips, hand-feeding her in a way no one ever had. She hardly noticed the distinctive salty flavor of the olive.

"It has a pit."

She had an overpowering urge to leap on his lap and smother him with kisses. Instead she bit down harder and made him pull his finger away with an "Ouch."

"Thank you," she said, eating the olive with exaggerated relish, then removing the pit as delicately as possible.

The lunch was probably delicious, but sharing it with him felt more like foreplay than feasting, not that she had much experience with the former.

Joel carried the conversation. He read a lot of books—wonder of wonders—and liked music, but especially he loved sailing. He described his boat so vividly she could feel the wind in her face and the motion of the waves. Or maybe three glasses of champagne were more than she could handle.

She ate as much as possible, as slowly as possible. The air was hot, even in the shade, and she knew her face must be shiny with perspiration. Her tank top was sticking to her back, and her lids drooped, making it an effort to stay alert. Joel cleared the remnants of the meal and stowed everything back in the cooler, setting it aside on the bleacher below theirs.

"Want to look at the papers now?" he asked in a low, caressing voice.

"Sure, why not?"

She gave herself a couple of mental slaps and tried to jumpstart her brain. Trouble was, she was remembering Debbie Wooster. The high school football team, which also played in this stadium, had voted Debbie the cheerleader "most likely to." And she did, under the bleachers after every game, a reward for victory or solace for defeat, depending on the score. She favored the bleachers on the visitors' side because out-of-towners always left quicker—or so she claimed.

Katy tried to peep down at Debbie's infamous love nest, but all she could see was a sliver of dirt and a discarded beer can. It would be cooler under there and private, wonderfully isolated from the busy little town and its army of wagging tongues. Even if someone came into the stadium, they'd never see under the bleachers. But she'd never know how it felt to make love with a virtual stranger in a clandestine place. No reckless adventures for her. She was fated to live an ordinary life, and that wasn't all bad, was it?

"I had a quick look at some of the papers last night," Joel said, "and I'm a little puzzled."

He stood and bent over the duffel, sorting out what he wanted to show her. His khaki shorts stretched taut over his backside, and she fervently hoped it was only the champagne that was making her so...so...

"Here's what's weird," he said, sitting so close his knee pressed against hers. "The town is celebrating its centennial this year, but it's only the ninety-ninth anniversary."

"What? That's not possible!" Suddenly, she felt very sober.

"Afraid it is. Look, here's the official charter, and here's the newspaper with the announcement."

She read.

"Hiho was official in 1904."

"Yes. This earlier article explains," he said, handing it to her. "Unfortunately, Hortense goofed on the application and had to file a second time. The town was officially incorporated on February 10, 1904."

"This is terrible! The college has already broken ground for a new building. What will happen if they don't get the endowment from the Pawley Trust this year? And the poor library! We're desperate for money to renovate and update. It's too late to postpone the Centennial Celebration!"

"I don't think one year matters all that much," he said mildly. "The town's attorney can sort out the legalities."

"It matters a lot! You can't tell anyone about this!"

"Someone else may read the papers." He took the one she was holding and put it back in the bag with the others.

"Have you told anyone else about them?"

"I may have mentioned I was bringing them."

"Pretend you forgot them! No one will get excited about a bunch of old papers when there's so much else going on. Just don't talk about them!"

Now she knew why he'd brought her here. He wanted her in the contest, and he had to know she'd want the papers to stay secret. If word of the mistaken date leaked out, the centennial would be ruined. The college and the city wouldn't get the trust funds for another year, which could even mean the library would have to cut her job. Joel was smart enough to guess the trouble leaking the information could cause. He didn't need to spell it out. It was blackmail, plain and simple. She was trapped!

"Aren't you overreacting?" he asked.

"Easy for you to say! It will be a catastrophe if this leaks out. I'll do anything to keep it quiet. Anything! I'll even be in the stupid beauty pageant if you won't tell anyone about the date."

"You'll enter the contest?" He sounded incredulous, but she wasn't buying his innocent act.

"If you'll swear, hope to die if you tell a lie, and promise not to mention a word about this, not even a hint to anyone. You have to lose the papers, burn them, never let anyone see them."

"That's a little drastic."

"Well, don't burn them, but keep them yourself for a couple of years until the money from the Pawley Trust has done some good for the town."

"I guess I can hang on to them." He stood to leave, frowning as though he was the one with the really big problem.

"Do we have a deal?" she asked insistently.

"I said I'd keep them. No one needs to know about the date." He started down the bleachers with the cooler thumping his leg and the duffel slung on his back.

She was probably saving his job as well as the centennial, but she didn't feel noble. She felt rotten. He'd only brought her here to drop his bombshell, not because he wanted to be with her.

"Aren't you coming?" he asked over his shoulder as he walked across the playing field.

"I'll walk home."

"Katy, let me drive you."

"No, thank you."

"Well, suit yourself."

He didn't look back a second time. Obviously he had what he wanted, her participation in the beauty contest.

JOEL MADE HIS second trip to the quaint old Keystone Inn, this time to keep the dinner appointment with the chamber-of-commerce guy who was in charge of his participation in the centennial. Joel didn't have to worry about finding him. Petey Louden pounced the instant he opened the door, introduced himself and pumped Joel's hand in a viselike grip.

"Really a pleasure meeting you, Joel. The whole town's excited having you here for the big event. Ain't this restaurant something? Started as an inn before the first world war. Now the owners live upstairs. Sam and Sarah Rosen bought it about ten years ago. They've really spruced up the place and improved the menu, but kept the homey look. It's a showcase of Hiho history."

The walls were crowded with photographs and

memorabilia of the town's past, too cluttered for Joel's taste, but he couldn't fault the food he'd bought for lunch.

"Sorry my wife couldn't make it tonight," Petey said. "Her sister's having a baby over in Mayville. No one in her family can do anything without a gathering of the clan. Well, what do you think of the town your ancestors founded?"

"Looks like it's thriving," Joel said, doubting that Petey even heard his answer.

He was chatting up the hostess, who then led them through several small dining rooms in what was actually a Victorian house converted for commercial use. Joel and Petey were the first diners in a cozy room with high bay windows and dark burgundy wallpaper. The round tables had starched white tablecloths and napkins folded to stand up at every place setting. There was enough glassware and flatware for a seven-course meal. It was going to be a long evening.

Petey was probably in his late twenties. He had thin strawberry-blond hair cut short and a round face with a florid complexion. Most likely, he'd beefed up to play high school football, and the extra weight had turned to flab.

"We'll be having a dinner for you with the whole chamber later in the week," Petey promised. "I'm president of the board of directors this year. We're a pretty active group. Ordinarily I'd wear my red welcome jacket to meet an honored guest. Chamber tradition. But my wife, Peg, forgot to pick it up at the cleaners. I didn't realize it until I went to the closet to get it."

Petey was wearing a green plaid sports jacket that

could've started its useful life on the back of a horse and a bright-yellow knit shirt. Joel felt overdressed and conservative in a charcoal suit and pale blue shirt and tie.

They ordered drinks from a waiter Petey knew by name, a student at the college. Joel asked for a beer, and Petey ordered a Bloody Mary.

"Gotta get my vitamins," he said, using the oldest bar joke in existence.

With the formalities over, all Petey wanted to talk about was cars, cars and more cars. Joel was able to hold up his end of the conversation without much mental effort. He tried to steer the conversation to the town and its library, more specifically the librarian, but if it didn't have wheels, the car salesman didn't know it existed.

Finally they ordered dinner, ribs and fries for the chamber man, a steak and mashed sweet potatoes with ginger for Joel. He tried to concentrate on Petey's opinion about what sells a car, but he couldn't get Katy out of his mind. She was entering the beauty contest. He should be happy about it, but he wasn't.

Joel was aware of the hostess leading another pair of diners into the room, but he didn't glance at them until Petey stood up.

"Rob, Katy, come meet Hiram Hump's descendent in the flesh."

Joel looked up and instantly loathed the weak-chinned man with prematurely thinning light hair and sharp features who had his hand on Katy's waist.

"I'm the welcoming committee tonight," Petey explained. "Can't have the guest of honor eating takeout in his motel room. Joel, this is Rob Pawley and Katy…"

"We've met," she said, sounding a little breathless. He felt as if he'd been kicked in the solar plexus.

"Rob's an attorney," Petey said enthusiastically. "Head of the Pawley Trust."

The faucet-family man, Joel noted sourly, automatically offering his hand because it was what men did. Katy kept hers clenched at her sides out of reach.

"Nice to meet you," Rob and Joel said almost in unison.

"Hey, why don't you two join us?" Petey suggested.

"Fine with me," Rob said.

The guy was crazy. He could have Katy all to himself, and he was willing to eat with Petey.

"They've probably already ordered, Rob," she said without acknowledging Joel.

Was she angry at him? He'd had no way of knowing the family papers would shake her up so badly. She'd volunteered to be in the contest. His conscience was clear there. But what the hell was she doing with Pawley? He was too short for her, no doubt also too dull. She could do better, but maybe not in Hiho. So was she settling for what was available?

"Rob and Katy have been friends forever," Petey said, finally hitting on a subject that got Joel's full attention.

"Just good friends." Katy finally looked directly at Joel as if challenging him to make something of it.

"No reason why a man and a woman can't be friends," Joel said, wondering if he'd blown his chance with her.

Rob was discussing some city business with Petey and not paying any attention to Katy or him.

"If you have any regrets…" Joel whispered.

"No, I said I'd be in the stupid beauty contest, and I will."

"What's that?" Apparently Rob was tuned into their chat after all.

"I'm entering the Miss Hiho pageant," she said as if daring Rob to find something wrong with the idea.

"You're kidding. Why do you want to do that?" her "friend" asked.

"Don't you think I have a chance?"

There was a question that could sink old Rob's ship. He did what lawyers do. He covered his own ass.

"It just doesn't seem like your style," he said blandly.

"She's almost a sure winner," Joel said.

"Yeah, sure," she groused.

She was beautiful even when she was being sarcastic. Tonight her hair was half up, half down, a cascade of raven waves falling to one shoulder, another look that didn't work. Trouble was, everything about her was a turn-on to him, even the little oddities like the purple nail polish she wore with a plain blue cotton shirtdress, short but not skimpy enough to be interesting, and stubby-heeled white shoes.

"So you and Rob have known each other a long time," he said as quietly as possible while Rob and Petey were absorbed in a debate over funding for a sewer project on Bigelow Street.

"Yes."

"About the makeover for the contest…"

"I'm stuck with it, I guess."

Damn, he wished she'd be just a little bit enthusiastic. Instead she was surly, he was jealous, and she should be having dinner with him.

When the food finally came, his seemed tasteless, and she picked at a dinner salad as though every lettuce leaf would make her bulge with extra pounds. This wasn't what he wanted, wasn't what she wanted. He wanted to be alone with her, and she clearly wanted not to enter the contest. Apparently neither was going to be satisfied.

Katy and Rob left first. They were going to a movie. Petey launched into a lengthy explanation of how vans should be changed to give them more macho sales appeal. Joel nodded agreement at widely spaced intervals, but he was occupied with tormenting himself.

How good a friend was Rob? Would their date end at Katy's door, or would the weasel get to stay overnight? It was none of his business, but Joel was so jealous he hardly recognized himself.

"BETH, I'M IN TROUBLE. Do you still have that sack of stuff I gave you for the church rummage sale?"

Katy took a deep breath to get her wind back from sprinting to her sister's new two-story pseudo-Victorian house across from the elementary school on Maxwell Street.

"What kind of trouble? Something to do with the beauty pageant?"

"How do you know about that?"

Unless her sister was suddenly psychic, the news was probably all over town.

"Petey Louden told me when he called. He has a client who wants to test drive a car this afternoon, so he needs Doug's key."

"On Sunday? I thought the dealership was closed."

"You know my husband. If someone wants to buy a car, Doug will open up in the middle of the night."

"What about my stuff?"

"It's in the closet in the guest bedroom, but why on earth…"

Katy was already dashing upstairs, taking the beige carpeted steps two at a time with her older sister trailing behind.

"It's a joke, right?" Beth insisted. "You loathe beauty contests. You weren't even sure you wanted to be a backstage helper. They're sexist and demeaning, remember? Only an exhibitionist could possibly enjoy being in one. I'm quoting you here.''

Katy hurried into the spare room, lugged a big black plastic bag out of the closet and dumped the contents on the embroidered comforter on the double bed. This room, like all those in Beth's house, was a mix of country and modern. Her sister had never met a bunch of weeds she couldn't turn into a wreath or a wall hanging.

''I can't explain,'' Katy said. ''It's just something I have to do.'' That explanation would satisfy her nosy older sister for less than a second.

''What are you looking for?''

''Oh, look, my old Pearl Jam CD from my teenage rebellion,'' she said, trying to avoid explaining.

''I didn't know you had a rebellion. You were the perfect child,'' her sister pointed out.

''You probably missed it. Only lasted a week. I wasn't much of a rebel. Here it is!''

She plucked a hot-pink tank suit from the jumble of outgrown clothes and cast-off junk. The ruffle around the neckline was hanging loose, but that was easily repaired.

''You can't be serious,'' Beth said. ''You wore that suit when you were fifteen.''

''Seventeen, but I don't want to buy a new suit for the competition. Bathing suits are too expensive to wear only once.''

''What's wrong with the one you're using now?''

''Nothing if I wanted to enter the Olympics. Navy blue, one piece, excessively modest. I bought it to swim, not be seen.''

''This is just a temporary aberration, right? You'll

wake up tomorrow morning and forget all about being a beauty contestant.''

"I've already called Mrs. Melbourne. *She* doesn't think I'm crazy. I left my entry form in her mailbox on the way over.''

"Just because she was your cheerleading coach doesn't mean her opinion counts. She may be running the beauty pageant, but she's no judge of talent.''

"You're still mad because she gave you a C in phys ed for not climbing the ropes,'' Katy teased.

"She ruined my straight-A average three semesters running. But that has nothing to do with you as a contestant. What's your talent?''

"I'll think of one.'' Katy was peeling off her gray cotton running shorts and red T-shirt. "Hey, I smell something wonderful. You're baking your famous cinnamon buns, aren't you?''

"They'll be done in ten minutes. Stay for lunch. We'll talk about this insane idea of yours.''

Katy tossed her bra on the bed and peeled off her panties, then started tugging the old swimsuit up her legs.

"Be careful or you'll put your finger through the material,'' her sister warned. "It's probably rotten by now.''

"You don't have to supervise.'' She gingerly began working the old suit, faded by sun and chlorine, over her hips.

"See, it still fits,'' she said, triumphantly sliding the straps over her shoulders.

"Check it out in the mirror.'' Beth pointed at a full-length one on the door to the adjoining bathroom.

Katy stepped up to the glass and worked some wrinkles out of the suit by pulling on the bottom.

"Wonder if I could perk up the color by dyeing it."

"You may not want to," her sister said dryly. "Check the rear view."

"Oh."

Katy tugged on the back, but the suit wouldn't stretch to cover the eight-year expansion of her buns.

"My butt is fat!" she wailed.

"Oh, don't be silly," her practical sister scolded. "No one can wear a bathing suit they wore in high school when they're twenty-five. You were a skinny kid then."

Katy was too depressed to argue. She stared morosely at the big expanse of flesh left bare by a suit that had once modestly covered her bottom, and admitted to herself it was miserably uncomfortable besides looking tacky.

"I won't eat all week," she vowed. "I'll use my grocery money for a new bikini."

The door slid open a crack, but she was too agitated to walk over and close it all the way.

"You hate bikinis. Let's think this out, little sister. Why are you going against your principles to parade half-nude in front of the whole town?"

"I think Brandi should have some competition." She started peeling off the suit. Getting out of it wasn't any easier than getting into it.

"Yeah, right, that's a big worry of yours."

"Why shouldn't an intelligent woman be a contestant?" Katy said petulantly. "After all, Miss Hiho has to represent the whole town."

"Mommy!" The door flew open and both twins

rushed into the room. "The timer rang. Can I frost the cinnamon buns?" Ari asked.

"Daddy took them out," Haley said, making it sound like a condemnation of her mother's baking skills. "Why is Aunt Katy bare naked?"

"You two, shoo. I'll be right down to help you frost the cinnamon buns. Aunt Katy is having trouble with *her* buns."

"Oh, thanks a lot," Katy said when the door slammed behind her nieces. "Hold my flabby body up to the derision of three-year-olds."

"Don't be silly. Your body is great. It's your mind that's wacky. You have to have an act of some kind. You can't sing, dance or twirl a baton."

"I can't do worse than Sadie Smithson and her flaming baton," she protested. "I have a week. I'll research some ideas in the library."

"Remember, Brandi started dance lessons while she was still drinking milk from a bottle."

"Brandi's mother is a manipulative b—"

"Katy! Just give it some more thought. Come have brunch with us. Hot cinnamon buns, fresh strawberries, breakfast casserole with eggs, cheese and sausage."

"I'm not eating this week."

"You can't skip meals. You get light-headed. Hurry up. We'll wait for you, but the girls are hungry."

Katy dressed, weakened by the heavenly smell of hot cinnamon buns. Cooking could be her talent. She could make chocolate chip cookies and pass them out to the judges. Of course, she'd probably leave out the sugar and burn the bottoms.

She might as well have one more decent meal before she started fasting. She walked downstairs pretending she never again wanted to see Carter, the man who had gotten her into this mess.

At the bottom of the stairs she heard men's voices coming from the back of the house where the family room, kitchen and dining area shared one large open space. When she recognized one belonging to Petey Louden, she was tempted to bolt out the front door. Hopefully he hadn't been persuaded to stay for Sunday brunch.

On second thought, she had a few things to say about his big mouth. When he left, she'd follow him out to his car and…

Do what? There was nothing secretive about the contest to be Miss Hiho. The *Herald* would undoubtedly print every tedious detail. The whole town would be watching the contestants. Because no one expected her to be one of them, she'd be scrutinized like a bug under a microscope. Probably her sanity would be called into question.

Did she want a cinnamon bun badly enough to eat with Petey if he was staying?

She did.

She walked into the kitchen and wished she hadn't.

There were men's voices all right, three of them. Her brother-in-law, Doug, was assigning seats at the scrubbed pine table in the area off the cluttered, countrified kitchen. Beth had been on a barnyard kick when she decorated the less-than-two-year-old house, and black-and-white cows abounded from the curtains to the calendar and cookie jar.

Petey was bending Beth's ear about using automobile upholstery on household furniture, citing its greater strength and longer life. Beth, of course, preferred flowery chintz.

The third man had his back turned, but Katy knew that dark brown hair and broad shoulders. He turned when one of the twins yelled, "Aunt Katy, sit by me!"

"Hello," Joel said with a little smile that made her knees go weak. "I didn't expect to be invited to eat with your family."

"I always make a big Sunday brunch so anyone who drops by can join us. We're delighted to meet you, Joel," Beth said, overplaying the hostess role. Or so Katy thought.

"I've been giving Joel a tour of the town. Took him out to see where the college has broken ground for the new science building," Petey said, hovering over the rolls on the cooling rack like a hound over a bone. "Mighty nice of you folks to ask us for brunch."

Katy wondered how Doug could work with Petey day after day after day? Must be because Petey sold more cars than any other salesperson at Fillmore Motors, the dealership that had been in Doug's family for three generations. He'd make her crazy!

"Well, what do you think of the town, Joel?" Katy's brother-in-law asked as he dished egg casserole onto plates and passed them around.

Joel hesitated an instant before answering. Katy wondered whether she was the only one who noticed.

"I imagine Hiram and Hortense would be proud of it," he said.

Beth offered a platter of warm cinnamon buns, splitting one in half for the twins to share.

"I want a whole one," Ari protested.

"Eat what's on your plate, then you can have seconds," her dad said.

"Aunt Katy is worried about her buns," Haley blurted.

"We saw her bare naked with no clothes on," Ari added for shock value.

"You two have to stop hiding behind closed doors and bursting in without knocking," their mother said, reprimanding them. "Katy was trying on an old bathing suit for the beauty contest."

Katy wanted to crawl under the table, especially when she saw Joel watching her with an amused expression.

"Afraid you're going to be disappointed if you expect to win, Katy," Doug said sympathetically. "Brandi Rankin is a shoo-in for Miss Hiho. I've seen her in a bathing suit."

"Oh, and you're an expert?" Beth challenged her husband. "There's a lot more to winning than parading around in a skimpy suit. Miss Hiho has to have poise, personality and talent."

"What's your talent, Katy?" Petey asked as he reached for another cinnamon bun.

"I'm curious about that, too," Doug teased.

"Katy has lots of talent!" Beth said, rallying to her defense.

She might doubt her little sister's sanity, but Beth was quick to stand up for her if anyone else made negative comments.

Joel was sitting across from Katy. She kept her eyes down and concentrated on pushing food from one side of the plate to the other. Nothing like a family critique session to dull the appetite.

"I'll worry about the talent competition later," she

said when everyone at the table stopped talking and looked at her for enlightenment.

"Aunt Katy knows where to put the books," Ari said, supporting her even if she didn't quite understand what was going on.

"Dr. Seuss is not Mother Goose," Haley said, giggling.

"Katy will do fine," Beth said. "It's not easy for anyone to compete against Brandi. She was taking dance lessons when other little girls were playing in the sandbox. Melinda is obsessed with making her a winner so she can take credit, but all the talent is on her ex-husband's side of the family."

"Beth, that's not very nice!" Katy said.

"It's true, though...."

"Well, folks, this sure was nice, but I have to meet a customer," Petey interrupted, standing up and popping a last chunk of cinnamon bun into his mouth. "Ready to go, Joel?"

"If you don't mind, I think I'll walk back to the motel," Joel said. "I need the exercise."

"Oh, sure, fine." Petey obviously found the possibility of getting from one place to another without four wheels an alien concept.

"Thanks for the tour," Joel added.

Even with Petey gone, the conversation turned to vehicles. The twins went out to play in the fenced backyard, Katy helped her sister clear the table, and the two men talked as if they'd known each other for ages. Joel was a big city boy now, but he had a gift for fitting in wherever he was, Katy noted. She was the one who was ridiculously out of place—in a beauty contest.

"Daddy!" Ari ran into the house leaving the

screen on the sliding glass door open. "Will you put water in our pool?"

With everyone distracted by the twins, Katy hurried upstairs without waiting to know whether Doug would fill the wading pool. She bagged her old swimsuit in a plastic sack from the grocery store, but her plan for a quick getaway was foiled. Joel was standing at the bottom of the steps, the twins hovering on either side of him, when she came down.

"We're going swimming!" Ari said, bubbling with excitement.

"At Joel's pool," Haley explained.

"Hold it a minute, kids. Katy hasn't said yes yet," Joel warned.

"Yes to what?" This was like playing a game where she didn't know the rules.

"I offered to take the girls swimming in the motel pool if you're willing to help. Two are more than I can handle alone."

If she refused, her nieces would be terribly disappointed. She looked at their eager faces and felt trapped. But then, she was already in over her head, entered in a beauty contest and worried about the ninety-ninth anniversary problem. The fact that she was attracted to Joel only complicated the whole mess. No wonder she liked her casual relationship with Rob. No strings, no great passion, no attachment.

No fun, no love and no future, a little voice whispered in her head. She was ready for a change in her life, but it wouldn't happen with a man who would leave Hiho and her without a backward glance. Joel was a reluctant visitor just killing time until the Centennial Celebration was over. She absolutely could not become interested in a man who would never fit into her hopes for the future. The prospect of falling for him was scary because nothing could come of it.

"It's okay if you're willing," Beth said, coming up behind the girls.

"I don't have a suit." She discounted the pink thing in the bag she was holding.

"You can borrow that green bikini I bought for our honeymoon. In fact, you can have it. I'll never wear it again. I should've thought of it when you were trying on your old suit."

"Thanks, but no. I'll stop home for my own."

Beth had been dizzy with happiness at the prospect of a Caribbean cruise when she'd bought the two tiny strips of green fabric laughingly called a bathing suit. Only Doug knew if she'd ever had enough nerve to wear it.

"No problem. Doug offered to drive us," Joel said. "I guess that's a yes from Aunt Katy, girls. Get your suits on."

They stampeded up the stairs on either side of her. Katy knew she'd been had. Beth and Doug got some free time, and the twins would love the motel pool. But what about Joel? Was he just being a nice guy? Was he repaying their hospitality or was he enchanted by the twins? They were at an adorable age with their fourth birthday coming up in August, but she wanted to believe he was a tiny bit interested in her.

"I hope you don't mind," he said as they wandered to the family room to wait for the girls.

He sat in her brother-in-law's spot, a huge lord-of-the-manor chair upholstered in brown leather. She and Beth teased him about being King Doug when he settled down in it to watch sports on TV. At least, unlike Petey, he wasn't so obsessed with cars he'd sit through NASCAR races until he became bleary-eyed. Katy actually liked car racing more than he did.

Both Doug and Beth disappeared somewhere. Were they being coy by leaving her alone with Joel? It wouldn't be the first time they'd tried to play matchmaker. In fact, Beth thought Katy was wasting her time with Rob when neither of them had any interest whatsoever in marrying the other.

"It won't take them long to get into their suits," she said, ignoring his question because she did mind being maneuvered into the outing. If he wanted to be with her, why not come to her first?

Obviously, he was only trying to fill some time rather than spend it hanging around with nothing to do in a strange town until his "civic" obligations started. He had what he wanted from her. She was in the contest. Wasn't that bad enough without the risk of falling for him? The less she saw him, the better.

After five of the longest minutes of her life, the twins came into the room giggling up a storm and loaded with equipment.

"Wow, can we get all the stuff in one little car?" Joel teased. "What's this thing?"

He grabbed the end of Ari's neon-pink noodle, a long foam tube for floating. Haley had a green one, plus a beach ball, a towel with purple, pink and yellow sea creatures, her goggles and water wings for safety.

"Do you like our new suits?" she asked.

Katy expressed admiration for Ari's electric pink and Haley's bright cobalt. They looked adorable in two-piece swimsuits, but why wouldn't they? The twins were cute and little. She was sure to bulge and look awful if she tried to parade around with a bare midriff.

"Ready to go?" their dad asked, appearing from wherever he'd been hiding.

Joel didn't have his car, so they all had to get into Doug's. Katy made sure she was sandwiched between the twins in the back seat.

AFTER DOUG STOPPED to let Katy get her suit, he dropped them off at the motel. Joel let her use his room first to change. He tried not to imagine her stripping off her shorts and top, then peeling down her panties and unsnapping her bra. He tried to concentrate on keeping the twins out of the water until she came out, but it was hard. He wanted to be in the bedroom with her, but she'd probably deck him if he even tried to move to first base.

Whatever chance he'd had before he told her about the papers was gone. She felt blackmailed into the pageant, and he felt like a jerk for not letting her off the hook. He tried to excuse his unplanned extortion, but he squirmed with guilt for letting her enter the contest. Was his job worth that much? Couldn't his brother finish dental school without any more help from him? What meant more, his promise to his sibling or his integrity? Or Katy?

She joined him and the girls poolside and started rubbing sunscreen on the them.

"I'd better do your back before I change," he offered, surprised by how badly he wanted to run his fingers over the smooth, flawless skin between the navy straps of her tank suit.

"The girls can do it," she said coolly.

"Well, I'll get into my suit then."

He went to his room hoping her clothes were lying in disarray on the bed. Silly as it seemed, he wanted to touch a garment that had touched her. He'd never before felt this way about a woman's possessions, and he certainly didn't have an underwear fetish. This urge to feel close to her was totally irrational and unlike him.

He was disappointed by her neatness. Everything she'd brought with her was tucked into a red-and-white striped canvas bag propped against the side of the bed. Tempted as he was, he always respected other people's privacy. He undressed and got into his light blue boxer trunks so he could join them.

When he got back, the four of them had the pool to themselves. The motel was pretty much deserted this weekend, probably serving mostly as a business traveler's destination. No doubt they'd enjoy a boom when the centennial was in full swing next week. Former residents of the town would treat it as a homecoming. Petey told him no less than fourteen high school class reunions were scheduled to coincide with the festivities.

Katy was already hip-deep in the shallow end helping Haley float using her noodle. Ari was hanging on the side of the pool and kicking water in their direction.

These girls played rough. He slipped down into the water, and the twins converged on him, splashing and giggling until he was as soaked as they were. Katy laughed and egged them on.

"Let's play a game," he suggested. "Do you know how to play Marco Polo? It's like hide-and-seek."

He explained the simple rules. The person who was it—that was him—closed his eyes and counted to ten, then without opening them, tried to find someone.

"When I say 'Marco,' you say 'Polo,'" he said. "I have to find you by following your voices."

"No fair peeking," one of the twins said.

He started counting slowly. The girls were giggling, making themselves easy prey, but he was after bigger game.

"Nine, ten, Marco!"

"Polo," the three of them said in unison.

He waded after one of the twins, but made sure she escaped. "Marco!" he called again.

The twins squealed and yelled, "Polo!" Katy's response was low, but he had her. He dove in her direction and caught her in his arms when he came up.

"Gotcha!"

He held her captive in the circle of his arms while the twins hooted and splashed both of them. Water beaded on her skin, trickling out of sight under the demure neckline of her suit. For a moment her deep blue eyes sparkled with an intensity that matched his feelings, then she loudly called for a return to the game.

The twins played in the water until they wore out the adults. Their favorite game was bopping each other and him with their big foam noodles, but Katy put a stop to it. The two adults ended up sitting side by side on the edge of the pool while the girls, held afloat by water wings and noodles, paddled around the shallow end.

The sun was hot and Joel's lids drooped, but his awareness of Katy was total. He let his toes tease hers as they dangled in the water, his foot sliding over the top of hers as she halfheartedly tried to evade him. Their thighs touched, but she moved away, the bottom of her wet suit making a plopping noise on the concrete apron.

The twins had given him an excuse to be with Katy, and he enjoyed their antics. But he fervently wanted to be alone with her in his motel room, spending a lazy Sunday afternoon getting to know each other better.

Instead he waited while Katy got the three of them ready to leave, then dressed himself, loaded them into the Incline and treated them to cones at the Dairy Delite.

When he dropped the twins off, Katy wanted to walk home from her sister's house, but he was adamant about driving her. He wanted—needed—a few minutes alone with her. He drove to her place and parked in the alley beside her entrance.

Her hair was beginning to dry, forming tiny frizzy curls across her forehead, but even with a limp wet ponytail hanging down her back she seemed extraordinary to him. He was mesmerized by her natural beauty.

No one would call her cute. Her mouth was a little wide, her nose straight and classical. Her face was a little longer than a conventional beauty's, but when he looked into her vivid blue eyes, he was overwhelmed.

"The day doesn't have to end," he suggested with faint hope.

"Is this where I invite you inside and…" She shrugged and her cheeks flushed pinker than the sun had left them. At least she'd had the same thought he did.

"I think so," he said in a husky whisper.

"Goodbye, Joel. Thank you for letting the girls swim at the motel."

"Are you only thanking me for them?"

"Yes, they loved it."

He was pretty sure she'd had fun, too, but this wasn't the time to press the issue.

"I promised to help you get ready for the contest."

"Just how do you propose to do that?"

"I know what's involved in getting a model ready for promotional work. I think that experience will carry over into a beauty contest."

He sounded like a pompous ass, but Katy didn't always bring out the best in him. He'd gone from hot and bothered to arrogant in one easy step. He was beginning to believe only Big Bert was happy about her participation in the pageant. Joel wasn't sure he wanted her to go against her principles and participate in a cattle call for town queen.

"As if that takes genius," she said, getting out of the Incline.

He got out, as well, even though he was sure he wasn't going inside with her.

"Don't worry about a new bathing suit or evening gown," he said, standing in the alley as she went up her steps. "I'll help you."

She turned and stared at him, hands on hips.

"No way! I can make my own decisions and pay for my own clothes."

"What about your talent?"

"I'll think of something."

"Look, the contest is next Sunday. That's only six days to get ready. You volunteered to be in it. You want to make a good showing, don't you? Every contestant needs a coach, and I'm the only one who expects you to win. You'll have to live with your performance for a long time."

"Are you saying I'll be in a rocking chair at the old folks' home, and people will stop by to snicker?"

She made a joke of it, but he could tell she was worried.

"Let's meet tomorrow and see if there's anything I can do to help."

"I have to work."

"I'll meet you for lunch."

"Okay, twelve o'clock. Park in back this time."

She went inside, leaving him with a silly grin on his face. The woman was making him goofy.

This whole centennial business couldn't be over fast enough for him. He hated small-town politics, small-town social life and small-town mentality. It was crazy to feel the way he did about a girl who was totally entrenched in a place where he wouldn't dream of living. She was a white-picket-fence kind of woman, and he was light years away from wanting to settle down in a permanent relationship. He was on a testosterone high, but some hard jogging and laps in the pool would take care of that. He was too old for a crush and too young for till death do us part.''

7

By NINE O'CLOCK Monday morning Joel had gone through his e-mail, contacted his secretary in Cleveland and had a lengthy phone conversation with Big Bert.

His boss had spent the weekend at the new plant site making sure he got his money's worth out of expensive overtime labor. Joel fervently hoped Big Bert didn't get inspired again and decide to move the marketing department to Mayville. The city was at least triple the size of Hiho—close to 50,000 people—but it wasn't big enough for him. He'd gotten used to the amenities of big city life. He didn't live to sail his boat, watch professional sports and enjoy facilities like his fitness club, but they certainly made life pleasant.

He kept busy on his laptop but didn't accomplish much. For every missive he sent out, he wrote another in his head, all directed at Katy and destined never to be sent. He was eager to keep their noon date if only to bring his image of her back to reality. She couldn't possibility be as beautiful, as vivacious or as seductive as the fantasy that had kept him awake for hours last night. When he got to know her a little better, she'd lose the mystique and seem more like an ordinary woman. He hoped.

He gave up on doing anything constructive, sent

e-mail to his mother and brother, and surfed the Net, then started making The List. Katy had to win the contest. Big Bert was so enthusiastic about making her the Incline model, he'd sent his idea to the board of directors. Apparently they loved the idea, too. What their new line needed was a spokesperson women would want to emulate and men would dream about.

Joel had to copy his list in long hand on motel stationery because he didn't have a printer, but all in all, he was satisfied with his ideas for making Katy a sure winner. It was time to meet her at the library and sell her on the plan.

SCHOOL WASN'T OUT YET, so things were slow in the children's department. Katy had time to make a big poster for the summer reading club and check through the latest book reviews to make her order list, not that the library could afford anywhere near the number of books she'd like to add to the collection. Hopefully when the Pawley Trust was distributed, their budget picture would improve.

The thought of losing the endowment on a technicality made her side ache. Was she wrong to keep the mistake about the date a secret? Usually she could talk over her worries with Rob or her best friend, Judy Matthews, but the ninety-ninth birthday mix-up was one thing she couldn't mention to anyone.

Probably she'd been an idiot to rush into the beauty contest. Joel didn't think the birthdate problem was a big deal, and he hadn't pressured her in any way to enter in exchange for his silence. So why had she? Maybe it was her perverse way of doing penance for her silence. Or maybe she believed Joel was more likely to keep it secret if she did as he wished. Trouble was, she had a better chance of finding a lone bean in a corn silo than winning against Brandi Rankin. The only woman who might possibly beat the dancer was Judy, but she taught family living and home skills at the high school. Her ultraconservative, stuffy principal would take an exceedingly dim view of one of his teachers appearing in the contest, not that Judy liked them any better than Katy did.

She watched the clock, shelved some fire-fighting books in the crafts section, but caught her error and put them in the right place. Then watched the clock some more. She was so sure Joel would be on time, she ducked into the women's restroom and tried to do something with her heavy, unruly hair. Nothing worked, so she left it hanging loose, trying for a sultry look. Fat chance!

As least it would be a short work week. She had to be at the library all day tomorrow and Wednesday evening, but she'd already arranged to have Thursday through Saturday off as vacation time to help with the pageant. Little had she known she'd be using it to get herself ready, not that anything she did would be any more effective than spitting on a parched garden.

When Katy went to lunch, the children's room was unattended, so she locked the cash drawer to safeguard the bit of change in it. She was alone and so eager to see Joel she paced and fidgeted.

At eleven fifty-seven he came into the room.

All she could say was, "Oh."

"I parked in back, just where you told me."

He was drop-dead gorgeous in tan chinos and a dark blue-green golf polo.

Before she could make a witty, scintillating comment, her best friend came in behind him.

"Judy, why aren't you in school?" she asked with alarm, wondering if something really bad had happened.

"It's the kids, not the teachers, who can't leave the campus for lunch," she said with a small laugh.

"Joel, this is Judy Matthews. Joel is Hiram Hump's descendent, our guest of honor."

"It's a pleasure to meet you, Mr. Hump."

"Carter, not Hump, but call me Joel."

He took her hand and held it several seconds longer than a handshake required. Katy was used to the effect her petite, green-eyed blond friend had on men, but for the first time ever she really, really didn't like it.

"Joel and I are going to lunch. Want to join us?"

If Judy said yes to that unenthusiastic invitation, she'd throttle her, which was, of course, silly. Katy didn't have any claim on Joel, and he'd be gone after the centennial anyway.

"Sorry, I only have thirty-five minutes. I just came to talk."

That meant more trouble with her good-for-nothing boyfriend, Brett Howard. But Judy already knew what advice Katy would give: Dump him.

"I can see you're busy, though, so I'll call you later. Nice meeting you, Joel," she said as she left.

He put his tongue back in his mouth and grinned sheepishly.

"Is she in the beauty contest?"

"No." He didn't deserve an explanation.

"Good thing. She'd be real competition."

Like Brandi wasn't? She didn't want to point out another time that the dancer was a cinch to win based on talent alone. He'd only insist on knowing what Katy's nonexistent talent was.

"Where would you like to go for lunch?" he asked.

"The town square. I packed my own and extra for you."

She took her purse and the brown bag lunch from a book cart where she'd put them a few minutes earlier. How eager did that look?

"Ride or walk?" he asked.

"It's a block away." She raised one eyebrow, a little trick that made her look sardonic and, hopefully, exotic.

They walked there with the sun warm on their heads. The breeze felt like a big hair dryer, but it wasn't the weather that made her feel hot and bothered.

She led the way to a reasonably clean bench at the foot of Hiram's statue.

"I hope you like salad and rye crackers," she said, taking two plastic containers and forks out of the sack.

"Doesn't everyone?" He popped a cover and stared skeptically at the somewhat limp lettuce smeared with orange dressing.

Her salad was flavored with a few drops of malt vinegar, the closest thing to diet dressing in her kitchen. She wouldn't be surprised if Joel went for a real lunch after she went back to work, but he didn't complain.

"I made a list of what you need for the pageant," he said, getting down to business.

"A list?"

This was going too far. She grabbed it out of his hand and started reading it aloud.

"Buy swimsuit."

"Unless you want to wear the one your sister offered to loan you yesterday."

"Two pieces of string. No, thank you. Buy evening gown. Forget that. I've been a bridesmaid or maid of honor nine times. I have that covered."

"No frills or ruffles and hopefully not baby pink or blue. You need a dress with bare shoulders and back, something clingy and..."

She gave him the evil eye, and his voice trailed off.

"Appointments for hair, nails, hot wax," she went on. "Hot wax! I'm perfectly capable of shaving my own legs."

"I was thinking of the bikini." At least he looked uncomfortable. "I thought women, well, never mind."

"You left out the most important thing—lose ten pounds."

He laughed.

"It's not funny." She put aside the remainder of her salad, rejecting it as inedible.

"You don't need to lose ten ounces. You're perfect just as you are."

How could she argue with that even if she didn't believe it?

"Who will notice my nails?" she asked to change the subject.

He took the hand not holding his list and studied it, brushing his thumb over the inside of her wrist.

"You do have nice hands," he said softly.

It was practically an invitation to do something interesting with them. She let his list slide to the ground, then narrowly missed bumping his head again when they both bent to retrieve it.

"I don't know why you made a list," she said. "There's nothing on it I haven't already thought of."

"It's what coaches do."

"You're not my coach!"

"Sure I am." He smiled, not his usual cocky grin but one that melted her resistance. "Who wants you to win more than I do?"

"Because it's your job."

"No, because I think you're beautiful, and you're wasting yourself in Hiho."

"I am not!"

Just when she'd been ready to jump on his lap in the town square, he'd spoiled the moment.

"I put that badly. You should win the contest because you're gorgeous and charming."

With that comment it was hard to stay mad at him, but she tried.

"I notice you didn't say talented," she said dryly, standing to head back to the library.

"About your talent…" He stood, too.

"Let me worry about it," she said emphatically.

"Can I pick you up after work?"

"No."

"Then I'll see you at the pageant meeting tonight. The high school at seven, right?"

He would have the schedule.

"Let's get one thing clear. You are *not* coaching me."

"I want to help."

"You can help by not helping."

"Just a few suggestions?"

He leaned toward her, taking her by surprise, and kissed the corner of her mouth.

She forgot they were in the town square in plain sight of lunch-hour traffic cruising down Pawley Avenue and Main Street. Her lips parted in astonishment, and he kissed her again making her tingle with pleasure. His arms circled her shoulders, and his tongue slid between her teeth. She forgot about the Rainbow Day Care kids coming to the library for a visit at one o'clock and kissed him back the way she'd imagined doing a few hundred million times in the last two days.

"I will see you tonight," he said decisively, backing away and leaving her bereft.

They walked back to the library hand in hand, and she knew she was in big trouble.

JOEL WAS SO EAGER to see Katy again he blew off an invitation to the Elks pancake supper. He was tactful, not wanting to offend the lodge brothers, but he would've turned down the governor and the president to be with her.

He got to the gym before seven, but not before Katy and most of the other contestants. To his absolute delight, she rushed over, took his hand and dragged him over to a square-faced woman with salt-and-pepper hair and dark, sun-cured skin like old leather.

"Mrs. Melbourne, this is Joel Carter, our guest of honor."

Miracle of miracles, she didn't call him Carter-Not-Hump. He took the older woman's hand and tried not to wince as her paper-dry fingers squeezed tightly. What was it about people who thought hand-shaking was a strength contest?

"I've told Katy a dozen times she can call me Edna now."

"Mrs. Melbourne—Edna—is the high school gym teacher and cheerleading coach. She's in charge of the beauty pageant."

"Excuse me," Edna said abruptly, rushing off in the direction of a ruckus going on by the stage.

"She acts like a marine drill sergeant in class, but she's pretty nice outside of school," Katy said when the teacher was out of hearing. "Her husband is a major league baseball scout. They don't have kids, so she's sort of taken the whole town under her wing."

Joel wondered if that was a fate that Katy worried about for herself, but he had a hard time thinking insightfully when she was standing so close. Her hair, still hanging loose, was delicately scented with jasmine, and it was all he could do to keep from burying his face in it.

"Let's line up for roll call," the gym teacher shouted above the din in the gym.

"Line up?" Joel grinned at Katy and was rewarded by a smile.

"If I'm late, she may make me do push-ups." She smiled but sounded as reluctant to leave his side as he was to have her go.

She was wearing a little blue-and-white striped top

that didn't quite meet the waistband of her low-slung white shorts. It was the first time he'd been turned on by a belly button, but there was no part of her that didn't excite him. He found a seat on the bleachers close to the stage where he could watch her.

"All right, contestants, here's how we're going to do this," Mrs. Melbourne said in a parade-ground voice. "We put all of your names in a hat, and Mr. Wainwright, the retired high school principal, pulled them out in the following order, which was completely fair since his vision is failing. When I call your name, form a line here on the black line. That person will be number one in the talent segment. For the bathing suit competition, the first four move to the end of the line. Same with evening gowns and the question part of the contest. That way you'll get mixed around pretty well."

It was a workable plan, but stirred a lot of buzz among the sixteen contestants.

"First, Sadie Smithson."

She called all the names, putting Katy third from last and Brandi Rankin last.

"No, this isn't going to work," Melinda Rankin said tramping down from the top bleacher, her stiletto heels sounding like rifle shots on the metal stairs. "It's not fair to put Brandi last in the talent contest. She gets so nervous she'll throw up if she has to wait that long."

"Mother! It's okay!"

Brandi hurried over to pacify her black-haired mother whose dye job was scary with her colorless skin. A tailored fuchsia suit made her look wholly out of place in the gym.

Brandi was wearing shorts so skimpy they barely

covered her butt and a top that could double as a headband, but all Joel saw was competition for Katy. Would the judges choose her baby-doll cuteness over Katy's more substantial beauty? He didn't envy the panel that had to choose one winner out of sixteen hopefuls. He'd hate the job, and he was going to make it worse after Mrs. Melbourne—he couldn't think of her as Edna, either—sorted things out.

"There's a simple solution," Melinda said, taking on the stone-faced gym teacher. "Just let Brandi switch places with Sadie. It doesn't matter when *she* does her little act."

A little flame-haired dynamo exploded down the bleachers.

"It matters a lot. She's doing magic with a live rabbit. You can't make a poor little bunny wait until the last."

"Magic?" Melinda challenged. "She can't even catch a baton."

"She certainly can!" Kerri Smithson stood with her hands on hips, so angry even Mrs. Melbourne hesitated. "My grandmother's act is much better than all that jumping around Brandi does."

The little imp gave a couple of silly jumps in mockery of a ballerina until Melinda caught her by the back of her faded pink T-shirt.

"Don't touch me!" Kerri shrieked.

She twisted free, took a threatening martial arts stance, twisted, circled and let fly. Her foot, clad in a red canvas shoe with a rubber sole, connected solidly with Melinda's ample backside.

All hell broke loose. The contestants forgot about staying on their line and surged forward. Mrs. Melbourne whistled shrilly between her teeth calling for order, and Melinda grabbed Kerri by the shoulders. She tried to shake the girl and avoid another kick, but Sadie got between them.

"Don't you dare put your hands on my granddaughter again," she said angrily. "And you, Kerri, run on home right now."

Kerri stalked out, but Joel saw the smirk on her face. Her cause was just, and she didn't give a hoot whether she was in trouble or not. Little rascal, Joel thought, not blaming her for the outburst.

"Mother, how could you?"

The real casualty in the fracas was Brandi. She was crying, tears streaming down her flushed face. Katy was the first to offer comfort, putting her arm around her and speaking softly. Joel couldn't hear her words, but whatever she said must have given Brandi courage. The little dancer broke away and went up to Melinda.

"Go home, Mother. Or I quit the contest."

Melinda's mouth moved but no words came out. Joel almost felt sorry for her, but she'd brought it on herself. One of the things he especially appreciated in his own mother was that she'd always given her sons freedom to make their own decisions.

Katy began soothing Brandi again after her mother stalked out of the gym. Somehow she convinced her to stay and line up again. The gym teacher pulled rank and bullied the contestants back into a semblance of order.

Joel knew his time had come. He strolled over to Mrs. Melbourne and said a few words to her.

"Attention, please. You can chatter later, Amanda," she told a brown-haired girl in a white denim miniskirt. "Ladies, this is Mr. Carter, Hiram

Hump's descendent and our guest of honor for the centennial. He has some news for you.''

Her introduction had everything but a drumroll. The contestants stared at him with rapt attention making him wonder if Katy had leaked something about his company's plans. Her lips were parted slightly, and the expectant expression on her face almost made him forget what he intended to say.

''This is just between us,'' he said with a grin, knowing the whole town would know by tomorrow. ''The company I work for, Vision Motors, is launching a new economy-size sport-utility vehicle, the Incline. The market plan is to use a small-town girl—woman—as spokesperson. We're prepared to offer the job and a lucrative contract to the contestant who becomes Miss Hiho.''

He'd unleashed the dogs of ambition. One instant he was facing a line of calm, mildly interested women. The next he was mobbed, surrounded on all sides and fielding a barrage of questions.

''Will you consider a more mature woman?'' Sadie Smithson asked.

''Whoever wins will be offered the job. Naturally it's up to the winner to accept or reject it.''

''How lucrative will the contract be?'' the woman in the denim miniskirt asked.

''Our attorneys will work that out with Miss Hiho. It will be significant.''

''Can my boyfriend do it, too?''

''No, only the beauty pageant winner.''

''Will you use the runner-up if the winner doesn't want to do it?''

''You'll probably be fifteenth runner-up,'' someone challenged the girl who asked.

"Only Miss Hiho qualifies."

The group was pressing closer, vying for his attention. Behind him one of the little she-devils pressed her knee against the back of his. He turned his head, but couldn't tell who did it. Someone else pulled on the sleeve of his shirt.

"There's nothing more I can tell you now. Good luck in the contest, and I'll be talking to Miss Hiho when the contest is decided."

He tried to back away and accidentally stepped on a foot. The owner squealed then forgave him in a sugary tone.

"Let the man go!" Mrs. Melbourne bellowed.

The group broke up, releasing him. He waved thanks to the gym teacher, but was grateful he'd never had to be in her class. She was one tough female.

He looked around for Katy, expecting to see her with Brandi, but she was nowhere in sight. He questioned a couple of contestants, but no one had noticed her. After a couple of minutes he gave up. She'd ducked out on him again, and he wasn't going to let her get away with it.

8

KATY DIDN'T JOG HOME. She ran.

By the time she reached the sanctuary of her own kitchen she was breathless, light-headed and mad at herself. She sat on a chair until her breath came back, and she knew the cure for her semi-dizzy state: food. Except for a few bites of lettuce for lunch, she hadn't eaten all day.

Any way she looked at it, she was in a big mess. When all those women had surrounded Joel, fawning over him and vying for his attention, something snapped. She wanted to push them away, tell them to get lost because he was her man and, yes, she'd hurt them if they didn't buzz off.

She was possessed by the green-eyed monster, insanely jealous about a man she'd only known a few days. It was a humbling and very bad feeling. It gave her a whole new understanding of Judy's problem with Brett. Her friend must be an angel to be so forgiving with a cheating womanizer.

Maybe she'd be more rational when she was stuffed to the gills. She started with the stale remains of a box of little round crackers with peanut butter and had progressed to a pint of her favorite chocolate ice cream when someone knocked on her door. She saw him only as a shadow behind the curtain, but in her heart she knew it had to be Joel.

"Go away!" she yelled, sure that he could hear her through the flimsy wooden door with its curtained window.

"Why did you run away again?" he shouted.

Everyone on the south side of town would be able to hear him.

"I have a date!" She defiantly spooned another dab of ice cream from the carton to her mouth.

"You don't have a date. You're trying to avoid me."

"I do so! With Ben & Jerry," she insisted on naming the makers of her favorite ice cream. "And there's not enough to share."

The metal doorknob turned, and he slowly eased the door open.

"You forgot to lock it again," he said, stepping inside and filling the kitchen with his presence.

"No reason to," she mumbled.

"You're upset about something."

She wolfed down such a large spoonful of ice cream she couldn't answer. Somehow it seemed to have lost its flavor.

"Tell me what's wrong," he said.

It sounded like a desperate plea, but she wasn't processing words the way she should.

"Nothing."

"There's something."

He followed her around the cluttered kitchen, oblivious to the pitfalls of stacked magazines, a box of auction knickknacks she hadn't sorted yet and a black trash bag waiting to be put out for tomorrow's garbage collection.

What did he want, a confession? Did he expect

her to tell him she was madly infatuated, wildly attracted to...

No, she could never let him know. Her feelings were a thousandfold worse than they'd been during her one and only "fling" with a chemistry graduate student when she was getting her masters in library science. Their lovemaking had been interesting in a clinical sort of way, and they'd parted on reasonably amicable terms after realizing their relationship wasn't a grand passion for either of them. If she and Joel ever made love it would be explosive, combustible, all-consuming. She'd suffer the torments of hell when he left her. And he would.

"Did you happen to notice I'm the oldest contestant except for Sadie? Most of those girls were in high school a year or two ago."

"Do you want to back out? You can. I don't want you to be miserable."

"The papers..."

"Nothing is worth making you unhappy."

He was being kind and understanding. How could he? Antagonism was her only defense!

"It's too late. I'm stuck. Everyone will think I'm chicken if I quit now." Her voice dropped to a whisper. "And I don't want you to lose your job."

He laughed softly.

Oh, no! She knew that look men got. His face softened, his eyes were dark, mysterious pools, and his lips parted seductively.

"You're going to win," he said.

"You don't know that. You don't even know the judges."

"You're a shoo-in, and I'm going to help you, remember? Now put the ice cream down."

She clutched the cardboard carton to her chest, never mind that it was already soft since the freezer compartment of her fridge was not efficient.

"Give it to me, Katy. Please, sweetheart. Hand it over. You don't want any more."

He used a tone usually reserved to coax a cowering puppy out from under the bed during a thunderstorm.

"I'll trade you something for it," he offered.

"What?"

She sidestepped a stack of newspapers waiting to go in the plastic recycle bin in the garage.

"A ride in the Incline." He took keys out of his pants pocket and dangled them.

"No deal."

"I'll buy you a new bathing suit."

"Certainly not!"

Her hand was cold and wet. She had no idea why she was still clutching the ice-cream carton except that he wanted to deprive her of it. She avoided a pile of magazines on the floor, but several tumbled onto the old linoleum.

Before she could bend to pick them up, he lunged, making a grab for her ice cream. He lost his footing on the slick cover of a magazine and tumbled backward. She grabbed at his shirt instinctively to stop him from falling, but he took her down with him. The carton slipped from her grasp, and the contents shot forward and plopped out in a glob of chocolate mush on his forehead.

"Oh, I'm sorry," she gasped, laughing so hard she didn't even try to sound sincere. "Are you hurt?"

The melting ice cream was trickling down the sides of his forehead and dripping from his eyebrows to his lids. He swiped it away with the back of his hand.

"Serves you right for trying to take away my chocolate fix!"

She tried to shove herself off his chest, but he held her upper arms and pulled her closer. She pushed away the empty carton and felt his legs imprison hers. What was her motivation for trying to escape?

They kissed urgently, their mouths locked together as though they couldn't exist separately.

"We shouldn't do this," she gasped with no intention of stopping and no will to resist.

His hands were under her shirt, caressing her back and shoulders, and almost incidentally, unsnapping her bra. His tongue plunged deep into her mouth, and she'd never been so excited by a kiss.

Another dab of ice cream trickled down to his eye.

"I'll get you a towel," she offered. Instead of getting up to do it, she flicked her tongue to catch the offending droplet.

"Don't move," he said.

"Why would I want to? You're on the bottom." She wiggled her whole length against him.

"No, I really mean it, don't move," he whispered. "I see someone standing outside through the curtain on your door."

Even as he warned her, the doorbell sounded.

"Don't answer it," he said in a low, husky voice.

"What if someone needs me?"

"The town can get along without you for one night. I'm the one who needs you."

The bell rang again. She didn't really want to drag her chocolate-stained self away from where she was.

"It's not locked, is it?" Joel asked.

"You should know."

"Katy, you home yet?" a voice called through the door.

"It's Rob." Her lips were against Joel's ear, the better to be heard, of course.

"Don't answer." He squeezed her tightly as though he needed to constrain her.

"Do you think I want to explain the ice cream—and you?"

She could feel the beat of his heart against hers and the tickle of his breath on her cheek.

"Do you need to explain anything to Rob?" His voice was so soft she could hardly hear it.

He was jealous! It was liberating to know she wasn't the only one who'd succumbed to that green-eyed demon. She kissed him again, willing Rob to go away.

"He's gone," she said after several tense moments locked in Joel's arms, his lips moving against hers as though he had to silence her.

"Are you sure you're not hurt?" she asked.

"From the fall? Only my head. I should wear a helmet around you. But I do ache."

The last sentence was said in a hoarse, sexy voice.

Did every woman have an epiphany when only one thing mattered—the man in her arms? Could she forget about the danger of being abandoned and live for the moment?

He kissed her tenderly, gently stroking the back of her neck.

She could forget her worst fears if it meant being with Joel now.

"You're sticky," she teased. She wouldn't mind being in the bottom of a Dumpster with him, but she sensed the final leap had to come from her. "Would you like to wash up, take a shower?"

"You have a smear right here." He touched her cheek. "And here on your nose."

"I guess I'm a mess, too."

"Then we'd better shower together."

"It would be quicker." She was so excited she could hardly speak.

She scrambled to her feet and offered him her hand. He took it and sat up.

"You're sure?"

She only nodded.

"We should leave our clothes in the kitchen. Not get chocolate in the rest of the house," he said.

"Good idea."

He got to his feet and walked to the door, turning the key and testing the handle to be sure it was locked.

She didn't want to be the first to start removing clothing. She watched, enthralled while he peeled off his stained shirt, the same dark blue-green that suited him so well. His chest had a silky mat of dark hair between coffee-brown nipples.

"You next."

She slithered out of her top, glad the kitchen was dim now as the late-spring sky darkened.

"More," he pleaded.

Her bra was already loose. She let it fall down her arms to the floor.

There was nothing like the sound of a man unzipping. She wanted to hear it again, *zip, zip, zip,* but how silly was that? It was only a symptom of a sudden attack of shyness. She unzipped her own shorts and let them slide down to her ankles, at which point the sandals had to go.

He was barefoot now, too, his navy briefs bulging in a way that fascinated and awed her. She'd hadn't seen all that many naked men—well, only the chemistry student, actually. Was that any reason to shake and shiver?

"Come on," he said.

He must know she was nervous. She took the hand he offered and let him lead her through the living room, into her warm, dim bedroom. He stopped before they reached the bathroom door on the far side of the room.

"You can change your mind."

She shook her head so vigorously he probably thought she was too aggressive. Or maybe not. He knelt in front of her, hooked his thumbs in the elastic of her boring cotton panties, and slowly peeled them off her. She thought he'd expect her to do the same for him, and then she wouldn't know whether to touch him in a private way or not. But he stripped off his own underwear in one rapid movement.

He was the one who adjusted the water in the shower stall, found a washcloth and took one lavender bath towel from the metal cabinet that served as her linen closet.

Whatever she'd expected—with good reason because he had an erection large enough to be a teeter-totter—it wasn't the gentle way he washed her face and then his, letting the water stream over them while he held her close and kissed her deeply.

"Not in the shower the first time, I don't think," he said, kissing her closed lids as lukewarm water cascaded over her head.

Anywhere, she was shouting in her mind, but he led her from the shower and stepped back to turn off the water.

He dried her with a tenderness usually reserved for babies, toweling her hair with the top of her head pressed against his chest.

"I have a problem," he said as he dried himself on the same towel.

Oh, oh, there was reality popping up at the worst possible moment.

"You're not…" She grasped for the current buzzword, difficult given her lack of participation in man's favorite sport. "Prepared?"

"Yes, I am. That's the problem. If I retrieve my very recent purchase from my pants' pocket, will you think I came here to seduce you?"

"Well, yes. You stopped on the way here?"

"No, after lunch."

"Well, I guess you'd better get it."

He left, which gave her a chance to admire the adorable way his bare buns flexed when he walked. She arranged herself on the bed and draped a sheet over her hips but no farther. Her heart was pounding so loudly she could hear it, an unnerving sensation, but not as disturbing as the tightness between her thighs and the fluttery feeling low in her belly.

When he came back, he tossed a long strip of foil packets on her nightstand and turned on the little reading lamp with a shepherd girl in a pink gown as the base.

He sat beside her and pushed away the sheet, then kissed her with an intensity that made her tremble. He left her lips to lavish attention on her throat and breasts where her nipples were stone-hard and aching with desire.

"You drove me nuts with that outfit you wore tonight," he said, nudging her so there was room to stretch out beside her. "You have a very erotic navel, Katy."

She didn't believe him at first, but he gave a convincing demonstration with his tongue.

"Now," she said, sure she'd never be more ready for lovemaking if she lived to be a hundred.

"Not even close."

She was going insane. The human body wasn't meant to be wound up like an old-fashioned clock, but she wanted this to go on forever. She loved the man. She was completely besotted, desperately eager to make him as happy as she was.

Every kiss, every touch seemed to be for her arousal only, until his body was hot and moist from the exertion of pleasing her. He groaned with something between agony and ecstasy, then took precautions at last. He parted her thighs, reached under her to lift her buttocks, and squeezed delightfully hard as their bodies joined.

She was on the roller coaster of love, the peaks and valleys coming in such quick succession she could hear herself shrieking. They rocketed home together and stayed locked together in a trance that could've lasted minutes or hours.

"Wow."

"I'll take that as a compliment." He rolled to her side and nuzzled her ear with wet little kisses. He brushed his lips over hers while his hand nestled between her thighs. He was sweet and gentle, and she cuddled against him, sighing with contentment.

Was this the way sex was supposed to be? She felt limp, languid and terribly seductive. She didn't want this magical time to end.

"Joel?" Her voice was a tentative whisper.

"Um?"

"Is it just in books that men can, you know, perform beyond expectations?"

He roared with mirth and rolled to his back, pulling her on top of him.

"Let's see what happens in the next chapter, little librarian," he said.

JOEL AWOKE SLOWLY, content to take in the fragrance of Katy's hair on the pillow beside him and listen to her soft rhythmic breathing. The clock on her nightstand had big red numbers, and he didn't like what he saw. It was past 8:00 a.m., and there was no way he could avoid everything he had scheduled for the day.

He left the bed as quietly as possible. Considering how many times they'd made love during the night, he was doing Katy a kindness to let her sleep a little longer.

After he was dressed in his chocolate-stained clothes, he rummaged in the kitchen and found what he needed to make coffee. He liked to wake up to the aroma of the freshly brewed beverage, and he hoped it would awaken Katy. Meanwhile, he wiped up the ice-cream mess on the floor with paper towels, gathered the magazines from the collapsed pile, and confirmed that the trash bag contained garbage. He could tell by looking out the back door into the alley that it was pickup day, so he carried it out and put it beside a neighbor's garbage can.

Katy still hadn't stirred. Common sense told him to leave before she woke up. The temptation to kiss her awake was great, but neither of them had time for what might happen if he did.

He went into the bedroom where she was still curled on her side with her dark hair fanned out. There were no lipstick smears or other blotches on the white pillowcase, and he loved that her beauty didn't require full makeup.

"Katy," he whispered softly, unable to resist seeing her before he left.

"I'm awake," she mumbled without opening her eyes.

"I have to leave. Don't you need to get up for work?"

She opened one eye and squinted at the clock.

"Shoot."

"I made coffee."

"Smells lovely."

"I'll be tied up all day. Will I see you tonight?"

"Tied up how?"

She rolled over onto her back and stretched lazily, then realized he was staring at one exposed breast, creamy and lush with a sultry dark nipple. She pulled up the sheet to cover herself and flushed becomingly.

He forgot the question.

"What are you doing all day?" she asked, sitting up and holding the sheet in place.

"Lunch with the Kiwanis, dinner with Rotary Club, and in between I have to go to the ground-breaking ceremony at the college."

"They broke ground as soon as the frost was gone."

"Well, this is the official kickoff. It's not where I want to be."

"And where would that be?" she baited him.

"Right here."

He sat beside her and gave her a morning kiss that threatened to loosen their teeth. Not by accident the sheet fell down to her lap. He softly kneaded one breast and felt her tiny tremor of desire.

"I have to get ready for work," she whispered.

It was a plea. He backed off reluctantly and stood to put space between them.

"Tonight, after I do my civic duty?" he asked.

"I promised Judy we'd do something, then I'm staying overnight at her house. What I'm really supposed to do is keep her worthless boyfriend away. He works for the railroad, and he'll be in town tonight. I can't let her down."

"Tomorrow then." He said it decisively, and she didn't object. "Oh, I forgot something that should be on your list."

"What?" She didn't sound enthusiastic.

"Makeup. You'll need a professional job for the contest. Maybe you can get a facial, too. Is there a place in town?"

"Maybe Shear So Dear." She sounded dubious.

"I'll see you Wednesday then. I don't know how I'll be able to wait until then."

"No doubt you'll manage," she said crisply, pulling the sheet off the bed to wrap around herself.

"I'll need to look at those bridesmaid dresses, too. Most of the weddings I've gone to had the attendants wearing little capes or ruffles. Frilly stuff that won't work for the contest."

He couldn't resist one more quick kiss, then he

had to leave. Big Bert was scheduled to phone at nine, and every call from his boss was top priority.

"Wait!" she urgently insisted.

"What's wrong?"

"Your car—where did you park?"

"In the alley, blocking your garage."

"Oh, boy. Well, maybe no one noticed. Let me check the alley before you go out."

Wrapped like a mummy in the sheet, she padded barefoot into the kitchen and pushed aside the curtain on the door.

"Good thing I checked. The paper boy is coming."

"I need to leave. My boss is going to call me at the motel."

"Just a second. Okay, he's gone. Go quickly before anyone else comes."

She practically pushed him out the door. He grumbled but hurried to save her reputation. This could only happen in a backward little burg like Hiho.

His phone was ringing when he walked into the motel room.

"How are things progressing with the beauty contest? My girl will win, won't she?" Big Bert asked without preamble.

His girl! That rankled, but Joel stifled his annoyance.

"She has a good chance. There are a couple of others who look promising for the ad campaign if she doesn't come in first." He believed in preparing his boss for unpleasant developments well in advance. "I made the announcement to the contestants last night. Took a press release over to the paper."

"The brunette has class. I don't want to see some brainless bimbo representing the Incline."

That would pretty much eliminate Mrs. Big Bert Edson, Joel thought but didn't say.

"How are things going in Mayville?" he asked.

"Right on schedule. Pop over when you get a chance."

Casual as it sounded, it was an order. Once again, Joel began to worry that marketing might be transferred there. But how practical would that be? His department needed the convenience of the Cleveland airport and access to big-city resources.

Big Bert hung up with his usual abruptness.

If Katy won the contest and signed on to promote the Incline, she'd have guys ogling her, lusting after her and fantasizing about her. Could he live with that? More to the point, should he do anything to prevent it? What was best for her?

9

JOEL WANTED HER, but who was the her he wanted? Or, in plain English, he'd said she was beautiful, so why worry about a makeover? It was futile anyway. She had as much chance of winning as she did of going to Mars.

Wednesday morning she got home from Judy's with only minutes to spare before Joel was due at her place. At least the sleepover had helped her friend get rid of that cocky womanizer, Brett Howard. When he saw Katy, he turned tail. She was proud of Judy for not listening to more of his lies, but why did Katy scare men off so easily? Talk about dubious gifts!

Was she—horror of horrors—only a one-night stand for Joel? She didn't know whether to scream, weep or jump his bones when he arrived at ten, exactly when he'd said.

At least he did a better job of saying "Good Morning" than he had the day before. He took her in his arms and kissed her so enthusiastically she began to hope he'd forget his list for the day.

"You're all I can think about," he said, keeping her close by locking his hands on her waist. "You look great in red."

He slid two fingers under a strap of her cherry-red tank top, and she wished she'd had enough nerve not to wear a bra. Maybe he'd forget about appointments and…

But no such luck! He stepped back and looked at her appraisingly. She wanted to say, "Hey, it's only a denim skirt I've had for ages," but his expression was so pensive it seemed better to keep quiet.

"We have time to look at your bridesmaid dresses before our consultation at Shear So Dear."

"They don't do consultations! They do hair as in cut, perm, style, dye, that sort of thing."

He ignored her and walked into her bedroom, heading straight to her closet and opening the door of the roomy walk-in storage space. He was invading her turf as casually as…as a man who'd heard her shriek during sex. She flushed remembering he'd seen parts of her she'd never seen herself.

"Here they are." He grabbed the whole collection carefully stored in plastic garment bags and dumped them on the bed.

"This one isn't a possibility," he said. "I hate chartreuse."

"It's luscious lemon-lime from Betsy Fiddler's wedding," she said a trifle indignantly even though she loathed the dress herself.

"This one's not any better."

He tossed aside the pink crepe her cousin Susan had made her wear. It was ruffled from the neckline to the floor and made Katy look like a stalk of holly-hocks.

"Try on this one." He unzipped a clinging turquoise dress with spaghetti straps.

"No."

"Katy, I've already seen…"

"It's not that. I wore it in high school. I didn't have hips then."

This was too embarrassing. She grabbed the next gown—a ballerina gown from Gayle Henderson's wedding—away from him.

"The skirt has twenty yards of cloth, and I look sallow in pale blue." She tossed it on the reject pile. "This is the one I'm wearing."

She plucked a long yellow jersey from the bed and held it up defiantly. Admittedly, she looked like a banana in it, but it didn't matter. The whole town had already seen it when she'd been one of eight attendants at Megan Graham's huge wedding.

"Convince me," he said. "Try it on."

"No, I've made my decision."

Just because he looked as handsome as any male model in his khaki walking shorts and a black knit shirt didn't mean he was her fashion consultant. He took the bag away from her, opened it and took out the dress.

"Much as I'd like to watch you try it on, there's no need to bother."

He slid his hand up under the skirt, a gesture that seemed erotic, and spread his fingers to show her the stain she'd forgotten.

"Purple frosting on the cake?"

"Purple punch. I forgot the dry cleaners couldn't get it out. I never intended to wear it again anyway."

"Why keep it?"

"The good part of the skirt might make a nice bathroom curtain some day, if I ever learn to sew."

He thought that was riotously funny. If he had a big belly instead of that flat, sexy tummy, it would've wobbled like a bowl of gelatin. Would he forget all this makeover nonsense if she slid her hands under his waistband and played fish? There had to be a better way to spend the day than going through her gowns.

"I'm buying you a bright red dress to knock the judges for a loop. Don't worry about the cost."

"I'm not impoverished. I work!"

"Yes, but if I pay, I get to choose. Come on, Cora is waiting."

"Her daughter, Sandy, cuts my hair. Cora Talbot is the owner. She only does her regulars."

"Not anymore."

He grinned and gave her a playful swat on the bottom to shoo her toward the kitchen door.

"You are way too cheeky," she protested, hoping he'd never find out how much she loved everything he did—except manage her career as a beauty queen.

When they got to the beauty parlor, Cora hustled out from the back room and greeted them as if they held the mortgage on her shop. Well, she greeted Joel. Either the fifty-something woman was smitten with him or she'd had way too much coffee. Cora was a poster image for the mature woman—slim, energetic and, in her own eyes, elegant. Her strawberry-blond locks were perfectly coifed, the elaborate coils heavily sprayed so no hair dare escape.

On the infrequent occasions when Katy felt in need of a trim, she went to Cora's daughter, Sandy, because they'd been in the same high school class. Alas, Sandy—plain and practical with blunt-cut light brown hair—was up to her elbows today doing a color job on old Mrs. Botts, who believed bright auburn dye could disguise her age.

The inside of the beauty parlor was a pink nightmare. The walls were the shade of stomach medicine, the chairs were covered in flamingo-pink leather and the floor had rosy-pink-and-white squares.

"Sit down in my chair, honey," Cora said.

Unless she actively hated someone, as was the case with her rival, Thelma Jean, at the Snip and Clip Salon, Cora called everyone "honey." Katy suspected she couldn't remember names.

"Honey, I've wanted to cut this hair for years. There's enough here for two people." Although her comment was about Katy, she directed it at Joel. "It needs thinning, trimming and a total reshaping to soften and flatter her face."

Cora whipped out a slinky pink cape and fastened it around Katy's neck, then ordered her to the sinks. While the beautician shampooed, rinsed, shampooed again, rinsed, conditioned, rinsed and sprayed some mysterious substance, Cora and Joel discussed what needed to be done to her.

"I want a light trim, that's all," Katy said, groping her way back to the chair, her head swathed in a big white towel that drooped over her eyes.

"We'll do something about the fingernails, of course," Cora said with professional briskness. "A pedicure, too, don't you agree, Joel?" His name she remembered. "What do you think about some highlighting?"

"No blond streaks."

"Oh, no, nothing obvious. Just some subtle tinting."

Katy watched her hair fall in suspiciously large clumps on the checkered floor. She felt like crying, but not over her massacred locks. Joel was all business, impersonally masterminding the makeover.

This was what it was all about, making her eligible to win the contest because his boss had some weird idea about her posing for pictures with the chunky Incline.

She was sitting with her hair in goo-covered spikes when Petey Louden and his dad, Pete Senior, came into the shop. Nothing like an audience when you've been publicly slimed.

"Cora, I wanted to see how you like your new car," Petey said in his heartiest salesman voice.

"I meant to bring it in. There's a little rattle."

"You do that! We stand behind everything we sell one-hundred-and-one percent. Is your sister still thinking of buying the same model?"

"She hasn't decided yet," Cora said. "Joel, have you met…"

"Yes, how are you, Petey?"

They did the handshake thing, then Petey introduced his father, calling him Pete Senior.

"I tried to give Petey a partnership in my shoe store—that's Louden's Bootery at the mall—but with this boy it's always been cars. He sells so damn many no one wears out shoe leather anymore. Hell on my business." He grinned with fatherly pride.

With thin pale hair plastered to his scalp, a round ruddy face and a waistline the circumference of a barrel, he was a walking prediction of how his son would look in twenty years.

Katy had heard him say the same thing about his son numerous times—every time she couldn't avoid him, actually. She smiled weakly, the best she could manage even though he was one of three judges for the beauty pageant.

In fact, Pete Senior might actually vote for her. He

belonged to the Friends of the Library and had complimented the way she kept the children's room. The second judge, Harold Jones, was the high school speech and drama teacher. He was the town expert on talent since he'd sung in the chorus of an off-off-Broadway musical back in the dark ages. His wife, Lorelei, owned Light on Your Feet School of Dance and had been Brandi's instructor for years. Of course, Brandi took lessons in Mayville now. Would Harold's wife want to see a former student win, or was she mad because Brandi had changed teachers? There was no predicting what a judge would do, especially the third judge, Eloise Smathers. She owned the local florist shop and sat on the chamber of commerce board. She was pleasant to everyone, but didn't seem to have any favorite among the contestants.

The Louden men left, Cora directed Katy back to the sink, and Joel finally stopped hovering and instead paced the cozy waiting area. He wandered back when Katy returned, drenched and disgruntled, to Cora's station to be blow-dried, brushed, sprayed and fussed over.

In the end, she had to admit the soft waves and sable highlights were flattering, but gone were the days of carefree ponytails. She'd rather have her hair back, but Joel's rapt expression certainly warmed her.

When she went to pay, Cora waved her away. Joel looked sheepish and quickly ushered her out of the shop.

"You can't pay for my haircut!" she sputtered.

"We'll settle up later."

JOEL DROVE THEM to the mall; their schedule didn't allow for leisurely strolls today. He wanted to shop before he did something really stupid like dance in the town square with Katy, beautiful Katy, in his arms. She didn't need a makeover to be the loveliest person he'd ever known, but he'd take her to a dozen pink hair parlors if it meant staying close.

He was in trouble. Not only wasn't he the settling-down type, he just couldn't bring himself to return to a town like Hiho. He'd promised himself that years ago, but could Katy be happy anywhere else? Could he do what it would take to *make* her happy? Could he actually spend the rest of his life in a small town? He knew the answer was no.

For now, he needed to invest energy in getting her ready for the pageant, although he knew he wasn't doing all this just for Big Bert. Joel wanted to be near her on any excuse.

"Let's look at bathing suits first," he said as he parked the Incline a comfortable distance away from other vehicles so he wouldn't have to return it to his boss with a scratched door.

"I have that covered. I'll wear my sister's bikini. How bad can it be? I'll only be on stage for a few minutes."

A few memorable minutes that will haunt my dreams for many nights to come, Joel thought. But he wasn't ready to tell Katy that, maybe never would be.

"Then let's look for a long gown," he said. "Where's the best place?"

"I guess it can't hurt to look. Wanda's Wedding World has a good assortment."

She led the way to the tasteful little shop where, of course, she knew the clerk.

"Hi, Erika," Katy said with a low-watt but charming smile. "This is Hiram and Hortense Hump's descendent, Joel Carter."

"Hi, Erika," Joel said. "Is Wanda in today?"

He wanted to work with the owner. There wasn't much merchandise on display in the shop, and it would save time if they could go directly to the racks in back if that's where the better gowns were kept.

"She sold out ages ago," the tall clerk said, brushing long black spiky bangs away from her eyes. "Anastasia owns it now, but she's on a buying trip. She has to pick out stock for the Christmas formal, that's how far ahead a person has to plan in the dress business."

This was more than he wanted to know about the shop, but before he could open his mouth, the clerk started talking to Katy.

"My brother saw a strange car parked by your place when he was delivering his papers this morning. Said it looked sorta like a van but boxy and smaller."

"Really?" She did absentminded disinterest well. "I didn't notice."

Small towns! If the mail carrier picked his nose on his route, the whole town would be able to describe it before dinner.

"I bet you need something for the beauty pageant," Erika said. "Brandi Rankin and her mother were in earlier. Brandi was determined not to wear sequins, but Melinda insisted she needed to shine. So guess what they bought? Yellow sequins. If I had a mother like her, I'd run away to someplace wild like Bora Bora or Vegas.''

Joel finally persuaded the chatty clerk they were there to buy, and she disappeared through a curtained doorway.

''Can we have lunch after this?'' Katy asked.

''Whatever you want.''

Erika returned with an armload of gowns, everything from pale aqua sequins to yards of pink netting. Twenty minutes later he'd talked the clerk into letting them see the hidden racks for themselves. There wasn't a red dress in the place, and darned if he'd settle for anything else.

''This one's not bad,'' Katy said, holding up a bright green gown with long, matronly sleeves.

''You'd look like the Grinch,'' he said dismissively.

They walked out of Wanda's Wedding World empty-handed. Who knew buying a dress could be so complicated?

''Erika's little brother is a blabbermouth,'' Katy said unhappily.

''Does it matter so much whether people talk about us?'' he asked.

''No, but Rob should find out from me first.''

He didn't like the sound of that.

''I thought there was nothing between you.''

''There isn't, not, you know, the bedroom part. But we've been friends a long time. Rob might have assumed that some day, that is...''

Joel needed to hear this even though he hated every word.

''I just should have the decency to tell him myself.''

"I see." He didn't see. "Tell him what?"

"Oh, nothing!" she said with a flash of temper darkening her vivid blue eyes. "Let's eat."

"Is the food court all right for lunch?" he asked using the grandiose name for the few fast food stands in the main concourse.

"Oh, my gosh!"

She stopped and grabbed his arm. "There's Pete Senior. Over there, at the table partly hidden by the potted plant."

Joel looked without interest toward the Subs and More sandwich shop where she was pointing, then spotted the reason for Katy's surprise.

"Isn't that…"

"Yes, Sadie Smithson. Look, they're holding hands across the table. She's feeding him a fry."

Did Katy share the town's mania for trivial gossip?

"I seem to remember Petey saying his dad is a widower."

"Yes, but he's also a judge, and Sadie's a contestant in the beauty pageant."

"It's a small town. Lots of people are connected to the contestants."

"Yes, but they're not judges. It's obvious she's trying to influence his vote. Oh, my gosh, he kissed her fingertips!"

Joel wouldn't mind sucking a little salt and grease from any part of Katy's body, but it didn't seem polite to say so.

"This isn't a situation like the judge who's married to Brandi's former teacher. This is undue influence, conflict of interest. I'm really glad I don't want to win," Katy said.

"Sadie won't win," he said, although he didn't trust any small-town panel to be impartial.

"Oh, no! Here comes Melinda and Brandi. Melinda's seen them."

"Worse, she sees us," Joel said dryly.

"Do you see that?" Melinda said stalking over to Katy. "If that isn't influencing a judge, I don't know what it is. You come with me, Katy. You're a witness."

For an instant Joel thought Katy might refuse, but Melinda grabbed her arm in a scarlet-nailed grip and practically dragged her toward the cuddly couple by the potted plant.

Brandi looked at him with resigned misery and followed. Whether he liked it or not, he couldn't walk away from the confrontation.

It took all of two seconds for Melinda and Sadie to start shouting at each other. The couple stood, and Pete patted Sadie's shoulder trying to calm her.

"There's only one way to settle this!" Melinda said, furiously digging her cell phone out of a huge red brocade purse that matched her too-short shorts and blue halter.

Joel protested when the enraged stage-mother insisted they go with the others to Mrs. Melbourne's office at the high school, the official headquarters of the beauty pageant. It was her free period, and she wanted them to hustle over. He wanted to refuse, but Katy pressed his hand and his resistance wavered. Anyway, if he didn't join the parade, Melinda would probably have a full-blown fit and foam at the mouth.

When they got to the gym teacher's office, Mrs. Melborne was sitting behind a gray metal desk covered by files, papers and the paraphernalia of running physical education classes. She made navy shorts and a white blouse look like a uniform. Joel hoped she wouldn't blow her steel whistle, but it might be the only way to silence the woman howling for Pete Senior's blood.

"The rules are pretty clear," Mrs. Melbourne said, tapping her fingers on a photocopy of the pageant regulations. "If a judge allows any undue influence to be exerted on him or her, it means the judge is disqualified. I assume Sadie didn't have him tied to a chair."

Pete Senior's face had gone from light pink to alarming red. All his bluster petered out when Mrs. Melbourne asked him point blank, "Were you behaving improperly with Sadie at the mall?"

"We're just friends," he said weakly.

"Do you think you should resign, Mr. Louden, or would you like to have a hearing with the pageant committee?"

Joel gave her high marks for leaving the aging Romeo some options.

"I'll resign. No problem. It's not really my thing anyway."

"Anything Melinda wants, she gets," Sadie said indignantly. "It's bad enough she tried to rough up my little granddaughter..."

"That's settled then," the gym teacher said in a voice that brooked no dissension. "Mr. Carter, would you stay, please? The rest of you may leave."

He didn't want to stay. This was worse than being called to account in a principal's office, and the atmosphere was about the same, with institutional green walls, an overloaded bookcase with physical education texts and training manuals, and plastic baskets of athletic equipment. It was crowded but not cluttered. Mrs. Melbourne was definitely master of her domain.

"I'm afraid we're short one judge." She smiled, but it didn't soften her face, only rearranged the web of tiny lines etched in her skin.

"I imagine a lot of people would like the honor," Joel said, ill at ease because he was afraid he knew what was coming.

"You'd think so, but people are too chicken to make a decision. The pageant committee scraped the bottom of barrel when they decided to let Pete Senior serve."

"Maybe a woman…"

"Not a good possibility. You're ideal. You don't know most of the contestants, and as guest of honor, you'll raise the status of the contest. You're the perfect replacement judge."

"You're forgetting," he said, grasping at his one hope, "my company wants to hire the winner. I'd have to consider our own criteria which wouldn't exactly make me impartial."

"No one's impartial," she said. "But if I let Sadie get away with using her wilting charms on a judge, the whole contest is suspect. I'll call the other committee members, but they'll be delighted to have you as the third judge."

Did he say yes? His assent didn't seem to matter.

"There must be someone else."

"There isn't. Congratulations, Mr. Carter. I'm sure you'll do a fine job."

"I really don't want to…."

"I won't put the notice in the newspaper until I go through the formality of speaking to the other committee members, but between you and me, I'm running this pageant."

He hadn't felt so trapped since his peanut-butter-sandwich-in-the-face days, but he didn't know how to get out of it without jeopardizing his role as guest of honor—and his job. The only upside was he could help Katy win by voting for her. He couldn't imagine any other contestant outshining her, but if her talent act fizzled, he'd have to give her a low score. It was a no-win situation.

"I guess I'm your new judge," he said with resignation.

"Good. Here, you'd better have a copy of the rules and judging criteria. You'll need to report at least thirty minutes before the contest begins."

"Fine." He turned to leave.

"Oh, and one other thing, Joel."

She stood for the first time and forced him to look into her small black eyes.

"The locals are obviously pretty touchy about judges canoodling with contestants. You'll have to keep your distance from Katy until the contest is over."

Canoodling?

"I'm her coach," he insisted, picking his battleground and loading his ammunition. "Let's forget about me judging."

"Katy doesn't need help." She laughed, but it sounded more like marbles rolling down a flagstone path. "She has more friends than you can shake a stick at, not to mention her sister. Beth was lousy in gym class, but she's pretty smart otherwise. If this thing you have with Katy is personal, the contest is only four days from now. How long is that?"

An eternity if he couldn't see Katy, but there wasn't much point in protesting. He nodded dumbly and started to leave the gym teacher's office.

"And don't park that vehicle of yours by her place until the pageant is over."

He hated small towns. There was more privacy in a nudist colony.

Katy was waiting outside.

"What's wrong?" she asked.

She could read his face even if she didn't know he was mourning for the wasted days when he'd have to stay away from her. Not for an instant did he think they could fool the whole town by meeting secretly.

"I'm a judge."

"Oh, no! Did you volunteer?"

"I'd sooner volunteer to pick up trash along the highway with a prison chain gang. I won't be able to coach you."

"Oh, Judy will help me. And my sister."

"I'm supposed to stay away from you until after the contest."

"Oh."

No forced cheerfulness from her, at least.

"Bummer," she said.

"Yeah, bummer."

"But it's only—" she counted on her fingers "—four days."

"Yeah, four days. Do you want a ride anywhere?"

"No, I'm fine. Not a good idea, anyway, I guess."

A bunch of high school girls sauntered past them, heading for the door of the girls' locker room. Free period was over.

"I guess I can't kiss you," he said wistfully.

"No."

"Well, see you Sunday." She turned to go, and he watched her hips sway as she walked down the hallway.

Small towns! Canoodling!

He felt like kicking a few lockers on his way out.

10

KATY HAD TO HAVE a new coach if she was going
to stay in the contest. She still didn't know what her
talent would be or what to wear. Her choice was
Judy, sweet and uncritical, but it was the last week
of school. Her friend was bogged down with grading.

Beth assumed it was her responsibility to whip
Katy into shape. She descended on her Wednesday
evening after work with the string bikini in hand.
Even though it was past their bedtime, the twins
trailed behind their mother in yellow print dresses
just like hers. Sometimes her sister overdid the
mother-daughter dress-alike thing.

"You haven't thought this through," Beth said in
her most annoying sisterly voice.

The girls rummaged through Katy's pile of magazines looking for people to cut out as paper dolls.
Katy knew there was a reason why she'd saved them.

"I have thought. I'm quitting."

It had been all about Joel anyway, an excuse to
spend time with him. She saw that now. The mix-up
on the centennial date had only been an excuse, sort
of. She wanted to be with him so badly it was like
a toothache in her heart. No matter what else she was
doing, she was only going through the motions.

"It's too late to quit," Beth said, not unkindly.

"Anyway, someone needs to give Brandi a run for her money."

"I want her to win. She deserves it." Katy said.

"She probably will win. That's not the point. You signed up to participate. What will your nieces think if you're a quitter?"

Low blow. Whenever Beth had trouble getting her own way, she managed to throw her daughters into the equation.

"Now what should we do about your talent?" she asked.

Katy glanced toward her phone on the kitchen counter but couldn't will it to ring. Even if it did, she couldn't see Joel, not if she stayed in the contest. But Beth was actually right. She'd gotten herself into this mess, and she needed to see it through.

That meant not seeing Joel, but agonizing over the separation didn't make much sense. He'd be gone after the centennial festivities. He couldn't wait to blow this burg. He refused to see the good side of small-town life, the sense of community, the closeness of people...

Oh, who was she kidding? She ached to be held in his arms. Four days without him seemed like an eternity. She was overwhelmed by the prospect of living the rest of her life without him.

But he would leave Hiho and her.

She hadn't heard a word Beth had been saying.

"Sing, Aunt Katy," Ari said.

"Mommy says you have to," Haley insisted.

"You have a nice enough voice," Beth said. "All you need is one short song, something easy."

"I can't sing in front of people."

"You have to have a talent. What's that song you like to hum?"

"'The Battle Hymn of the Republic.'"

"Be serious. I'm trying to help you. Pick one you can talk your way through the way actors do when they can't sing."

Katy was annoyed enough to try. She blurted out a tuneless rendition of an old Beatles song.

"Don't sing, Aunt Katy," Ari protested vehemently while Haley covered her ears with her hands.

"Maybe singing isn't a good idea," Beth admitted.

"No maybe about it," Katy groused.

The phone mocked her with its silence, then she remembered how busy Joel was. Tonight he'd had to attend a meeting of the county historical society. Every group in town wanted a piece of him. She wanted all of him, but there was a better chance Hiram would clink down off his pedestal and clunk through town in all his bronze glory.

"I have it!" Beth clapped her hands with enthusiasm. "Not for nothing did we take tap dancing lessons when we were kids. We'll work up a little dance for you, something lively and cute."

"I only took six lessons. You're the one who was good at it. Why don't you take my place in the contest?"

"Don't be silly. Married women aren't eligible. Now try this."

She demonstrated a little soft-shoe routine, but didn't quite manage to click her heels together.

"Naturally it works better with tap shoes. Maybe we can borrow some. Oh, don't worry about the dress. I went to the Retro-Fashion shop in Mayville and found a stunning gown in your size. I forgot to bring it here, but you'll love it.''

''It's orange,'' Haley volunteered.

''Orange? I'm not running for pumpkin queen.''

''It's a deep, vibrant orange, perfect with the tints in your hair. Now, let's try that dance step.''

''You kids want some ice cream?'' Katy asked, ignoring her sister. ''Chocolate.''

She started getting out their favorite bowls.

''None for me,'' Beth said.

Katy sat three plastic dishes with cartoon faces on the counter.

''None for you, either. Don't forget the fitness competition.''

''You mean the swimsuit competition,'' Katy said reluctantly putting the third dish back into the cupboard.

''No, I've been reading up on beauty pageants. The proper term now is fitness.''

''Fitness, schmitness.'' Katy put the dishes of ice cream on the table for the twins and licked the serving spoon. ''I quit.''

''No, you can't. Promise me you won't. The girls have been so excited about seeing Aunt Katy on the stage with all the other pretty women.''

''I have no talent.''

''Try the dance. I'll show you again.''

''You know that won't do. I'll read something.''

''Dramatic readings always tank. They're too melodramatic.''

''It's not as if I want to win!'' She said it so loudly her nieces looked alarmed. ''I'll think of something,'' she said morosely.

She did think a lot after Beth and the twins left,

but not about her talent or lack there of. She wanted to talk, but missed Joel too much to cry on Judy's shoulder about it. The night was long and lonely.

The phone, treacherously silent all day Wednesday, rang while she was still in her pink shortie pajamas getting a bowl of corn flakes for breakfast Thursday morning.

"I've missed you," Joel said as soon as she said, "Hello."

Wonderful words for her lovesick psyche, but what should she say back?

She tried for a tentative tone.

"That's nice."

"Not nice, terrible. This is ridiculous. I got roped into being a judge, and I hate not being able to see you openly."

"There's no way to meet secretly in this town," she said.

"I'll leave my car on Main Street and walk over. People must have lives, go to work. They can't spend all their time spying."

"You make the town sound like a nest of secret agents. Even if no one sees you come here, I'll know. I hate being in the contest, but as long as I am, I'll play by the rules."

She wanted him to tell her to quit because being together was more important, but he didn't. Of course, he wouldn't. His boss wanted her to win for reasons that totally escaped her. It was Joel's job to see that she did.

"I'm not sure it's ethical for you to be a judge anyway," she said, "since you're so gung-ho that I win."

"I told Mrs. Melbourne that. She said there are no

impartial judges. Anyway, I've read the rules, and it's all a matter of points. Even if I give you ten, the highest score, in all the other events, you still have to come up with a talent. Even I can't give you a ten for sucking your thumb.''

''I haven't done that since I started kindergarten.''

''Sorry, it was the only thing that came to mind. Guess I saw one of the twins doing it. If I can't come there, where can we meet?''

''Nowhere.'' She felt despondent.

''If we bump into each other in a public place, that's certainly circumspect.''

''I guess. Only I have to be with someone else.''

''Tell me it won't be Rob.''

''No, I'll call Beth. I guess she and the twins will do as chaperones.''

''When and where?''

''The town square at ten. I'm on vacation the rest of the week. I'll call back if I can't make it.''

''I'll give you my cell phone number.''

She scribbled down the numbers on the back of the cereal box, but she was sure they were unforgettable. Everything about Joel was.

Beth made it sound as if she was doing the favor of the century, but she and the twins met Katy in front of the General Store on Main Street and walked over to the town square with her. Her sister had insisted on knowing why, but was surprisingly sympathetic.

''He is a hunk,'' she said. ''If I weren't a happily married woman…''

With a twin on each side and her sister hovering behind, Katy crossed the street. At first she thought he wouldn't show, but the Incline pulled up by the curb on Main Street less than a minute after she got there. Ari started to scale the pedestal, no doubt intending to ride piggyback on Hiram's shoulders, spotted with pigeon droppings. Her mother started coaxing her down while Haley offered sage advice on how to entice her to level ground.

"Hi," Joel said, strolling up with a casualness Katy didn't share.

"Good morning."

"It is now." His voice was so soft not even Beth's dog ears could hear him. "I've missed you."

"I can't stay long. I have to go home, get my car, go to the mall."

"What do you drive?"

Odd he didn't know, but, of course, she didn't drive it much in nice weather. She described her little red compact. He seemed impressed by the color choice, but didn't bring up a red dress again.

The twins were temporarily entertained by hiding under one of the green slated benches, so Beth walked over to them.

"Hi, Beth. Good to see you," Joel said. "I want to talk to you about Katy's makeover. I made appointments and told Cora to put them on my tab since they're my idea. Tomorrow she's scheduled for nails, eyebrows and a wax job."

They were back to detailing! She'd like to wax him!

Katy looked around the empty square and wished the two of them were alone on a deserted island. Partly because her new haircut called for a more sophisticated look, she was wearing a sleeveless sheath dress, a red cotton knit that hugged her in all the right places and ended at mid-thigh. The V-neck dipped low, and she was wearing her second-best bra which gave her enough lift to look downright buxom.

Eat your heart out, Carter, she thought, wondering if he'd worn tight-fitting black shorts and muscle-hugging white T-shirt to impress her. Even if he hadn't, she loved the bad-boy look, so masculine it made her toes quiver.

She tried to tune out the clinical discussion of her dubious assets, but not even the twins demanded her attention. Seeing Joel without being able to throw herself in his arms and kiss him silly was almost as bad as not being with him at all. His back was turned, and she remembered how smooth and well-muscled his back was from his shoulders down to his spectacularly cute buns. She loved the little bit of fuzziness at the end of his spine and the way he'd moaned with pleasure when she ran her fingers down...

Her eye caught his sorry excuse for a car parked a short ways away by the curb, and something was going on. Someone was fiddling with the antenna, but Katy could only see his—no, make that her—back in standard Hiho garb, jeans, high school T-shirt and navy baseball cap. The culprit ran away before Katy could see who it was.

"Joel, someone's done something to your SUV," she called, interrupting his conference with Beth.

All of them trooped over, the twins hanging on his hands like the women-in-training they were. Joel extricated himself from their affectionate grips and crouched to examine the Incline for damage, but he was looking too low.

Katy's first reaction was a boisterous laugh that got his attention. The "vandal" had attached a pair of very skimpy black lace panties and a heart-shaped note to the antenna with a red ribbon. She grabbed the paper missive first and ripped it free.

"Listen to this," she read. "'Hey, Stud'—that's stud with a capital *S*. 'There's more where this came from when you identify my lip print.'"

She held it up to show him an exceedingly bright red-orange lip print.

"Tacky," Beth said. "Who would wear lipstick that color?"

Katy didn't point out that she probably would if she could bring herself to appear in public in an orange dress.

"Someone who wants to influence a judge," she did say. "No doubt she'll reveal herself and try to leave her lip prints where they'll do her more good."

"I don't need this," Joel muttered under his breath.

He tried to untie the ribbon, but it had been knotted too tightly too many times. Beth did the job for him by digging a nail clipper out of her tan saddlebag purse and snipping until the ribbon was shredded.

He fingered the panties and pursed his lips. He didn't look nearly as outraged as Katy felt now. The nerve! When she found out who did it, she was going to… What? Have a catfight with the culprit? Tattle to Mrs. Melbourne? Make a big issue of it like Melinda would?

Darn! A nice girl didn't have many options for revenge. If she were lucky, she'd win the stupid contest just to eliminate the panty-pusher.

Of course, there was the little problem of the talent competition. Maybe she could read a fairy tale like *Little Red Riding Hood* and act out all the parts. She could make masks on sticks to hold up when each character spoke. One little problem. The rules said the contestant had to do everything involved in the act. If she tried to draw a wolf, it would look like a goose with ears.

Suddenly she'd had it with the whole charade— Beth and Joel both being so darn eager to make her over, the silly things women would do for attention and the way Joel made her forget who she really was, a small-town librarian who was content with her life the way it was.

"I have to go," she said.

"I'll walk you home." He crumpled the panties, note and ribbon into a ball in his fist.

"You can't. Against the damn rules."

She started off, not even apologizing to the twins for using a naughty word.

KATY CROSSED OFF the last item on her list, a new
bra she could wear under the plunging neckline of
the orange secondhand gown. She didn't care that
she'd be parading in front of the whole town in cast-
offs her sister provided, but she wasn't going to do
it with sagging boobs.

Now, armed with new white spike-heeled sandals,
panty hose, deodorant, lipstick and a pair of silver-
plated hoop earrings that hopefully wouldn't tarnish
until after the contest, she was more than ready to
leave the mall. The only good thing about her shopping spree was doing it alone. Beth had hair appointments for both girls, and, given the sudden rush of
business at the town's two beauty parlors, she
couldn't hope to reschedule until after the pageant if
she cancelled to supervise her sister. Katy had made
her purchases without any coaching, and she'd handle the talent alone, too—if she ever thought of
something to do.

She carried her purchases across the asphalt of the
parking lot to her car, which was parked at the end
of a row where she'd found a spot in relative shade
beneath a tree.

Rather than bother putting the sacks in the trunk
for the short ride home, she opened the back door.

Her primal instinct kicked in and she shrieked in

fear before her eyes sent a more benign message to her brain.

"You scared me!" she accused Joel.

He was hunched down on the back seat, and she wanted to pummel him for giving her the fright of her life.

"What are you doing here?" she demanded to know.

"Roasting. Do you know how hot the interior of a car gets? We have to do heat tests on our car upholstery before…"

"Joel!"

"You really should lock your doors. Get in and start driving before someone sees you talking to your packages."

He took them away from her and stowed them on the floor, all the while staying hunched down where he wasn't likely to be seen.

"We need to talk," he said urgently.

"My phone isn't tapped, you know."

She wasn't big on cloak-and-dagger games, and she still hadn't forgiven him for making her heart pound double-time in her chest.

She opened the driver's side door, got in and started the car.

"All right, I'll fess up. I want to be with you. I can't think of anything else. I checked every red compact in the parking lot until I found yours."

"How did you know it was mine?"

"Doors unlocked, windows rolled down and a stack of kids' books on the floor."

"I keep them handy in case the twins ride with me."

"I figured. Drive, will you?"

"Where's your horrible box-on-wheels?"

She was still upset from the scare and in no mood to pull her punches.

"At the motel. I walked over."

"I'll take you back there," she replied, starting the car.

"Contestant seen at motel with judge. There's a cute headline. There must be somewhere we can talk in privacy for a while, say, Cleveland."

"Be serious!" She began driving toward the nearest exit.

"How about Mayville? I have to go there anyway to see how the new plant is coming. We can pick up my car..."

"No, I'm still not supposed to be with you."

"Tell me you don't want my company, and I'll get out here."

"I didn't say that. It's just..."

"Do you want me to drive or will you?"

"Oh, all right. It's one way to avoid Beth's coaching for a few hours. She's determined to find a talent the way she found a dress for me. I'll drive."

"So you miss your old coach?"

She snorted rather than admit that she did.

"Put on your seat belt," she said crossly, mad at herself because she didn't have it in her to stay away from him. "Even the twins know you have to do that."

"Are you going to make me ride in the back seat all the way?"

"I suppose I could stop at the fairgrounds and let you come up front."

They stopped and made the change, then she went

on her way again, not admitting to herself how much
she wanted him beside her.

Katy knew Highway 42 to Mayville well enough
to drive on autopilot, a good thing because her mind
was a churning mass of contradictions. She wanted
to be with Joel more than anything in the world, but
the temporary, insubstantial nature of their relationship was making her crazy. Maybe a quick, clean
break was best, but when she was with him it seemed
impossible.

She should have kept him in the back. He didn't
exactly interfere with her driving, at least not after
she strayed across the center line while he was fon-
dling her thigh, but she was constantly aware of the
slightest movement he made and the way he sat,
knees apart and hands locked together on his lap.

They rode with the window open. She didn't like
the car air-conditioning any better than she did the
unit at home, and he didn't object. The gently rolling
farmland was planted mostly with corn not much
higher than her ankles, and she liked the pungent,
earthy smells of the countryside—most of them anyway. On the fifty-mile trip they saw only a few people, those moving on the streets of the two small
towns they passed through on the way. It was a
sleepy part of the state, but she liked the rural qui-
etude and the lightly traveled road.

They entered Mayville through suburbs of spa-
cious new homes, then drove through a downtown
district that seemed booming compared to Hiho's.
Joel directed her to the eastern outskirts of the small
city where Vision Motors was turning farmland into
an industrial site.

''The last time I was here, the buildings were only

steel skeletons,'' Joel said, after directing her to stop in an area of flattened grass and weeds.

The site was vaster than she'd expected and swarming with activity. She couldn't begin to guess the function of all the construction equipment sitting around, although books about monster machines were favorites with the preschool boys in her story groups.

They got out and walked the perimeter of the site taking care to keep out of the workers' way. She was impressed in spite of herself by the patterned brick walls and looming cranes.

''I guess it will be good for Mayville,'' she said, wondering how long she and Joel could be together without talking about anything important.

''Lots of new jobs.''

''All this hinges on the success of the Incline?''

''Not entirely, but good sales in that line would help keep it running.''

Eventually they wandered back to her car hand in hand, not talking much because there was an uncomfortable constraint between them.

''Want to drive?'' she asked.

''I will if you're tired,'' he said. ''But you're a good driver.''

''I'm worn out from trying to be a beauty queen. I wanted to quit, but Beth thinks it's too late. The programs have been printed. We have our spots in the talent competition. I suppose quitting now would be more conspicuous than sticking with it.''

She got in when he held the passenger door open for her, then watched him walk around to the driver's side.

"Maybe you feel you owe it to the town," he suggested.

"I wouldn't do anything to spoil the celebration."

She was thinking of the papers he had, the proof that Hiho was only ninety-nine years old. Joel needed her to be in the pageant. How far would he go to make her participate? Would he really lose his job if she dropped out?

"Based on beauty, brains and personality, all the things that count, you should win. I want you to."

She noticed he didn't say talent. Had anyone ever won a beauty contest with zero points for that?

"You have so much unrealized potential, Katy. It bothers me that you're indifferent to it. You're wasting your life in a small town like Hiho."

"I love the town! I love my job!"

"There are libraries everywhere, any one of which would be fortunate to get you."

"You're making it sound as if I'll need a new job—and I might, you know, if the Pawley Trust withholds funds until the real one-hundredth anniversary next year."

"That doesn't need to happen."

"Are you going to show anyone else the real town charter?" she asked even though the answer could devastate her.

"That's not my plan."

It might not be his intention, but what would any man do to save a really good job?

"I'm not wasting my talents in Hiho," she said.

"Aren't you ever curious about the way people live in other places?"

"I read a lot."

It wasn't a satisfactory defense for staying in the

town where she was born, but there was nothing to say that he would understand. He hated small towns. He didn't try to hide his distaste from her, even though the people of Hiho were doing everything possible to welcome him and honor his ancestor. Joel didn't understand loyalty to a place and probably never would, no matter what she said.

"Life isn't something you read about. You have to experience it," he said.

"And the way to do that is live with a couple million strangers who don't give a damn about you?"

"That's small-town mentality if I've ever heard it. Do you have any idea how closed-minded you just sounded?"

"You, of course, don't need to be open-minded because you know everything already, right?"

They drove back in stony silence. This was their first fight, and it would probably be their last and only one. There was a wall between them, an impassable chasm. She didn't really believe he'd ruin the centennial by producing the real charter, but she wouldn't give him an excuse for doing it. She was in that contest to the bitter end.

After the longest ride of her life, she asked him to pull off at the fairgrounds and get out. She wasn't going to be disqualified now. She'd like to win just so she could shove the Incline job in his face.

"Goodbye, Judge Carter."

"I'll see you at the pageant?"

"You'll definitely see me. I'll be the one dressed like a pumpkin."

SHE BURNED RUBBER when she hit the highway. Joel knew he'd goofed badly with Katy. There was so much he wanted to say to her, but instead he'd made her furious by denigrating Hiho and her reasons for staying there. He'd only wanted her to know how special she was, but his bias against small towns had made him behave like a jerk.

He trudged back to the motel, liking himself even less than small towns. Why had he brought up the centennial date? She probably thought he was trying to blackmail her into staying in the contest and saving his job. Nothing was farther from his intentions. He only wanted her to put him before her allegiance to the town.

The realization hit him like an eighteen-wheeler barreling down the highway. He was jealous of a town! He wanted Katy to be totally his, and it would never happen as long as she was married to her little niche in Hiho.

Suddenly he was bone-weary, but not from the walk back to the motel. It didn't matter whether Big Bert fired him. He'd lost his heart to a small-town girl, and he didn't care whether he salvaged his career with Vision. There were other jobs, but one thing was sure—he couldn't spend the rest of his life in Hiho. He had too many bad memories of his childhood spent trying to fit into one small town after another. If he ever had kids, he didn't want them to grow up in one.

The gray clouds gathering in the west perfectly matched his mood.

He reached the motel parking lot and remembered he'd left the windows on the Incline partly open. No point getting the upholstery soaked when it rained, as it certainly would.

He walked to the SUV and noticed with relief it wasn't adorned with more suggestive underwear. He opened the driver-side door to raise the windows and nearly put his hand in a huge pie with cherry juice bubbling up around the edges of golden-brown crust. It came with a note.

"Thank you for considering a mature woman to represent your lovely vehicle. Respectfully yours, Sadie Smithson."

He carried the pie to his room.

12

JOEL WALKED into the high school gym early on Sunday evening. Not only did he hope for a front row seat, he had to see Katy before the beauty pageant began.

Many of the closely packed folding chairs assembled in rows all the way to the back of the gym were already occupied, either by possessions people left to stake claims or early birds so eager they were willing to sit on butt-numbing metal seats until the contest began. No one had told him where the judges had to sit, so he found a single seat in the third row next to a chair reserved by a briefcase. He had a duffel with him, so he dropped it on the seat, took out the plastic laundry bag he'd found in his motel room and stuffed what he needed into it. Thus armed, he went looking for Katy.

There were exits on either side of the stage. He picked one at random, guessing they both led to the backstage area. The heavy green metal door shut itself behind him, and he looked around at a scene of pandemonium. For every potential queen, there were a dozen people doing who knows what, and they all seemed to be milling around in the area to the side and rear of the steps that led up to the stage level.

He looked around for Katy—and saw Big Bert.

"Joel, the lady with the whistle has been looking

for you. She's rounding up the judges." His boss lowered his voice to a conspiratorial whisper. "Good move getting yourself on the judging panel. I've been checking out the candidates. Our favorite's only real competition is the little blond dancer."

"I went over to Mayville to check out the plant," Joel said to change the subject because he didn't want to discuss Katy with the man who insisted she had to win.

"Later, Carter, later." Big Bert went over to glad-hand a guy Joel recognized as one of the committee members.

He didn't see Katy, but he did see more trouble between Brandi and her mother.

"I can't dance without it," Brandi heatedly argued. "My ankle has been bothering me all week."

"Darling, be reasonable," Melinda coaxed. "You don't want to spoil your routine with that unsightly brace."

"It's only a piece of elastic."

Joel walked away without waiting to hear Brandi lose another battle with her mother and nearly collided with a contestant in a purple robe. She puckered her lips, painted in a familiar bright orange-red shade, and that was one mystery cleared up.

There was one more thing he had to do, and the time was right when Sadie Smithson sashayed through the crowd carrying a cage with a cowering white bunny.

He reached into the plastic bag, took out the empty pie tin, and called out loudly, "Great pie, Sadie. I enjoyed every bite."

She tittered. Heads turned. Melinda exploded between them.

"You accepted a bribe from that aging phony?"

Melinda snatched the pie tin and turned it over to read the masking tape label on the bottom.

"Sadie S!" She practically shrieked. "Judges cannot accept favors from contestants. It's in the rules."

"It was only a pie. Delicious, too," he added for Sadie's benefit. Truthfully he hadn't had enough appetite to sample it before he wrapped it in newspaper and disposed of it.

"What's going on?" Mrs. Melbourne asked, although she'd undoubtedly heard Melinda's tirade.

"Sadie did it again! She should be disqualified."

"It was only a pie," the grandmotherly contestant said, feigning innocence.

Edna—now he remembered her first name— looked at him with disappointment.

"True, Joel?" she asked curtly.

He nodded assent.

"I'd like to kick you out of the contest," she said to Sadie, "but the rules are clear. It's the judges responsibility to refuse gifts and bribes. It's undue influence and you're out, Joel."

"Out of what?" Bert's voice boomed as he approached the knot of people.

He was trying to look casual, but his orange-flowered Hawaiian shirt, white rayon slacks and Italian loafers were more out of place than his usual business suit.

"I have to disqualify Mr. Carter as a judge because he accepted a bribe," Mrs. Melbourne said.

Joel could've made a good argument for himself. He had found it on his car seat and hadn't eaten any of it, but he'd staged this scene to get off the panel.

He couldn't vote against Katy, and he couldn't vote for her, not when winning would mean she belonged body and soul to Hiho for a year.

"Who'll take his place?" Big Bert asked, not looking at Joel.

Joel could see his job being downsized and his career fizzling like a wet firecracker, but it just didn't matter anymore.

"There's no one," Mrs. Melbourne admitted.

Even in prim navy slacks and a long-sleeved white cotton shirt, she looked as if she were unraveling. She fingered the silver whistle around her neck, and her face seemed to crumble.

"Well, it's a little out of my line," Big Bert said, "but if you're really in a spot, I could help out." He was beaming with delight.

"Consider yourself on the panel, Mr. Edson," the pageant director said.

"Just call me Big Bert. I forget to answer to that mister stuff."

Joel turned away, half of his objective realized, and came face-to-face with the most gorgeous woman in the world. For a few moments he was too awestruck to speak.

"You got yourself disqualified. You did it on purpose," Katy accused him in a husky whisper.

She was wearing a flowery aqua-and-blue robe that didn't quite come to her knees. He wondered whether she was wearing the bikini under it.

"Where can we talk?" he asked.

His disgrace had created a buzz. Too many people were watching him, including the girl with red-orange lips who looked furious enough to bite his head off. He needed to get away before she demanded her panties back, which had gone the way of the pie.

"Be serious," Katy protested. "It's a zoo back here."

"Where are the contestants getting ready?"

"The classrooms in that corridor," she said, pointing at a door to the rear of the backstage area.

"Let's check it out."

He took her arm and hustled her down a locker-lined corridor.

"Is there a door that goes outside?"

"To the right at the end, but if we go out, we can't get back in."

"Come on. I'll handle it."

"Oh, yeah, you've really been handling things well. Why did you do that thing with the pie tin?"

He grabbed her hand and sprinted toward the exit, then stepped out, catching the door with his foot before it closed after them.

"I have to go back in," she said.

"I'll hold the door so we're not locked out. This won't take long. Here." He handed her the plastic bag.

"What is it?" She took it but didn't look inside.

"The town charter, the newspapers, everything sensitive. They're yours."

She was so stunning he felt breathless. He took in all the little touches, the dramatic lines of her plucked brows, the elaborate stage makeup and her sable hair teased to perfection. Her perfume was heady stuff, and it was all he could do to keep from taking her in his arms and making a shambles of the makeover. Changing her was like gilding a lily. She didn't need improving, and she couldn't possibly be any more beautiful than she naturally was.

"I can't accept them. There's no reason to give them to me," she said.

"Take them for your peace of mind. I want you to know I would never show them to anyone but you."

"I never thought you would. You keep them."

"After the pageant..."

"I don't want them then, either, but I do want to know why you got yourself kicked off the judging panel. I didn't expect you to be biased in my favor. I don't even want to win."

"I know, but if I were still a judge, you'd get all tens."

"Yeah, right, as if I have more talent than Brandi. She lives in dance studios."

"I'd give you a top score in talent if you rode a broomstick across the stage, if you plucked a chicken, if you whistled Yankee Doodle..."

"Joel!" She laughed so hard her eyes were teary, threatening a mascara job that was totally unnecessary to enhance her baby-blues.

He carefully blotted first one eye, then the other, with his hand, not minding the dark smear on his skin.

"I'm supposed to do relaxation exercises before the pageant starts," she said.

"I hope whatever happens, it's what you want," he said softly taking her hand in his and kissing her fingertips.

"Thank you."

She pushed past him and went inside, running

down the corridor without him. He didn't try to catch up.

Joel went back to the chair with his duffel, stuffed the papers back into it and dropped the bag to the floor where he held it secure between his feet. A few minutes later Rob Pawley claimed the chair with the old-fashioned leather briefcase. He was the last person Joel wanted to sit by, but it was too late to move. Not only would it be too conspicuous, there wasn't an empty seat in the place. Latecomers were standing at the rear of the gym leaning on the cement-block wall or sitting in the aisles until the local police had to shoo them away to enforce the fire code. Hiho didn't lack enthusiasm for the pageant.

The preliminaries dragged, and Joel paid little attention to the mayor's welcome, the introduction of the judges or the other ego-stroking that went with most public events. Petey Louden was acting as master of ceremonies, but Mrs. Melbourne kept control of one podium herself. She was the one who introduced the contestants.

The swimsuit competition, make that fitness, was first.

"If Katy doesn't win this, something's wrong," Rob said. "That girl is stacked."

Joel didn't answer. He wouldn't get high marks as guest of honor after the pie-bribing scandal broke, and decking the head of the faucet-factory trust wouldn't help, either, even if it was a tempting idea.

The women came out one at a time while Mrs. Melbourne introduced them with a little background information. Each candidate's supporters had to hoot and howl before the program could proceed. Edna blew her whistle when the cheers lasted too long and kept things moving.

Joel held his breath when Katy slowly and gracefully walked on stage, made a slow stately turn, and took her place in the semicircle forming across the stage.

"I'm a butt-man myself," Pawley said, sharing confidences without any encouragement from Joel. "Look at that backside on Katy. Pretty luscious. Not many girls can wear a thong without looking lumpy."

Shut up about Katy or I'll be forced to mop the gym with your scrawny carcass, Joel thought sourly.

Of the sixteen candidates, only three were as tall as Katy. One had skinny legs, and the other didn't quite fill the top of her suit. Some of the other girls were cute and curvy, but there was only one winner in his eyes.

Mrs. Melbourne ran the contest like an Olympic competition. After all hopefuls came out, the judges marked their score sheets and handed them to a runner. A couple of eager girls too young to be in the contest posted the scores on a green chalkboard at the side of the stage. The audience could see but the contestants couldn't, probably on the theory that a bad score would discourage the person in the next segment. Of course, all over the gym, supporters were holding up fingers to flash point counts at their favorites.

Katy got all tens, one from each of the three judges who were sitting at a table in front facing the stage so they had the best view of the proceedings. Brandi received the same score, and two others lacked only one point of a perfect rating. Thankfully, the judges weren't being harsh.

Joel spotted Beth and her family in the bleachers. Mrs. Melbourne had wisely banned all coaches and supporters from the backstage area during the contest, relying on committee members to help with clothing changes. One of the twins was trying to climb down under the seats, a drop of maybe eight or nine feet, and the other conscientiously clapped as each score was posted.

Joel was nervous, not knowing whether to hope Katy would win. He wanted what she wanted, but he didn't see how anyone could not pick her as the winner. It had to be devastating for a woman to stand in front of a mob and be judged like horseflesh, but she was a class act and didn't seem at all rattled.

The contestants left the stage using the runway-walk they'd been taught. The only one who didn't look stiff was Brandi. Her contest experience made a difference, but Katy had natural poise when she wasn't trying to strut in that artificial way.

The fitness segment was over. Next came talent, then evening gowns and the final question. There was no space on the board to score the question. Apparently the judges would hold back those scores to make crowning the winner more dramatic.

Joel thought the talent presentations would last forever. Sadie lost the rabbit on her first magic trick and got more laughs than points for her flowers-up-the-sleeve bit.

By the time Katy's turn came, his breakfast bagel had turned to concrete in his stomach. Rob, sitting beside him in the aisle seat, allowed no act to pass without his caustic comments. Joel didn't even bother grunting when Rob described a nervous young singer as a sow in heat. The lawyer couldn't possibly be this jerky around Katy. This must be his idea of man-talk, but Joel thought he was an egotistical idiot who tried to sound clever and sophisticated by knocking other people. Joel had met more than a few like him, and not just in small towns.

At last everyone but Katy and Brandi had performed with uniformly low scores. Apparently talent was going to be the make-or-break segment.

Mrs. Melbourne looked at the notes in front of her and paused as though she couldn't read what was written.

"Next on the program is Katy Sloane," she said slowly. "I'm not quite sure what her talent is, but the title is, Put Me Here, Put Me There, Put Me Gently If You Care."

Katy ran on stage pushing a dolly with a bookcase and a stack of books on it. She positioned it sideways so she was standing in profile to the audience as she faced it.

She deserved a ten for costume alone, skimpy red shorts, a sleeveless white blouse with a blue sailor's collar and a little white navy hat.

"Now, boys and girls—and big people, too— here's how we put our friends on the shelf so we can always, always find them."

She snatched a book from the pile, did a little high-stepping dance step, and held it high above her head.

"Do we drop it?"

"No!" A chorus of little voices came from the audience.

"Do we scribble on it?"

"No, no!" Even a few adults joined in.

"Do we ever tear a page?"

"No, no, no!" The whole audience got into the swing of it.

She started shelving books, whipping them off the dolly with the grace of a juggler keeping balls in the air, all the while doing a little ditty in a singsong voice.

"Dr. Seuss doesn't go by Mother Goose. *The Bad Cat* goes before *The Cat in the Hat. A* before *B, B* before *C,* and so on and so on until you get to *Z.* And here we are with my favorite still, the *Little Blue Engine* that chugs up the hill."

She'd done it! Katy had taken what she did best and turned it into performance art! Joel stood and clapped wildly, and he wasn't alone. She got a standing ovation. He wasn't sure how she'd done it, but the town loved the act and loved her. She pushed the stacked bookcase offstage and got called back for three more bows.

Edna had to blow her whistle to cut off the applause, and the judges didn't hesitate to hand over the scores.

Katy had a boardful of tens, not a single glitch. But Brandi did, too, so far the only other contestant with a perfect score. She was the last to show her talent, but there wasn't much doubt she'd get high marks. Then it would all come down to the evening gown segment and the question.

Joel had to gulp air. His future and his happiness were at stake, and he didn't know how things would play out.

"Nothing like ballet to show what a girl's made of," Rob said with a leer in his voice.

"Shut up, shut up, shut up," Joel mouthed silently, but Rob wasn't one to gauge other people's reactions.

Joel knew virtually noting about ballet, but Brandi came onstage looking like a professional. Her taste must have prevailed over her mother's because she was wearing a swirly white costume, no ruffles or frills. She warmed up with a some subdued movements, did some graceful steps, then dashed around the small stage and went into a leap—

And fell.

She cried out and crumpled into a heap. The audience gave one big collective gasp, and Melinda sprinted up the steps to the stage and helped her red-faced, angry daughter limp off.

"I told you I needed an ankle brace," Brandi accused her mother.

Petey Louden declared the talent portion of the program finished on the opposite side of the stage from Mrs. Melbourne, who hustled after Brandi, probably with first aid in mind.

"Now for the part you've all been waiting for," he said. "Our lovely ladies will return in their evening gowns and answer a question drawn at random from this bowl."

Petey pointed at a young girl who'd materialized from backstage, but the audience was more interested in what was happening at the judge's table. Big Bert himself stood up and addressed the audience, no mike needed. When his voice boomed, it rattled the rafters.

"Ladies and gentlemen, the judges have decided to award Brandi Rankin a collective score of eighteen even though she was unable to finish her presentation. That's six points from each judge for her dramatic beginning, costuming and obvious talent.''

The audience applauded politely. The town might be proud of Brandi's talent, but she didn't seem to have a large cheering section.

The scoring was fair both to Brandi and to the other contestants, although most got scores of threes and fours. Brandi had no chance of winning unless Katy goofed badly, but she was still a contender for first runner-up. The contestants who'd done well in their swimsuits had tanked in the talent segment, earning scores as low as two. Katy had soared ahead of the pack, but Joel knew, she wouldn't be happy winning because Brandi was injured and couldn't complete her act.

Petey killed time with corny jokes, then the contestants filed out in their long evening gowns. Joel had to admit they all looked beautiful, even Sadie who'd wisely muted her hair color and chosen a pale blue dress with long sleeves.

Katy took his breath away. He smiled broadly at the gown hugging her like a second skin. Her vibrant pumpkin-orange dress stood out like a highway flagman's vest in the sea of pastels, but she was a total and complete knockout.

He hardly listened as a parade of contestants gave pat answers about world peace, the environment and the need for a new sewer system on the west side, the latter coming from Sadie in answer to a community-needs question.

Brandi managed to limp up to the mike and give a poised, very acceptable answer. Katy followed her.

''Katy, what is the most important thing you have to offer the town of Hiho?'' Petey asked.

Joel had long ago gotten over public-speaking jitters, but he was a nervous wreck for Katy's sake. He suffered for nothing. She answered in a clear, melodious voice without a moment's hesitation.

"Kindness. Most of us never have an opportunity to make big, important contributions, but everyone can make life a little better by showing courtesy, consideration and kindness to others."

The town loved her answer, they loved her, and the judges had to love her. More importantly, Joel loved her. He'd probably loved her since the minute she'd conked heads with him.

The decision came quickly, handed to the master of ceremonies by one of the scorekeepers. One by one the four runners-up were called until Katy was left standing alone, the winner of the beauty pageant.

Joel's eyes were damp when she stepped up and received an armload of red roses and a delicate gold crown from Petey.

"Ladies and gentlemen, may I present Miss Hiho, Katy Sloane. She'll preside over the centennial festivities next week, serve as Miss Hiho for one year and be eligible to participate in the Miss Ohio contest."

Katy wasn't crying. Beauty contest winners always bawled, but she was dry-eyed and wearing only a tentative little grin. Brandi, the runner-up, hugged her, and Katy whispered something that brought a weak smile to the little blonde's face.

Big Bert ambled up to the podium, obviously confident he was the one handing out the most important prize. He gave Katy a big hug over the top of her bouquet, then took the mike away from the red-faced, perspiring master of ceremonies.

"Congratulations to all you lovely ladies and to Katy Sloane, Miss Hiho. As you know, one little perk of winning this honor is that Vision Motors is offering you a one-year contract to represent our new model, the Incline. Katy, we'd be honored to add Miss Incline to your other title."

Katy's mouth was open, but she didn't look overwhelmed with joy. Would she tell Big Bert what to do with his butt-ugly vehicle?

Joel knew his moment had come. He stood up.

"There may be one little problem," he said in a voice loud enough to quiet the audience.

"What's that, Joel?" his boss asked, a scowl on his face.

Big Bert did not like problems.

"The rules stipulate that Miss Hiho must be single during her reign. I have reason to hope Katy will be a married woman soon."

"Just a minute," Rob said. "I know we've been keeping company for a while, but I'm not quite ready to..."

"Sit down and shut up," Joel said with as much restraint as possible in the circumstances.

Rob sat and shut up.

"Do you mean that?" Katy asked.

She gave him the radiant winner's smile she'd been holding back.

"I do." The audience was so quiet he could whisper and be heard, but he spoke loudly and firmly. "I love you, Katy Sloane."

"Whoopee!" she shrieked.

She thrust the huge bouquet into Brandi's arms, snatched off the crown and planted it on the little dancer's blond curls, lifted her skirt and catapulted down the steps to the gym floor.

Joel remembered to hoist the duffel to his shoulder, climbed over Rob's legs to the aisle and opened his arms. Katy bounded into them, and their lips collided. He hardly heard the collective sigh of approval from the audience.

They raced hand in hand for the door at the back of the gym and didn't stop until they were outside in the hot sunlight, kissing as though they could meld together.

"You mean it?" she gasped.

"Oh, yes."

"I never thought you were the marrying type."

"I wasn't until I met you. You're sure you don't want to go back and claim your crown? You haven't known me very long."

"Do you have deep dark secrets I should know?"

"Well, maybe one," he admitted. "I'm probably out of a job. Big Bert wanted you as the spokesperson."

"But I want you! I love you! Do you really love me?"

"I love you!"

It took a few more kisses to convince her.

"I'll live anywhere with you," she said, hugging him so hard he wanted to be anywhere but in front of a high school where the whole town would soon swarm out.

Over his shoulder he saw the first person emerge from the building.

Big Bert.

"I'll save you time," Joel said. "I resign."

"Why would you do that?" Big Bert screwed up his beefy face in puzzlement.

"So you don't have to fire me."

"Hell's bells, why would I want to do that?"

If he didn't know, Joel wasn't going to give him an itemized list.

"I came out to congratulate the two of you," his boss said.

"But, you wanted Katy as Miss Hiho." Now Joel was the one who was puzzled.

"The little blonde will do fine. I know how to handle her momma."

Joel wasn't often speechless. He was now.

"When you get the time," Big Bert said, "we'll talk about moving your department to Mayville. Eventually I want the whole operation there."

"To Mayville." One short week ago he would've been depressed by that news. Now he wanted to jump for joy, click his heels and make love with the woman he adored beyond reason.

Big Bert left them and went back into the building.

"Mayville," Joel said again.

"Are you upset? Did you think we'd be living in Cleveland?" Katy asked with a worry line creasing her smooth, flawless brow.

"No, I couldn't be happier! We'll live midway between Hiho and Mayville, maybe in the country. You won't have to quit your job. I'll be a gentleman farmer in my spare time."

"But you love big cities. You hate small-town life."

"That was Carter-Not-Hump. I love Hiho. It brought you to me."

"My sister will say no one should get engaged

after one week. She's probably on her cell phone now trying to get my parents to fly here."

"Time isn't everything. This is the tenth day we've known each other, and I've loved you my whole life. I just hadn't met you yet."

He swept her into his arms in spite of the duffel bumping against his back and carried her to the Incline while she whispered wonderful words in his ear.

After they were settled on the seats, the motor started on the first try. Today that was what counted.

"I could learn to love this vehicle," she said, cuddling against his arm. "Your motel room or my place?"

"Let's see where the Incline takes us."

NO POSTAGE
NECESSARY
IF MAILED
IN THE
UNITED STATES

BUSINESS REPLY MAIL
FIRST-CLASS MAIL   PERMIT NO. 717-003   BUFFALO, NY

POSTAGE WILL BE PAID BY ADDRESSEE

HARLEQUIN READER SERVICE
3010 WALDEN AVE
PO BOX 1867
BUFFALO NY 14240-9952

If offer card is missing write to: Harlequin Reader Service, 3010 Walden Ave., P.O. Box 1867, Buffalo NY 14240-1867

Get FREE BOOKS and a FREE GIFT when you play the...

LAS VEGAS GAME

Just scratch off the gold box with a coin. Then check below to see the gifts you get! →

YES! I have scratched off the gold Box. Please send me my **2 FREE BOOKS** and **gift for which I qualify**. I understand that I am under no obligation to purchase any books as explained on the back of this card.

311 HDL DUYR

111 HDL DUY7

FIRST NAME

LAST NAME

ADDRESS

APT.#

CITY

STATE/PROV.

ZIP/POSTAL CODE

(H-D-05/03)

7	7	7	Worth TWO FREE BOOKS plus a BONUS Mystery Gift!
🍒	🍒	🍒	Worth TWO FREE BOOKS!
🔔	🔔	♣	TRY AGAIN!

Visit us online at www.eHarlequin.com

Offer limited to one per household and not valid to current Harlequin Duets™ subscribers. All orders subject to approval.

The 100-Year Itch

Holly Jacobs

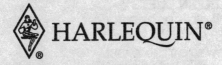

HARLEQUIN®

TORONTO • NEW YORK • LONDON
AMSTERDAM • PARIS • SYDNEY • HAMBURG
STOCKHOLM • ATHENS • TOKYO • MILAN • MADRID
PRAGUE • WARSAW • BUDAPEST • AUCKLAND

Dear Reader,

I have this friend Pam. She shares my joys and is
always there if I need a shoulder. Pam's only flaw
is she doesn't share well. I keep trying to steal her
mom, Barbara, but for some reason Pam just won't
let me have her. I guess it would be a shame to break
up their writing team, because I've been a fan of
Jennifer Drew's work for so long.

That long-abiding appreciation of their work is
one of the reasons I was so excited to be asked to
write part of this 100th volume of Duets. Working
with Pam and Barbara was so much fun, and writing
about Hiho, Ohio's centennial-that-wasn't was a blast!
This is my first book for the line that's set outside my
hometown of Erie, Pennsylvania, but since I did bring
the hero to Hiho from Erie, I hope my fellow Erie-ites
won't mind. And when we set the book in Hiho,
Ohio, none of us realized that 2003 was really Ohio's
bicentennial. Happy bicentennial to my neighboring
state, Ohio, and happy birthday, Duets!

Holly Jacobs

P.S. I love hearing from readers. You can contact me at
www.HollysBooks.com, or snail-mail me at P.O. Box
11102, Erie, PA 16514-1102.

Books by Holly Jacobs

HARLEQUIN DUETS

43—I WAXED MY LEGS FOR *THIS?*
67—READY, WILLING AND...ABEL?
    RAISING CAIN
84—HOW TO CATCH A GROOM
92—NOT PRECISELY PREGNANT

SILHOUETTE ROMANCE

1557—DO YOU HEAR WHAT I HEAR?
1653—A DAY LATE AND A BRIDE SHORT

To Pam Hanson and Barbara Andrews, aka Jennifer Drew,
two of the loveliest ladies around!
And to Kathryn Lye—
thanks for this wonderful opportunity! You're the best!

1

"Hiho, Ohio, a quiet, lovely town. Hiho, Ohio, where no one wears a frown...."

Zoe Wallace grimaced.

The fact that Hiho, Ohio's name made comedians within a hundred-mile radius happy was one thing. But the fact that the official town song was enough to make dogs howl was another thing. A terrible thing.

The song was horrible. Worse than nails on a chalkboard.

Oh, the singers were enthusiastic and even close to being on key, but even Pavarotti would be hard-pressed to make this particular song sound good. As a matter of fact, the only way it did sound good was when it wasn't being played.

Zoe had yet to meet a townsperson who liked the song, and she had yet to meet one who wouldn't defend it, or the town's name, to any outsider who dared mock them.

Zoe realized the chorus was silent and watching her expectantly. As chairperson of Hiho's Centennial Celebration it was her duty to encourage the chorus. She forced a smile and clapped. "Excellent. Just excellent, everyone."

The director beamed. "And from there, we thought we'd sing a birthday song. After all, it's not every day your town turns one hundred."

The chorus started singing again and a voice behind her said, "*Psst,* Zoe."

She turned and saw Bertram Barky hiding in the shadows behind one of the auditorium's columns.

Bertram used to work for her aunt at Hiho's weekly newspaper, *The Herald.* At seventy-something, he had long since retired, but he still liked to pass on juicy tidbits to Zoe, whom he'd adopted as a surrogate granddaughter when she took over the paper.

Oh, sometimes those tidbits were more gossip than news, but they were always interesting.

She smiled. "Hey, Bertram. What's up?"

"Shh," he said, a finger pressed against his lips. "Come with me. We can't talk here. Someone might overhear us."

"But I'm in the middle—"

"It's important. The biggest scandal to rock Hiho since Tabitha Carter from the bar ran off with Pastor Mitch." Bertram was pulling at her arm. "Come on."

Zoe gave the chorus a wave, not interrupting their singing, and allowed Bertram to pull her out of the Middle School auditorium into the bright May sunshine.

"Now, what is it?" she asked when the big door to the auditorium slammed shut behind them.

"Not here, someone may see us. They'll try to stop me. They don't want me talking to you or anyone from out of town. Come on."

Bertram often had tips, but he'd never played this cloak-and-dagger kind of game before.

Not knowing what else to do, Zoe followed him into the alley at the side of the building. "Okay, spill it."

"It's all a lie," Bertram said, excitement evident in his voice.

"A lie? What's a lie?"

"The whole thing. The centennial."

Zoe shook her head. "I'm not following you."

"Hiho, Ohio, isn't one hundred years old this month."

"It's not?"

"No."

He waited, and finally Zoe asked, "So how old is it?"

"Ninety-nine."

"Are you sure? Everything I've read indicates that the town is one hundred this year. Hiram and Hortense Hump filed the papers early in 1903. It was official May 1903. It's on our charter."

"But what you haven't heard is that something

went wrong." He pulled a small notebook out of his pocket and consulted it. "Hiram told the town the paperwork was approved, but really, they had to refile everything and the town wasn't official until February of 1904."

"Well, that's interesting, but still I don't think it warrants this spy treatment."

"Don't you see?" he asked. "They want to keep it quiet."

"Who is *they?*"

"They. The mayor, the chamber of commerce…everyone. You have to break the story in the *Herald.*"

"This is just hearsay, Bertram. You know that. That fire fifty years ago destroyed almost all the official documents. The town's charter says May 1903. So, as far as anyone is concerned, 1903 it is."

Bertram looked as if he was going to argue, but Zoe held up her hand. "Let's say you're right. Let's say it really was 1904, not 1903. It's just not that big of a deal. I mean, if we'd known, I'm sure we'd have put off the Centennial Celebration until next year, but still—"

"It is a big deal if we want that endowment from the Pawley Family Trust. The terms were it was to be awarded to the college and the library *on our centennial.* If it's not our centennial, they'll pull it and the college has already broken ground on the new building. It's borrowed against that money. But the news is the news. Tell me you're not going to let them cover this up. This is big, Zoe. I held the proof in my hand. A letter from the newspaper's archive, but they took it and *lost* it and—''

''Uncle Bertram, there you are,'' Pete Matthews, Bertram's nephew, said as he headed down the alley. ''Alice has had me looking for you for almost half an hour.''

''See, they're trying to keep me away from reporters, even you,'' Bertram whispered to Zoe as Pete approached.

''Come on, Bertram, it's time to go home. Alice has dinner waiting on you.''

He practically pulled Bertram out of the alley and down the street.

''Pete, wait a minute, I'd like to ask you some questions—''

''Later, okay, Zoe? I've got to run. You know Alice, if I don't get back she'll have my hide.''

Zoe did know Alice Matthews, and Pete was right, she ran their restaurant and their family with an iron fist...tempered by a loving heart and some of the best food in the state.

''I'll catch you later then, Pete,'' Zoe said.

''Zoe, don't you forget what I said. The truth is out there,'' Bertram called as Pete practically dragged him down the street.

Zoe felt an old familiar burning in her stomach. When she first started working in New York she thought the sensation was the mark of a good reporter who sensed a story.

Now she knew it was an old ulcer flaring up, something that rarely happened since she moved to Hiho.

She didn't want a big story—didn't want a scandal. She'd like to sweep the centennial issue under the rug and ignore it, but she couldn't just let it lie. She'd have to check this whole thing out. It would be like having an elephant under a carpet—as much as she tried to ignore it, she'd know it was there, wiggling just beneath the surface.

Great. Another item on her list of things to do.

As coordinator of the Centennial Celebration, the list was already long and only getting longer. The first events started in a week and there were still hundreds of details to attend to.

Zoe pulled out her list and scribbled *Bertram* at the bottom.

As she wrote it down, she saw what headed her list for tomorrow and groaned. There, in black and white it said, *Thelma Jean.*

Oh, how could she have forgotten? Probably a mental block. She'd promised Thelma Jean from the Snip and Clip she'd get made over.

Not that she wanted to get made over. She sort

of liked her look as it was. Easy to maintain. Comfortable.

But Thelma Jean was giving away a makeover as a prize at the Centennial Celebration and wanted to take some digital photos of Zoe's before and after, then distribute them at the festival in a flyer.

Zoe had felt as if she had to say yes. But she had a feeling she wasn't going to like it.

Not like it at all.

"...AND THIS IS Mace Mason, here at WMAC News, where nice news matters."

Theodore Mason—Mace to his friends and fans—felt as if he were practically shouting. It was hard, even with a microphone, to be heard over the wails of the baby he was holding.

"And cut," the cameraman said.

As if he were playing the childhood game, hot potato, Mace handed the crying infant to its anxious mom and put down the mike.

He turned to the cameraman, "I think that's a wrap."

"Great story, Mace," Kip said.

Mace didn't even bother to answer the man. Not that he didn't like Kip, but *Great story, Mace?*

The story was sap.

Pure sentimental drivel.

Mother of triplets at home with a second unexpected batch of triplets...that wasn't news. His assignment editor wanted to use it for a Mother's Day tribute. "A Montage of Moms," she was calling it.

She thought it was a great idea.

Mace thought it was dreck. Pure and simple drivel.

He was a reporter. Not that anyone would know it from the stories he covered for WMAC. How was he ever going to jump to a bigger, harder-hitting station if they kept giving him these fluff pieces?

He made quick work of the drive back across Erie, Pennsylvania, to the office, ready to head to his small cubbyhole of a cubicle, when Stephanie Cooper, his assignment editor, snagged him.

"Mace, come on back here," she called.

Mace reluctantly headed into her much-larger-than-a-cubbyhole office.

"Sit down, Mace."

He'd have preferred standing so he could make a quick getaway, but he sat. Stephanie was the boss. Despite the fact that the station's hallmark motto was her idea, Mace liked her...most of the time.

Today, after spending almost an hour with triplet infants and their triplet toddler siblings, wasn't one of those times.

"I have a new assignment for you," she said happily.

Too happily.

Mace was suspicious whenever an editor seemed this pleased with an assignment.

"I still have to edit that triplet piece," he said cautiously.

She waved the comment aside. "You'll have time. I want you to leave tomorrow on assignment."

"You're sending me out of town?" Hope surged to life.

He'd always dreamed of going out on assignment. Foreign countries, world hot spots. He wasn't talking about a quick trip to Edinboro, but something out of state.

The short-lived hope popped like a bubble. Somehow he didn't think foreign locales was what Stephanie had in mind.

"I've got a new idea for *Erie Chronicles*," she continued.

Chronicles was Mace's baby. Mini-documentaries on the town's rich history. He'd found that digging into local legends and personalities fascinated him. So far he'd done eight half-hour episodes and hoped to do more. It was his favorite part of the job. *Chronicles* was the reason he was still here at WMAC.

They tied clips from the show into the news

program and the viewers' and, more importantly, advertisers' response had been good.

"And the idea is?" he asked, cautiously.

"Hiram Hump."

"Pardon me?"

"He was cursed with a horrible name, but went on to do great things. He wrote *Erie, A History* back in 1896, before moving. That book is considered a priceless jewel of our city's history. There's a first edition at the library on display. They even have a statue of him. Hiram moved to, and founded, Hiho, Ohio, which gives us a bond to the town. This is their centennial. I want you to cover it. Collect some bits on Hiram's years in Ohio, and cover their centennial celebration. We'll use some pieces on the news now, and use the others for the next *Chronicles.* Spend the week and relax. Think of it as combining work with a small vacation."

"What do you mean by relax?"

"I mean, you're tense and irritable. Everyone at the station's noticed." Stephanie sighed. "Mace, you're a great reporter. You have a great eye for gathering unrelated bits of information and putting the pieces together in a relatable way, which is why your *Chronicles* series has taken off. We're lucky to have you. But you're not happy. I don't know if it's the job or something personal, but you need to fix it. Your attitude is interfering with your work.''

"I'm a professional. Nothing interferes with my work," he said between gritted teeth.

"You're terse with the staff and they've noticed. I've had complaints.''

Granted, he wasn't as sunny as *Pollyanna* Paige Montgomery, who gave the term *chipper* a new standard to live up to. Her terminal good mood was even worse since her marriage.

He might not be Pollyanna Paige, but he wasn't mean. No, not mean. Terse. That's what Stephanie said.

"Who says I'm terse?" he asked.

"It doesn't matter. What matters is you're going to cover the Hiho centennial. You leave tomorrow and will be there for the entire week, right through the firework finale.''

He was going to find out who thought he was terse. Not that he'd do anything to them. No, he wouldn't do anything except kill them with sweetness. He'd be so sappy and gooey with it that even Paige would look *terse* next to him. And his target would probably overdose on pleasantness.

Visions of vengeful niceness danced through his head as he asked, "Are you sending a cameraman?''

"No. You'll do your own camera work.''

This wouldn't be the first time he'd done his

own camera work. Mace prided himself at being a jack-of-all-trades. He shot a lot of his own footage for *Chronicles*.

"And while you're putting together this piece," Stephanie said, her voice serious, "I want you to think about what it is you want. You're valued here, but I don't know if WMAC is where you want to be. You have options."

"I—"

"We'll talk when you get back," she said, the conversation obviously over.

Mace left the office. He was going to Hiho, Ohio.

What a horrible name for a town.

He had a feeling this was going to be the longest week ever.

MACE MENTALLY REVIEWED his notes as he pulled up in front of The General Store on Main Street, Hiho, Ohio, late the next morning.

Hiho, Ohio. Population 15,000. Named after *Hi*ram and his wife *Ho*rtense.

Hiho.

Mace had a small notebook of facts he'd pulled together before he'd even left Erie. He wasn't sure he liked a man who was so vain he'd name his town Hiho just to immortalize his name.

Of course, good ol' Hiram could have named it Humpsville.

That would be worse…much worse.

A small town in the middle of nowhere, celebrating its centennial.

When Mace dreamed about being a reporter, he dreamed about busting drug rings, reporting on mob activity. And here he was covering a small town's centennial, and doing a documentary on a man named Hiram Hump who wrote an obscure, yet acclaimed, book of history. He was working at a station that didn't want hard-hitting stories. No, they wanted the nice news—it mattered.

Mace sighed. Maybe Stephanie was right. Maybe it was time to move on.

But first he had a story to report. It might not be a story he particularly wanted to tell, but Mace was professional enough to finish what he started.

He was supposed to meet his contact, Zoe Wallace, here in The General Store. The two-story building had a huge wooden porch, lined with rocking chairs. It was pretty much the center of Main Street.

Main Street. Not an overly creative name.

Neither was The General Store.

But Mace guessed if you lived in a community called Hiho, you probably wanted to keep everything else as simple as possible.

He glanced at his watch. Eleven-thirty. Right on time. He prided himself on being punctual and professional.

He got out of the car and went into the store. A bell rang as he pushed open the door.

It was like stepping back in time.

A huge fireplace. Checkerboards, one with two older men playing a game. They didn't even look up as he came in.

More rocking chairs. And stuff. Lots and lots of stuff on shelves. Touristy looking stuff. Jars. Candles. Quilts.

A tall, blond woman stood behind a counter, an old-fashioned cash register between her and Mace. She smiled and asked, "Can I help you?"

"I'm supposed to meet Zoe Wallace here."

"Oh, you're just in time, which will annoy her. She was hoping you'd be late. Let me tell her you're here."

Why would this Zoe want him to be late?

The woman went to a door just beyond the counter and called, "Zoe, your appointment is out here. Best not keep him waiting."

A moment later, a woman emerged from a back room. He assumed it was Zoe Wallace and he suppressed a groan. It took every ounce of professionalism that Mace possessed to keep a straight face. She looked like… Well, he didn't even have a frame of reference.

Her hair was big and he didn't need to be a hairstylist to know it was about twenty years out of style.

And her makeup...

Mace might know less about makeup than he did about hairstyles, but he knew that slashes of blue over eyelids were no longer considered eye shadow. And the garish shade of red on her lips would look right at home on any hooker.

But worse than the makeup or hair, it appeared she'd tried to put on fake eyelashes, and one was drooping at the edge. He couldn't believe it wasn't making her crazy, tickling her eyeball as it wiggled with every blink of her eye.

Mace never noticed how much a person blinked, but either most people blinked a lot, or this Zoe was a compulsive blinker, but either way, the eyelash wiggled way too much.

"Um, Zoe Wallace?" he said, proud at how his voice never wavered.

She nodded, which caused the eyelash to jiggle even more.

Mace watched it, waiting for it to fall off completely, but her head stopped bobbling before it did.

"Theodore Mason?" Her voice was low and cultured. It didn't seem to fit with her outward appearance. "Do people call you Ted?"

"No...ah, they call me Mace."

"Mace Mason. It does have a ring. I'm just plain old Zoe." She thrust out a hand.

He didn't have the heart to tell her there was

nothing plain about her. So, he simply took her hand in his and shook it. She had a warm, firm grip, but that eyelash wobbled as they shook. It was going to fall off. He was sure of it.

Forcing himself to ignore the eyelash, Mace said, "Nice to meet you, Zoe. I appreciate your taking the time to show me around the town."

He might be able to keep from laughing at her eyelash, but he wasn't sure he could keep the humor out of his voice when he said the town's name, so he planned to avoid saying the word *Hiho* at all costs.

"Your boss said you'd be spending most of the week tailing me, getting a feel for the town and some background on Hiram Hump."

She stared at him a moment, as if waiting for something, then suddenly she burst out laughing.

"Miss Wallace?" Mace said, not sure what she found so amusing.

"Call me Zoe," she gasped as she continued laughing. The woman behind the counter was laughing as well.

Darn. Did he have something stuck in his teeth? He ran his tongue over them, but didn't feel anything.

A hole in the seat of his pants?

No, Zoe was in front of him and wouldn't have seen it.

The women were both still laughing, one feeding off the other.

Oh, no. Was his fly unzipped?

Mace couldn't think of a circumspect way to check, so he glanced down.

Nope. The hatch was battened down.

"Is something wrong?" he finally asked.

Maybe the people in the town were as crazy as its name. That would be just like Steph to send him into the midst of an asylum.

"Oh, no," Zoe said, taking a deep breath and finally calming down. "I just have to say, you've impressed me in the first few seconds of meeting you, Mace. This should be an interesting week."

Impressed was better than amused, but still he didn't understand. "Impressed you how?"

"You didn't laugh."

She grinned at him, as if not laughing was some huge accomplishment. "You didn't crack a smile, even. Clover—this is Clover Addison, by the way—and I had a bet at how long you could go without laughing, and I won. I said you were a professional and that you wouldn't laugh. And you didn't. Guess I'll have to spend my winnings buying you dinner."

"I still don't think I understand," Mace said.

"This," she said, waving at her hair and face. "You're the first person who's seen my *new look* and not laughed."

"You mean, this isn't your normal look?"

"Oh, I think I'm going to like you, Mace Mason. I think I'm going to like you just fine. If you don't mind a quick trip to my house before we get started so I can unmake the makeover, I'd appreciate it."

"Sure," he said, not sure what else he could say.

"Come on." She held her hand out to Clover who slapped a ten-dollar bill into it.

"Come back in anytime, Mace. It was a pleasure to meet a real gentleman." Clover shot a look at the men at the checkerboard and Mace assumed the comment was for their benefit.

"I might as well start your tour as we walk down Main Street," Zoe said. "I live two blocks from here."

She started down the street, still talking, and Mace followed.

Her makeover might be atrocious, but his view as he followed her was fine.

Mace gave his head a little shake. The last thing he needed was to be attracted to a small-town girl. He preferred his women a bit more sophisticated.

He caught up with Zoe, and walked right next to her.

She smiled at him and said, "Hiho, Ohio, was founded by Hiram and Hortense Hump. The name came from the first two letters in their respective first names.''

She must have seen him grimace, because she added, ''Here in Hiho we say it could have been worse. It could have been—''

''Humpsville,'' he supplied.

She laughed again. ''Right. Anyway, the town was incorporated in 1903. Our two biggest employers are Cloverleaf College and the Pawley Faucet Factory. We have—''

''Zoe,'' two voices cried in unison behind them.

She stopped and turned, and Mace followed suit. Two older women took one look at her and both cracked up.

''See what I mean,'' Zoe said. ''That's been the normal response to my makeover, which is why you impressed me so much. Mace Mason, let me introduce Ida and Cora MacIntosh. Two pillars of our community.''

She turned back to the women. ''Ladies, what can I do for you today?''

''Tom Walters,'' Ida said.

''What about Tom?'' Zoe asked.

''You have him scheduled to judge the pie contest in the festival,'' Cora said.

''And the problem is?''

''He doesn't have any teeth. Cora and I are known for our apple pies, and they have walnuts in them. How on earth is Tom supposed to judge something like that fairly? He'll be predisposed to like the cream pies. And you know Betty is entering her chocolate-caramel pie. It's stiff competition in its own right, but with a toothless judge? We don't stand a chance."

"Ladies," Zoe said, in a voice designed to soothe. "I'll see to it that Tom wears his false teeth for the competition."

"But he hates them," Ida practically wailed.

"Regardless, if he wants to be a judge, he has to wear them."

"And if he won't?" Cora asked.

"Then I'll find a replacement."

"Fine. We trust you to see that the competition is fair, Zoe."

"I'll do my best, ladies. Now, if you don't mind, I think I need to turn back the hands of time and return to my usual self. Only don't tell Thelma Jean, okay?"

"Oh, we'd never hurt the old dear's feelings," Cora said.

"Thanks."

Mace grimaced as he listened to the ladies' emergency. A pie-judging scandal? He could just see the headlines now: The Great Pie Dilemma.

Nice news?

This didn't even qualify as drivel.

How on earth was he going to survive a whole week of this?

2

"THIS ISN'T WHAT I EXPECTED," Mace murmured when he walked in her living room.

Zoe looked around the room, trying to decide just what he didn't expect about it. It wasn't as if there was anything that unusual about what the room contained. There was a couch, a couple of chairs, bookshelves and a TV. Nothing special or out of the ordinary.

Okay, so the room was done completely in shades of white. White walls, furniture, carpeting. Some people thought white was just one color, but there were shades and nuances. She wanted this room to emphasize that.

Everything was white except the arrangement of lilacs on the table. Deep and purple, they stood out in the room, giving it a focus. Fresh flowers were her one indulgence.

"Are you surprised in a good way, or not?" she asked.

He shrugged. "Just surprised."

"What did you expect?"

He shrugged again. "Something more...well, more country-ish I guess."

"Ah, you expected Aunt Bea to be cooking in the kitchen baking cookies...she'd be wearing an apron, and would decorate with lots and lots of gingham, eh?"

Another shrug. Zoe was ready to staple down his shoulders if he did it again. She wondered if he was shrugging as a gesture or maybe he had some kind of nervous tick.

She shrugged back at him, wondering if he'd notice she was mocking him.

He didn't seem to.

Men could be so dense. Even men who were reporters.

Since he didn't notice her mockery she settled for saying, "Sorry to disappoint."

She thought about trying to explain the effect she was going for, but decided against it. After all, she didn't care what Mace thought.

Instead she said, "Make yourself at home while I go change."

Aunt Bea indeed.

She walked through the dining room and into her bedroom, shutting her door with a little more force than it required.

She could have told Mace Mason that it wasn't all that long ago that she was living in a trendy section of Greenwich Village, working at a New York paper.

She could have told him about the people she'd met, the hard-hitting stories she'd broken…and the world-class ulcer she'd developed.

She unmade her over-made makeover as quickly as possible. She pulled her big hair into a ponytail, pulled off the fake eyelashes and washed her face three times before she felt like herself again.

Feeling a hundred percent better, she went back out to her shoulder-shrugging guest.

He might be a big-city snob, but she was going to forgive his attitude because he hadn't laughed at her makeover.

He hadn't even cracked a smile.

So what if his surprise at her modern decor bordered on insulting? Maybe he didn't like modern decor and hadn't meant to be offensive at all. Maybe it had nothing to do with a big-city sense of superiority.

She pasted a smile on her well-washed face and went back into the living room. He was staring out the front bay window, a cell phone at his ear. "…I can't stay the whole week. So far the biggest story I've got is the pie-judging scandal."

He paused.

"You heard me. Some old guy with dentures judging—" He stopped abruptly and said, "Listen, Stephanie, it doesn't matter. What does matter is you have to get me out of here. I'll stay the next couple days, get some footage then come home.''

Another pause.

''I don't need to relax…. Don't you tell me I'm terse. If I am it's only because you've sent me out in the middle of nowhere to cover the most non-newsworthy piece of drivel the world has ever known. WMAC has hit an all-time low with this one…. Don't tell me it's my job to make it news. Stephanie, don't you dare hang up on me—''

He smacked his cell phone closed with an angry gesture.

At the moment Zoe didn't care that Mace hadn't laughed at her appearance. She felt as if she was actually shimmering with anger.

So much for forgive and forget.

''Non-newsworthy, eh?'' Zoe asked with a smile that threatened to break her jaw.

He whirled around. ''You eavesdropped?''

''Not really.'' She let the smile drop because otherwise she was going to hurt herself. ''You were just shouting so loud a herd of elephants could have walked through the room and you wouldn't have noticed.''

He had the decency to look embarrassed. ''Listen, it wasn't meant as a reflection on your town.''

''Sure it was.''

''It's just that this isn't what I imagined I'd be doing when I went into journalism.''

Despite her annoyance, she felt a spurt of connection with this aggravating man. Once upon a time she'd had plans for her career and working in Hiho hadn't been one of them.

"Let me guess," she said softly. "You wanted bigger, better. Something with more pizzazz and more acclaim."

He didn't answer.

Didn't even shrug.

"Listen, Mace, we haven't known each other long, but let me assure you bigger isn't always better. Happy is."

He made a little scoffing noise. "With an attitude like that, you should be working at WMAC and not some little Podunk paper."

"Pardon me?" The feeling of connection snapped. She was surprised he didn't hear the sound reverberate through the room.

"*WMAC, Where Nice News Matters.* Gag. You and *Pollyanna* Paige Montgomery would be best friends in no time. Want me to talk to my boss for you?"

"Listen, Mr. Mason, your first mild insult I put down to just…well, to your being a man. After you didn't laugh at my makeover, I figured I'd cut you some slack and overlook it. But this little town is my home and that *Podunk paper* you're referring to is my livelihood. I am not going to cut you any slack if you're insulting either of them."

He raked a hand through his hair. "Listen, I'm sorry. I'm taking my annoyance out on you and that's not fair."

"You're right, it's not. And I'm sorry as well. Sorry that I thought..." She left the sentence hanging.

"What?" he pressed.

"I thought you were a nice guy. Instead, I see you're like so many other guys I've met in the business."

"How were those other guys?"

She didn't answer, and he said, "Listen, I said, I'm sorry I insulted your paper and town."

"No, you're sorry *I heard you* insult my paper and town. There's a difference." She shook her head. It was like talking to a wall. "Never mind. We don't have to like or respect each other. I just have to show you around."

"You're still willing?" He sounded surprised.

"I told your editor I'd help you, and I will. I don't go back on my word just because someone is unpleasant, opinionated...and wrong."

"Hey, don't hold anything back. Tell me how you see it." He offered her a small, noncondescending smile that said he knew he deserved whatever she dished out.

She couldn't help offering him a small one in

return. "Hey, don't try and be funny now. You'll ruin my low opinion of you."

"Really, I am a nice guy. It's just that work isn't going the way I hoped and this trip just may be the final straw."

"I know," she said. "Bigger, better and all that."

She wished she could make him understand that if he got what he wanted he might find out he'd been wrong. Even as she thought it, she felt foolish. After all, maybe bigger and better was exactly what Mace Mason wanted. She'd known him for all of what…an hour? His dreams were his own and absolutely none of her business.

"So why don't I apologize again for putting my foot in my mouth." He shot her another one of those grins that the camera probably ate up. "I really am sorry and would like to start over, if that's okay with you."

"Apology accepted. I don't like seeing reporters make sweeping generalizations. You can't report accurately if you come into a story with a bias. And you, Mr. Mason, are biased against small towns."

He paused a moment, as if considering her words, then finally said, "So convince me I'm wrong."

"I will."

ZOE WALLACE WAS A BABE.

That much was apparent as soon as she unmade that makeover.

Black shoulder-length hair and her eyes...well, they were blue, but that just didn't seem like an accurate description. Mace could think of a bunch of adjectives that would clarify the color—robin's-egg blue, sky-blue, jewel-blue—but he wasn't about to use any of them. They sounded far too...just *too*.

No, black hair, blue eyes. That was as far as he planned to go with a description.

But he would allow that she was drop-dead gorgeous. Not only that, but she could hold her own in a fight. That might not seem like something that would impress him, but it was. Mace had dated too many women who couldn't, or wouldn't, take him on.

Women who wilted the first time he raised his voice. And truth be told, raising his voice wasn't all that unusual. Mace enjoyed a good verbal sparring now and again.

Zoe had been right to call him on the carpet for his unthinking remarks.

Oh, she was still mad, but he had hopes he could tease her out of her funk. He'd already gotten one smile, maybe he could get more?

Why he cared if she was mad at him, he wasn't sure, but he did.

His view was fine even if her gait was brisk and rippling with her annoyance. Time to try the old *Mason* charm.

"Hey, it's not a marathon," he finally said, in what he hoped was a teasing, endearing tone.

"It's late and it's been a long day."

"Yeah, but—"

"So, let's grab a quick bite, like I promised, and get you settled so we can make an early start of it tomorrow."

She stopped abruptly a few doors down from The General Store. "Here we go."

Obviously his tone hadn't been endearing enough because she was still annoyed.

He didn't know her well enough to tease her out of her snit, so he simply followed her to the diner. It was built into a long stretch of brick establishments. The window proudly proclaimed it, Pete's Eats.

"You're kidding, right?" he asked.

She whirled around, ready to fight, and Mace wished he'd kept his mouth shut about the establishment's name. "What?"

"Nothing," he said, hoping to stave off another battle.

Zoe sighed. "The owner's name is Pete, and…well, it's a great place to eat. Honesty in advertising, I'd say."

"But—"

"Listen, when you live in a town called Hiho—"

"You keep things simple." He grinned. "I'd already reached that conclusion."

Some of Zoe's icy demeanor melted enough to allow her to offer him another small smile in return. "You've got it. And you'll love the food here. Pete's wife, Alice, does most of the cooking, and I dare say there's nothing in a bigger city to rival it. Before the week is out you'll feel like a regular. Just wait and see."

She pushed open the door and led him into a small dining room. Red-and-white checked tablecloths, bright sunny yellow walls.

Mace took it all in and then stopped himself. Since when did he notice decor?

First at The General Store he'd noted the rustic-nostalgic look, then at Zoe's place he'd been taken aback by her decorative style. All that white had him thinking of ice—an ice princess just waiting for someone to thaw her out. When she emerged unmade over, Mace had actually thought he might enjoy trying to warm her up.

The thought had scared him—not the warming-Zoe-up part, but the noticing-how-places-were-decorated part. After all, what man noticed something like that?

Yet here he was looking at the interior of Pete's

Eats and he'd actually thought the words *sunny yellow*.

He was thankful he didn't say them out loud. And he was even happier that he was only staying through Sunday because the town was already messing with his mind. Pretty soon he'd be using words like *ambiance* and *accent*.

If he did and Steph overheard, no one would be able to save him. She'd have him doing an in-depth report on interior design. There was a relatively new designer in Erie who ran By Design that everyone was raving about. Steph would make him report on that.

Talk about a non-news story.

"Do you prefer a table or booth?" Zoe asked.

Mace realized he'd been lost in decorating thoughts, which was preferable to thinking about Zoe as an ice princess in need of waking.

"Doesn't matter," he said.

She led him to a corner booth and moments after they were seated, a small man approached the table. "Zoe, honey, how are you?"

"Just fine, Pete. How's Alice?"

"Fit as a fiddle. She says to tell you she's got your favorite back there."

"Then I don't even have to think about what I'm ordering." She looked at Mace.

"Ah, just what is your favorite?" Mace asked

as he glanced at the menu which was conveniently printed on the place mat.

"You won't find it on the menu," Zoe said. "It doesn't need to be advertised. Trust me, you'll like it."

"Fine. I'll have what she's having," he told Pete, who hurried back toward the kitchen.

"Daring, eh? Well, there may be some hope for you yet, Mace Mason," Zoe said, offering him a smile…a real smile.

"Seriously, I'm sorry you overheard me. It's really not the town. It's frustration. My boss sent me for the week to relax."

"You don't look very relaxed to me," she pointed out.

"Your observant nature must be what led you to reporting," he said, knowing that his tone had come out less than friendly—some might even call it terse.

Zoe tapped her fingers on the tabletop as she frowned.

"Sorry," he mumbled.

What was it about this woman that had him behaving like a buffoon?

"Listen," she said, her fingers still beating a fast rhythm. "I don't want to spend my week sparring with you. I have too much to do as it is. Let's just forget that I overheard you and that I now know you're not happy about being in Hiho. We'll start all over again.''

She held her hand out across the table. ''Hi. You must be Mace Mason. I'm Zoe Wallace of the *Hiho Herald*.''

''Nice to meet you, Zoe. You can't imagine how nice.'' Mace shook her hand and desperately tried not to notice how warm it felt in his. More than warm, it felt…

He dropped her hand as quickly as he dropped the thought. He didn't come here for a fling with some *Podunk* reporter.

Podunk. He felt better having thought the word. Not that he was ever going to say it out loud again, but he'd think it all he wanted.

Podunk.

Podunk.

Podunk.

Unfortunately this particular *Podunk* reporter looked just as good after he thought the words as before.

''So, where would you like to start?'' she asked. Before he could answer, she added, ''The real centennial festivities don't pick up until this weekend. By the way, you're invited to a dinner Friday night at the college. It will be a great opportunity to introduce you around.''

''Thanks.''

''But that leaves you a lot of time. You're welcome to follow me as I take care of the final arrangements, but that's not exactly news.''

"*Not exactly news.* That's exactly the kind of stuff WMAC covers.'' He sighed then, a sigh that spoke of frustration with work. ''But you're right, I don't want to spend the next few days dogging your every step. Maybe some of them, but not all of them. What I'd hoped is that you could hook me up with some of the town's archives. I don't know if Stephanie explained exactly what I do.''

"She just said you were doing an in-depth piece.''

"I am. I'll be shooting footage of the festival, but in addition I'm gathering background information about Hiram Hump for *Erie Chronicles*. *Chronicles* are half-hour segments about Erie's history. We tie our subjects to current events, things we can use on the news, and then run the specials. It allows us to crosspromote.''

Pete came over and put a mug of coffee in front of each of them.

"Thanks, Pete,'' Zoe said.

Pete gave a noncommittal grunt and walked back toward the kitchen.

"But why cover Hiram Hump?'' she asked.

"You do know he was from Erie, right?'' Mace noted that Zoe loaded her coffee up with cream and sugar. He realized he was paying attention to all sorts of small things about her. Not just how she took her coffee, but also the way she tapped her fingers against the table when he annoyed her.

That he noticed anything about her was disconcerting. He tried to tell himself that it was the reporter in him, but it sounded hollow even to him.

"Of course I know Hiram's from Erie. We value our history here, which is why this centennial is such a big deal."

"Well, he wrote some obscure, but valued history and my editor thought—"

A voice interrupted him. "*Psst,* Zoe."

She turned. "Bertram, I—"

"Don't turn around," the voice barked. "Don't let them know I'm talking to you."

She obeyed and swung back around to face Mace, who could see the back of the head of the man who was *psst*ing Zoe.

"So, have you found out anything?" the *psst*er asked.

"Not yet, Bertram, but I'm planning on checking. I promise."

The *psst*er turned around and Mace got a glimpse of a life-lined man with thin gray hair. A man—Bertram, Zoe had called him—who was studying him, suspicion in his narrowed eyes.

"Who's he? A spy for them?" Bertram asked.

"No. He's a...a friend."

"Okay." He gave Mace a quick nod, then turned back around and continued, "This is the biggest story Hiho has ever had. I tried to talk to Pawley about the endowments, but even he doesn't want to hear. Said he couldn't do anything without proof. We need to get that proof, and they don't want us to. So be careful. They're watching me all the time. I managed to sneak away, but it's only a matter of time until Pete spots me here and—''

''Uncle Bertram,'' Pete, the jovial waiter who didn't look nearly as jovial now, said right on cue. He swooped in like some angry hornet and set plates filled with meatloaf and mashed potatoes on their table with a decisive slam as he continued talking to the *psst*er. ''You know you're supposed to be in the back helping Alice today.''

''Just taking a break, Pete. Resting my tired old feet,'' Bertram said in a voice that did indeed sound tired.

''*Old* isn't the word I'd use to describe you,'' Pete said with an inflection that made Mace wonder just what word the waiter would use to describe his uncle.

Pete continued, ''Come on, let's go into the kitchen before Alice comes out.''

Mace thought he might like to meet this Alice who struck so much fear into grown men.

Or maybe he wouldn't.

''Hope he wasn't bothering you, Zoe,'' Pete said.

''Of course not,'' Zoe said. ''Why I didn't even

know he was back there until you said something.''

Pete looked as if he didn't quite believe her, but
finally nodded and said, ''Well, that's good. Enjoy
your dinner. Come on, Uncle.''

''Don't forget what I said, Zoe,'' Bertram whispered as he obligingly followed Pete into the
kitchen.

''What was that all about?'' Mace asked, not
sure what to make of the cloak-and-dagger foolery.

''Nothing. Bertram is a bit…eccentric.''

''Oh,'' he replied noncommittally, but he sensed
Zoe wasn't being entirely truthful with him. He'd
been a reporter for too long to miss that something
was up.

Granted, what he'd been doing lately wasn't
very good reporting, but that didn't mean he
wasn't a very good reporter. He sensed a story.

''Try your meatloaf,'' Zoe said.

Mace speared the meat, regretting he'd followed
her lead. He wasn't overly enthusiastic about
meatloaf as a rule. ''About that man—'' he started.

But she interrupted. ''Come on, try it.''

He took a small bite and knew at that moment
that no matter how scary Alice was, if her meatloaf
could taste this good, he could learn to like her.

''This is…'' he let the sentence trail off, not
how sure how to describe what he was eating.

"Yeah, it's that good. I think it's the mozzarella cheese that does it."

He grunted his agreement.

"About your schedule," she said.

Mace couldn't have proved it in a court of law, but he sensed Zoe was anxious to talk about anything except Bertram. "I'll get you settled for the night," she continued, just a little too hurriedly, "and we can get you started first thing in the morning. I'll take you over to the college and introduce you around. In addition to the campus library itself, they have an exhibit on Hiram that I think would be helpful to you. You can dig around for information there."

"That would be great. And the paper? Can I possibly have access to your archives as well?"

Zoe didn't look exceptionally pleased with the request, but she finally nodded. "Sure."

She dug through her purse and handed him a key. "You can use this for the duration of your stay. It's for the back door. Help yourself."

"Great." He took the key and pocketed it. "Thanks. So, how far is my hotel?"

She hesitated. "Ah, did your boss tell you that you were staying at a hotel?"

"She just said you'd get me settled."

"And I will, but you see, Hiho has one hotel and it's booked solid for the whole week. There's one back on the interstate about fifteen miles from here, but I thought you'd prefer to stay in Hiho.''

"So if not the hotel, where am I staying? Please tell me not with you.''

The minute the words were out of his mouth he realized they could be interpreted as terse, and wished he could suck them back in.

But Zoe didn't seem to take offense this time. In fact, she laughed. ''Don't worry. You're not staying with me. Your boss had me book you a room at Aunt Aggie's Bed and Breakfast. I think you'll like it there. In addition to making the best muffins in the world, Aunt Aggie has that *Aunt Bea* quality you seemed to expect to find in the women of Hiho....''

3

ZOE WAS RIGHT, Aunt Aggie made the best muffins Mace had ever tasted. It would have been the perfect place to stay if it wasn't for her evil-looking pit bull, Baby.

He was pretty sure that Baby didn't like him.

And he was more than sure that he wasn't fond of Baby.

But Baby wasn't the reason he was feeling quite out of sorts this morning.

Oh, his room was comfortable—even his bed was—but he couldn't sleep.

All because of Zoe Wallace.

Every time he closed his eyes he dreamed of her.

Laughing.

Sputtering.

Fighting mad.

He couldn't seem to shake thoughts of her.

And now, walking next to her on the way to Cloverleaf College he wondered if Zoe had a car, because she seemed to walk everywhere, and it wasn't improving his mood. The view was…distracting.

She kept a running monologue on the town's history. "…that Clover was a women's libber and intended to make the college women only. But then she met Lief Johnson and he convinced her to marry him and taught her men had their uses, so it was a co-ed college. The Clover you met at The General Store is their descendent…."

Mace was finding it hard to focus on what Zoe was saying because his attention was on her face.

It was an average face, as far as he could tell. A basic-looking nose. Two eyes. A mouth that hadn't stopped moving.

Everything where it should be. Fairly nice symmetry.

Nothing extraordinary.

And yet, even without a fake eyelash bobbling against her eye, he couldn't seem to stop watching her.

"…We had the centennial beauty pageant last week. Katy Sloane, the town librarian won, but abdicated her crown to Brandi Rankin. You'll meet Brandi at the dinner later this week. But watch out for her mom…when she finds out you're an out-of-town reporter you're going to have a hard time shaking her. Brandi will kick off the festival by leading the parade on Saturday morning. We'll wrap things up Sunday night with a huge firework display. The Centennial Celebration has been such an economic boon for the community—''

Her sentence stopped dead in its tracks and so did she.

Zoe was staring at something. Before Mace could turn and see what, she sprinted across the grassy park.

What was she doing now?

He'd known her less than twenty-four hours, but already suspected that she wasn't a normal sort of woman.

Bad makeovers. Cloak-and-dagger meetings.

Running across the park after a...

A bull?

Not just any bull.

A big bull.

Giant even.

Man, if you painted the thing blue it could have belonged to Paul Bunyan himself.

''Zoe,'' he cried, squeezing her name past the huge lump in his throat.

''Zoe!''

He sprinted after her, although he didn't have a clue what he could do to prevent the giant bull from attacking her and trampling her to the ground.

He didn't know anything about cattle and suddenly wished he did. What good was knowing about English literature or even journalism in a situation like this?

"Zoe, damn it, stop!"

His warning was too late. She had something in her hand.

It was her belt, he realized.

She'd taken off her belt and was going to lasso it around the bull's thick neck. It would kill her.

"Hey! Hey, bull," Mace called.

The stupid thing was probably going to gore him, but at least Zoe would get away.

"Bull!" he screamed, trying to get it to come toward him rather than Zoe.

He waved his hand, wishing he had something red. That was the color bulls liked, he was pretty sure.

"Bull!"

Visions of Zoe gored by the beast flashed through his head.

"Bull!"

The bull turned and just stared at him with a rather bored expression on its big, homely face.

If someone had asked him yesterday he would have denied that a bull could look bored, but this one did.

Zoe slipped the belt over its neck, then patted it and murmured something in its ear.

Mace approached more slowly, not wanting to

spook the giant beast now that Zoe was holding on.

"What are you doing?" he asked, trying to keep his voice soft and calm.

Other than being slightly out of breath, she looked none the worse for wear. As a matter of fact, she shot him a dazzling sort of smile. "You tried to save me. That's why you were shouting, right? To get the bull to chase you instead of going after me?"

Mace shrugged, unsure what to say. Zoe didn't look overly moved by his shot at heroics. To be honest, she looked slightly amused.

"Sorry if I scared you. There was nothing to worry about. Jed here is one step from the grave and doesn't have the stamina to chase after you. Where he gets the energy to walk to the campus every day is a bit of a mystery. If he was any other bull, Don David would have gotten rid of him long ago. But he holds onto him because he's sentimental. Don's sentimental, not the bull. Although, Jed may be as well."

"Well, this Don David should keep the beast locked up."

"Nothing Don does can keep Jed penned. No fence is high enough or strong enough." She covered the bull's ears. "You see, Jed has a crush on Bessie, the college's mascot. He likes to visit."

"Pardon?"

"The college's mascot is a bison—The Cloverleaf Bisons. They don't have enough money to buy one yet—though we do have a buffalo fund—so Don donated Bessie to sort of fill in until they raise enough for a real bison. And Jed misses her. Love's like that. Sometimes there's just nothing you can do to stop it. It will break through any obstacle."

"Oh, no," Mace groaned.

"What?" Zoe asked.

"Not only are you crazy enough to chase after a bull—"

"He's gentle as a lamb," Zoe argued.

Mace ignored her and kept right on talking, "—but you're also a romantic."

"So?"

"Honey—"

"Don't call me honey." Her terminal good cheer evaporated just like that.

"Zoe," Mace said with emphasis, "love is just an excuse to propagate."

A man came running up to them. His face lit up when he saw Zoe and the bull. "You got him."

"Yes. You know, you've really got to watch him this week, Don. It's going to be crazy what with the festival going on. I know Jed's sweet, but I'd hate to see him scared by the crowd."

"I'm taking him out to Old Mac's farm. Figure even if he gets out, we could catch him long before he gets all the way into town. Mac's a lot further out than I am. I was just getting ready to load him into the truck when he got away. Thanks for catching him.''

"Glad to help.''

He slipped a rope around the bull's neck and handed Zoe her belt before leading Jed, the love-lorn bull, down the street.

"Old Mac?'' Mace asked.

Zoe threaded her belt through the loops on her pants and a small sliver of her stomach showed. Just a tiny little band of skin. Nothing overt, not even overly sexy. And yet, Mace couldn't tear his eyes away.

She finished, tucked her shirt back in place—much to his disappointment—and looked at him and grinned. "Mac's last name is MacDonald and he—''

"Has a farm?'' Mace supplied.

"Yep.''

"This whole town is insane,'' Mace muttered. He felt rather proud that he didn't add, *and you're the biggest lunatic in this asylum.*

"Maybe...but we're happy. Can you say as much, Mace?''

"I don't know where you got the idea I'm not happy,'' Mace said, not caring if he sounded annoyed.

First Stephanie said he was terse and needed to

take a vacation, and now Zoe—an utter stranger—
was telling him he was unhappy.

Like he should listen to what a crazy woman
who lassoed bulls with her belt said.

"I'm deliriously happy at this moment in
time...happy you didn't get yourself killed by that
beast."

"Like I said, Jed wouldn't hurt a fly. He's sort
of a town fixture. And Mace, I know happy when
I see it, and you're not happy...delirious or otherwise."

"I am happy."

"Nope, you're not." She smiled then. It was the
same smile that had punctuated his dreams last
night. Hot dreams. A smile that begged him to do
just what he'd done in those dreams.

And before he could think about it and talk himself out of it, Mace did just what he'd done in his
dreams.

He kissed her.

Planted a hard kiss right on her lips.

It didn't mean anything.

Their lips remained closed, for pete's sake.

It was practically platonic.

Of course, *practically* was the key word.

Because he wasn't feeling totally platonic about
Zoe Wallace.

Not at all.

And that didn't make sense because she wasn't

the kind of woman he was attracted to. He wanted someone sophisticated, someone career oriented with goals and ambitions that went beyond some Podunk paper, someone...

Yet, he looked at her, standing there, looking dazed, staring at him, and knew that though it didn't make sense, though he barely knew her, he wanted her.

More than a sexual longing, he wanted to know what she was thinking because he didn't have a clue, he wasn't even sure what he was thinking, for that matter. He didn't ask her and he refused to analyze his own thoughts any further than he already had.

"Zoe?" he finally said.

She gave herself a little shake, as if she was coming out of a trance. "Why on earth did you do that?"

"I don't know."

"Well..." She paused a moment, then said, "Well, don't do it again."

"Okay. But only if you promise not to chase after any more bulls."

"Deal." She held out her hand, as if to shake on it, then dropped it immediately.

Mace was glad because he wasn't sure what would happen if he had to touch her again right now.

"Let's go and get you situated at the college,"

she said as she started walking toward the college
again. "I have stuff to do."

"Fine."

MEN!

That one word kept interrupting the thousand
things she had to do for the festival.

Zoe might be able to handle the paper and the
centennial details, juggling them all and so far,
dropping none. But she didn't know how to handle
Mace Mason. She couldn't keep up with him.

First he was nice and didn't laugh at her crazy
makeover, then he was a heel, referring to her paper as Podunk.

She wasn't sure precisely what *Podunk* was, but
she was pretty sure it wasn't a compliment.

Then he'd tried to save her from Jed, trying to
get the bull to chase him rather than her. Not that
Jed would chase anyone, but Mace hadn't known
that. He thought he was risking his life, pitting
himself against a giant bull to save her. That made
him a hero.

All the waffling to and from nice guy status, she
could deal with and almost understand. After all,
men were fickle creatures and no sane woman
could truly understand how their minds worked.

But then Mace had kissed her.

Zoe couldn't begin to understand that.

She couldn't decide if it made him nicer or a

bigger heel. So she forced herself to concentrate on the copy she was supposed to be proofing.

Someone cleared their throat and she just about jumped out of her seat.

"Earth calling Zoe," Clover said with a smile.

"Sorry. Just lost in thought. I didn't even hear you come in. Did you need something, or is this just social?"

"Maybe a little of both." She paused and looked around the small office. "Where's your hunky reporter?"

"He's not mine and he's not that hunky."

Zoe crossed her fingers beneath the counter. That was a lie—not the part about him not being hers...he wasn't. But the other part, the hunky part, well he was gorgeous, but she wasn't going to admit it to Clover.

"You haven't noticed the way his eyes are so brown they're almost black?"

"No. Brown is brown. And I think I read somewhere that it's the most common eye color, so his eyes can't be all that special if more people share their color than any other."

"I don't think anyone has quite the same color eyes that he does. At least not here in Hiho. I don't know if you noticed it, but there's a certain dearth in eligible men here."

"No, I hadn't noticed," Zoe said, though that was a lie as well.

"Come on, even Vic noticed, and she hardly ever knows what day of the week it is."

"Sure she does, she's the mayor after all. She's got a fine mind for details." Knowing Vicky, she'd probably not only noticed the shortage of eligible men, but had some new plan up her sleeves to get some to move to town. Vicky was a driving force in the town's recent growth.

Rather than look for new industry, she was encouraging people to look for ways to attract tourism to the area.

"Vic's got an eye for the job, but not much else. But it's that lack of eligible men that made me think about asking Mace out. But not if you're interested in him."

"Interested in Mace Mason?" Zoe laughed at the thought. Although the laughter sounded a bit odd to her ears. Clover didn't seem to notice. In fact she smiled, so Zoe continued, "What kind of name is Mace anyway?"

"A nice one?" Clover said.

"Pretentious, that's what it is. Mace Mason." She thought it was cute when she first met him, but since he'd kissed her she'd decided it was best not to think of Mace as cute in any way. "But that's not what you asked. To answer your question, no, I'm not interested in him. After all, he's only here for the week."

"A lot can happen in a week." The gleam in

Clover's eyes gave Zoe an indication about just how much Clover would like to have happen.

"I don't think a personality change can happen that quick."

"What do you mean?" Clover asked.

"He doesn't like our little *Podunk* town." She could feel herself bristle all over again as she remembered his conversation. Bristling over the conversation was better than melting over his kiss. "He feels that covering Hiho's little centennial is beneath him."

"Well, maybe I can change his mind."

"I doubt it." Short of having a brain transplant, Zoe didn't see any hopes for Mace's mind changing.

"But you don't mind if I try?"

"I already said I didn't," Zoe said. Even as the words came out of her mouth, she realized they'd sounded a bit abrupt, so she added a "Really," in hopes of softening them.

Clover studied her a moment. Zoe tried to resist the urge to squirm under her scrutiny.

"Really," she said again.

"You say you don't mind, but I'm not sure that's what you mean."

"I'm a reporter. I always say exactly what I mean."

Why would she care if Mace had dinner with Clover?

To be honest, she was more nervous that Clover was having dinner with Mace. Clover was so sweet, Mace could really hurt her. "Just be careful."

Clover laughed. "I think I can handle Mace Mason. And if you're sure you don't mind—"

Zoe interrupted. "I'm sure."

"—I'm going to ask him to dinner tonight, all right?"

"Sure. He planned on spending the day at the college digging around, then he was going to meet me back here at the office at four."

"So, I'll go catch him at the college, and if he's interested we can do dinner when you're done with him."

Done with him?

Zoe had been done with Mace Mason the moment he kissed her.

She was past done with him. She was...she couldn't think of an appropriate phrase, but she was way past being done with him.

"No problem. Just be careful," she warned Clover again.

"Why?"

"I wouldn't want you to expect more from Mace than he can give."

Clover looked at her for an inordinately long time. "Are you sure about this?"

"Sure I'm sure." *Geesh*, how many times did

she have to say it? I have absolutely no designs on Mace.''

After all, one quick bull-induced kiss didn't mean anything at all. Why, Mace probably kissed hundreds of women.

The fact her knees had practically buckled had more to do with the fact she'd sprinted after Jed, not the fact Mace kissed her. Okay, so maybe a little because Mace kissed her, but that was probably due to her rather lengthy dateless existence.

''Positive,'' she added when Clover still stood waiting.

''Well, okay. I'm going to go find him now.''

''Good luck. See you later.''

This was great. If Mace was occupied with Clover tonight, Zoe should have time to go dig around the paper's archives and see if there was any proof to substantiate Bertram's wild statements.

And if she found the proof, what would she do?

It would certainly be a big story, and as a journalist she'd be obligated to print it.

But the college had already borrowed against that endowment. If they had to wait another year for it to come through...well, Zoe didn't know what that would mean to them financially, but it couldn't be good.

Of course the library was counting on the money for renovations and improvements. Why, Katy Sloane had practically glowed last time they talked, as she speculated about all she could do with that money.

Zoe shook her head.

Maybe before she went digging she should talk to Rob Pawley, who was overseeing the endowments for the college and library, and see just what sort of implications Bertram's accusations could have on the entire community.

One more thing on her list of things to do.

Why, it was great that Clover was taking Mace out tonight because truly, she didn't have time to play nursemaid for him.

Yes, Zoe was thrilled that Clover was taking Mace off her hands.

MACE WALKED the four blocks between the college and the newspaper with long, brisk steps.

Some people might think they were angry steps, but of course they weren't. After all, what did he have to be angry about?

Zoe practically threw him at another woman, but the woman in question was gorgeous and ran her own successful business, which indicated she had a brain.

Beautiful and intelligent. A winning combination.

So Mace should be grateful for the fix-up.

But he wasn't.

He was annoyed.

After all, he'd kissed Zoe in the afternoon and, before he'd gotten himself back under control, she was throwing him at another woman.

It wasn't very flattering.

As a matter of fact, it was almost insulting.

Oh, Mace didn't suffer under any delusions that he was a ladies' man. But he also knew that he wasn't some boy-toy to be shared between friends.

Yes, Clover seemed nice enough and he'd said yes to her dinner invitation, but…

He wasn't sure just what his *but* was, but he knew that he was annoyed with Zoe, which he guessed was pretty fair since she seemed to spend a great deal of time annoyed with him.

He walked into Pete's Eats and couldn't even work up a good snicker for the restaurant's name. That was just another small indication of how deeply annoyed he was.

He looked around and didn't see Clover.

He glanced at his watch. He was early. He found it difficult to gauge how long it took to walk somewhere. Erie was a driving town. But here in Hiho, everyone seemed to walk everywhere.

He slid into a booth toward the back and settled in to wait.

Pete came over. "Waiting for Zoe?"

"No. For Clover Addison."

Pete studied him a moment and then said, "Well, can I get you something while you wait?

And I should tell you that you may wait a while so you probably should order something.''

He glanced at his watch again. "I'm not that early."

"No, but Clover tends to live in a different time zone than the rest of us. As a matter of fact, I don't recall her ever arriving anywhere on time. Why, her mother used to say when Clover was two weeks late being born it was just an indication of how the girl's life would be lived."

"Oh."

"Most of the town tells her to be somewhere at least a half hour before they need her simply because she's always late. I don't suppose you thought to do that."

"Why would I?" he asked.

"Well, yes, there's that. Well, you just sit back and relax. What would you like to drink while you wait?"

"Coffee."

Pete looked concerned. "Don't you think it's a little late for coffee? I mean, it's bound to keep you up. And if you don't mind my saying, you look like you could use a good sleep."

Mace wasn't going to ask just what Pete meant by that. He didn't want to know if the fact he'd spent last night thinking about Zoe was that evident, that he looked that tired.

"Coffee," he repeated and immediately realized how short he'd sounded.

Pete must have realized it as well, because he didn't argue further. "Far be it from me to interfere. Coffee it is."

He hustled away before Mace could apologize, then hurried back with the coffee, set it down with a distinct clunk, and left again.

Great. Mace was systematically alienating the town. First Zoe handed him off like a hot potato, and now Pete was annoyed with him as well.

Mace sipped his coffee and stewed over…well, over everything. His life was out of control and he wasn't sure how to reclaim it.

To make matters worse, Zoe's little, *bigger isn't better, happy is,* phrase kept running through his mind.

He was happy.

Almost on cue, Zoe entered the restaurant. She gave a little wave to a man and headed over to his table, her back to Mace.

All thoughts of happy fled as he watched her sit down with the guy.

Who was that?

The man was blond, and even from this distance, Mace could tell he had a weak chin. He didn't look like he could stand up to a Chihuahua, much less Zoe.

What was she doing with a guy like that? She'd eat him alive.

Not that Mace cared. But really, a woman shouldn't go around kissing men if she had a boyfriend. It didn't say much about her character.

"Hi, is this seat taken?" a voice asked, startling Mace.

A very female voice.

He looked up and Clover Addison stood next to the booth smiling at him.

"Oh, you're early."

She glanced at her watch. "Actually, I'm running a little late."

"But not as late I was told to expect."

He heard the words come out of his mouth and wanted to kick himself. What was happening to him? Terse was one thing, but rude was another.

Clover didn't seem to mind. She smiled as she sat down. "I see you were forewarned. I always mean to be on time, but life always seems to get in the way."

She waved at Pete and called, "Just an ice water with lemon," then turned back to Mace.

"You see, I was all ready to close the store and be here on time when..."

He glanced at Zoe. What was that? She passed some papers, or maybe a file, across the table to the man.

"...and the man said, 'But I need chains...'"

The blond guy was looking at the folder—it had been a folder—and slammed it back to the table, a scowl on his face.

It wasn't much of a scowl because it was hard to manage a good one with such a weak chin.

Mace didn't think he was conceited, but he knew he could outscowl that guy any day of the week.

Outchin him as well.

"...but his wife said that, vacation or not, she just wasn't in to that kind of thing..."

Zoe and the mystery man were exchanging heated words. Mace strained, trying to hear what they were saying, but though they were obviously disagreeing, their voices were hushed and he couldn't make out a thing.

"...So what do you think?" Clover asked.

"Think?" Mace asked, tearing his gaze away from Zoe and concentrating on the woman sitting across from him.

What had she been talking about? A man who wanted chains and a wife who wasn't inclined to play those kinds of games even on vacation.

"Yes, what do you think," Clover repeated. "Do you think I should expand my merchandise selection to include something like that? I mean, I know you're not in retail, but you're from a bigger city and I'd value your opinion."

"I'll confess I'm not into kinky things," he

said, glancing over Clover's shoulder to where Zoe and Mr. Weak-chin were still going at it.

"Kinky?" Clover asked. "You think antique light fixtures are kinky?"

"You weren't talking light fixtures, you were talking about chains."

"To hang wagon wheel chandeliers from the ceiling," Clover said slowly, as if he were just a little slow.

"Oh."

"Chains," she murmured and chuckled. "Yes, that would be a big change in my merchandise."

The laughter faded and she smiled at him as she said, "Mace, if you'd rather not do this, I understand."

"No, really, it's not that. It's just that… Who's that man with Zoe?" He pointed to the booth on the opposite side of the restaurant.

Clover turned around and looked. "Rob. Robert Pawley. He's a lawyer. His family's as much an institution in Hiho as mine."

"How is that?"

"His family came into town about the same time the first Clover did. The Pawleys started The Pawley Faucet Factory, though they gave up controlling interest a long time ago. Rob still manages the family trust."

"And he's seeing Zoe?" Mace asked and then wished he hadn't. He didn't want Clover to think he cared who Zoe dated. No, he simply wondered what was going on between them.

"No. Actually, he was dating Katy Sloane until last week."

"Katy Sloane?" He thought he'd heard the name, but with the way Zoe babbled great quantities of town information at him, he wasn't sure who she was.

"The town librarian. She won the beauty pageant, but abdicated to Brandi Rankin."

Aha! That's where he'd heard the name.

Zoe continued, "Katy's story is a fun one. You see—"

Mace interrupted her. "So if this Pawley and Zoe aren't seeing each other, what are they talking about? Almost fighting about, by the looks of things."

Clover turned around again and studied the pair a moment, then turned back and faced Mace. "I don't have a clue. Rob is in charge of the big endowment for the college and the library. He'll be presenting the checks at the festival's closing ceremonies. Maybe that's what they're talking about. It makes sense, since Zoe's in charge of the festival."

"But they're not talking, they're fighting," he said.

Oh, it wasn't much of a fight. He didn't imagine

a weak-chinned guy like Pawley knew much about the finer art of fighting.

Now when he fought with Zoe…that was fighting. He liked that she could stand toe-to-toe with him and not flinch. He liked that she could call him on things when he deserved it.

"Like I said, I can't imagine why they'd be fighting," Clover said.

"So, what will you have tonight?" Pete asked.

He shot a nasty look at Mace.

Yep, he should have listened to the waiter and skipped the coffee. Maybe if he left a big tip Pete would get over it.

"I'd like spaghetti," Clover said. "Ranch dressing on the salad."

"And you?" Pete asked Mace.

"Whatever she's having," Mace said not caring what he ate. He was far too interested in the situation at Zoe's booth.

"Mace, this was a mistake, wasn't it?" Clover asked softly when Pete left.

He forced himself to concentrate on his date. "What was a mistake?"

"I'd hoped that we could get to know each other while you were visiting, but that's not going to happen, is it?"

"Sure. I'd planned on coming over to talk to you about the first Clover here in Hiho who founded the college. I need background for my

Chronicles piece, and she seems to have had an important role in the town. After all, the college and the faucet factory are the biggest employers in the area and..."

He glanced from Clover to Zoe's table and his sentence trailed off.

That Pawley guy was getting up and stalking toward the door.

Stalking.

As if he was annoyed.

More than annoyed—mad.

Of course, with that weak chin he couldn't carry off anger any better than he could carry off a scowl, but he seemed to be doing his best impersonation of anger.

"I rest my case," Clover said.

Zoe was just sitting there at the table, all alone. Her back was facing him, so he couldn't tell if she was upset.

He'd go find that weak-chinned Pawley guy if he made Zoe cry.

Not that he cared about Zoe. At least not in any man-woman sort of way.

Of course there was that kiss.

But that was just the heat of the moment.

After all, she'd almost been killed by a killer bull. Of course he kissed her, just to make sure she was still alive.

"Earth calling Mace," Clover said.

"Sorry. Just wondering what was up with that guy and Zoe. He left and she's there all alone. Maybe she's crying. Maybe they were dating and you didn't know it. Maybe he broke it off, breaking her heart."

"He was dating Katy last week and, to be honest, Rob is sort of bland. I don't think he has it in him to be dating anyone else that fast, much less break her heart. Plus, this is a small town. If they were dating, then I'd have heard. Like I said, it was probably centennial business."

"I don't know." She was still sitting there. He wished he could make out her expression.

"Would you feel better if you went and checked on her?" Clover asked.

"You wouldn't mind? After all, I'm here with you."

"Mace, ol' buddy, you haven't been with me from the moment I walked into the room. Go check on her."

He thought about denying her statement, but instead just got up and started for Zoe's table, and could have sworn he heard Clover mutter, "This should be interesting," but he wasn't sure and wasn't about to ask what she meant by it anyway.

4

"IS EVERYTHING ALL RIGHT, ZOE?"

Zoe wanted to moan. She had a raging headache and the last thing she needed was Mace Mason making it worse.

"Fine," she lied. "Just fine. I thought you were having dinner with Clover?"

"I am. We're over there."

That would teach her not to check out the entire restaurant when she came in. But she'd spotted Rob right off and didn't need to check any further...or so she'd thought.

"Well, great. Have a good time. I'll see you at the paper in the morning."

"Your date left," he said, ignoring her not-so-subtle hint he should leave.

"Rob wasn't my date, and yes, he did."

"So now you're eating alone?"

She refused to answer his statement disguised as a question. Of course she was alone.

When she didn't say anything, he continued, "You could come join Clover and me."

"I don't think so. Three's a crowd and all that. I'll see you tomorrow though."

Mace didn't appear to get the hint. Instead of saying, *well goodnight then,* or even *see you in the morning,* he said, "I'm sure she'd love having you join us."

She pasted a smile on her face, sure that any reporter worth his salt would see how fake it was, then spoke slowly and clearly. "I don't think so, but thanks for the invitation. See you tomorrow."

"You seem upset."

Oh, what a brilliant, insightful man.

"I'm not," she assured him, even as she worried about straining a smile-muscle in her face.

"What's in the file?" he asked, an innocent lilt to his voice.

Zoe hadn't known him long, but she didn't believe Mace had ever been innocent. She picked up the file. "Nothing. Just personal business between Rob and I." There was nothing incriminating in the folder—old articles on Hiho and notes from her conversations with Bertram. Notes that contained questions on just what year Hiho was founded in. She didn't want Mace to see them and start digging around.

"You're sure about dinner?" he asked.

"Positive." Finally he understood at least that much. "But thanks for asking. Enjoy yourself and I'll see you in the morning." It was another dismissal, and she held her breath, waiting to see if he'd take the hint this time.

"Well, if you're sure."

"Positive. Good night."

She let out her breath when he walked back to his dinner with Clover.

She finished her coffee in two quick gulps and left the restaurant before Mace could come back and grill her some more.

What a night.

Rob didn't have much to say other than he wanted her to just drop the whole thing. No one had presented him with any proof that Hiho wasn't a hundred and he didn't want them to. He wanted to award the endowment to the college and the library this year.

He got mad when she pressed him.

Well, mad for Rob was sort of irked for the rest of the world, but it was the most worked up she'd ever seen him.

He didn't want to know. He'd made that clear.

No one in town wanted any proof brought to light.

Not that she blamed them.

She wasn't all that keen on bringing the information out in a public and unignoreable way either.

But first and foremost, she was a reporter. It was

her job to simply present the facts. Morally, she felt she had to look into this.

Sometimes she hated having scruples.

"Psst."

Zoe didn't even have to turn around to know who was *psst*ing her. "Bertram? Where are you?"

Though the street was well lit, the alley the *psst* had originated from was dark. Bertram was there, hidden in the shadows.

"Listen, I saw you talking to Rob," Bertram stage-whispered. "He doesn't want to know, does he?"

"No. He doesn't want to have to wait another year to give the college that money. They're counting on it."

"This isn't about wants, this is about the facts. We're reporters and we can't allow a cover-up."

She stepped closer to the shadow and could make out Bertram's form, a slightly darker blob in a dark shadow. "I know. But Bertram, I don't have any facts, any proof."

"You'll find it." There was confidence in his tone. He believed in her abilities as a reporter.

"What if I don't want to?" she asked softly, voicing her private thoughts.

What if she didn't pursue this story? Would it make her less of a reporter?

"You're too good a reporter to just sit on this, Zoe. If there's proof, you'll find it and report it. I found that old letter in the newspaper's archives. They never ran the story in the *Herald,* so even back then no one wanted this truth to come out. Fool that I was, I turned the original over and didn't make a copy. I'm getting sort of slow in my old age. But you're at the top of your game. You'll do better.''

"I gave up *better* years ago and opted for happy,'' she murmured more to herself than to Bertram. She'd been thinking about that a lot since Mace arrived. When she'd left New York she'd left bigger and better behind and it had worked. She'd been happy...until now.

Thinking about happy made her think about Mace, which made her head hurt worse than it had in the restaurant.

"And Zoe, I'm sure you'll be there looking for a solution when it comes out.''

"But—''

"I've got to get back. I'll talk to you later.'' The dark blob shifted and she could hear the soft patter of footsteps moving away from her.

He was gone.

Zoe wasn't cut out for all this espionage stuff. She didn't want to investigate something that could ultimately hurt the community.

And yet, Bertram was right, she was too good a reporter not to.

Worry about the whole centennial situation nagged at her all the way home.

Longer than that even.

She spent her night tossing and turning.

Sure, some of the tossing had to do with the whole Hiho problem, but a lot of it was Mace's fault. Every time she shut her eyes, there he was…kissing her.

Over and over again that night he kissed her.

And she'd wake up bound and determined not to fantasize about his kisses anymore, and then…she'd start to wonder just how much she had to dig into the whole age of Hiho thing. And if she found the proof how she could keep it from hurting the college.

She'd worry about that until she dozed off again and there he'd be.

Kissing her.

Every time it looked like her dream Mace might go beyond kissing, she woke up.

Thank goodness.

She'd rather worry about Hiho than about Mace Mason kissing her.

Zoe finally gave up on sleep at about six, which was an ungodly hour, in her estimation.

Really, the only thing that should be up at 6:00 a.m. was…she couldn't think of anything that should be up that early.

But she couldn't face going back to sleep. She

didn't want Mace invading her dreams one more time, so she got dressed and headed to the office. It wasn't as if she didn't have enough things that needed done. She'd use the extra hours to maybe get a bit ahead.

She ignored the fact that she felt tired. No, more than that, she felt haggard.

Worn and short-tempered.

It was all Mace's fault.

She made a huge cup of coffee and, because it was too early to start any of the hundreds of calls she had to make, she decided to do some digging through the paper's archives, looking for more proof.

Somewhere along the line she got lost in the research and forgot about Mace Mason.

"Zoe?"

Zoe almost jumped out of her chair at the sound of her name.

She didn't have to turn around and see who said it. She knew that voice. Had heard it whisper her name over and over again last night.

She whirled around. "Don't sneak up on me like that."

"I didn't sneak. I walked in. That bell on your door even jangled."

"Well, I didn't hear it."

"Obviously." He held out a cardboard tray with

a small bag balanced on it. "I have a peace offering."

She eyed it suspiciously. "What is it?"

Not that she figured he'd poison her. She was simply testy due to lack of sleep and since Mace was one of the reasons for her tossing and turning, her testiness was spilling over onto him.

"Aunt Aggie sent you one of her muffins." He handed her the bag.

Zoe couldn't help the muffled groan of anticipation as she took it. Aggie Watson's muffins were renowned in Hiho.

"And Pete assured me you had a fondness for French vanilla cappuccinos. Did he lie?" He shot her one of those one thousand kilowatt smiles. The type of smile designed to make women go weak in the knees.

Of course, his smile wasn't why her knees felt suspiciously weak. No. It was her state of utter exhaustion. Her sleepless night had weakened her.

But she did allow a small smile as she took the cup. "Thanks."

"You seemed a little short last night. I wasn't sure if I'd done something, so I thought a peace offering, just in case, was in order."

"Are you accustomed to annoying people and not knowing what you did?"

He shrugged. "It does seem to be a talent of mine."

She remembered she hated his shrugging tendencies and was thrilled to recall a flaw. Even if it wasn't much of one.

Feeling better, she said, "It wasn't you I was annoyed at last night."

No. It hadn't bothered her at all that Mace had dinner with Clover. She liked Clover and if Clover liked Mace...well, it might show a lack of taste, but it certainly didn't bother Zoe.

Nah. She didn't care who Mister-Big-City-Reporter dated.

She took a sip of the cappuccino, which tasted far better than her rather bitter coffee had. "But if I had been annoyed, I'd forgive you after the first sip. I wasn't, but thanks for the cappuccino."

"You're welcome."

"Now, about today. What do you want to do?"

"I thought I'd dig around in your archives, if you don't mind. I want to get a better feel for Hiram. After that, I was wondering if you'd take me on a tour of the town?"

"I have to go out to the fairgrounds later," she said, making it sound more like a statement than an invitation.

"I haven't been out there yet. Is it in walking distance?"

"Just about everything in Hiho is within walking distance. That's the way it was planned. Actually, Hiram had a vision for what he wanted this town to be, and keeping most of it within walking distance was part of it.''

"One of the first city design engineers?"

"Something like that. He was a man of vision and I think he's responsible for Hiho being the town it is now."

Mace nodded. "About last night."

"I thought we covered that. I wasn't mad about you dating Clover."

"Not that. You and Rob Pawley. You were discussing something, something that didn't make either of you happy. Care to tell me what?"

"I'm a reporter, too, remember. I know when someone's fishing for a story. There's no story between Rob and me."

"I'm not fishing. I'm just observant. Something was up. That's fact, not conjecture."

"No," she insisted even though she knew she wasn't a very good liar, and though it was technically true that there was nothing between her and Rob, something was in fact up and it didn't take much of a reporter to sense that.

"Yes, there is. And I suspect that the *psst*er the other day in the restaurant is part of it. Bertram. I bet it won't take much asking around to locate him. And when I do, I suspect he might be more forthcoming with answers than you are."

"Mace, there are no answers. Conjecture, but nothing solid enough for a story."

"So what's the conjecture?"

He wasn't going to let this go. He was like a dog who'd grabbed hold of a bone and was going to gnaw it to death until he got some answers.

Deciding that it would be better to have him as an ally than to have him as an opponent, Zoe decided to tell all. Maybe having someone else working with her would help. After all, two pairs of eyes were better than one, especially if one pair of eyes were a dark chocolatey brown that...

Zoe shut off fantasies about Mace's eyes, shut off any stray fantasy of Mace himself.

"If I tell you," she said slowly, "do you promise not to report on anything without proof? Irrefutable, solid proof?"

"Zoe, I realize you don't know me very well, but I can guarantee you I'm not in the habit of running unsubstantiated stories."

"This story could really hurt the town—a town I love. I was looking for something to refute it this morning."

"Tell me what it is and I'll help you get to the bottom of it. You know what they say about two heads being better than one."

Zoe studied him a moment. Could she afford to trust him?

She wasn't sure. She just knew that she couldn't afford not to, at least not to trust in his journalistic integrity.

Trusting him for anything beyond that would be foolish.

And Zoe Wallace might be many things, but she wasn't foolish.

"Okay," she said, "here's what I know…"

MACE LISTENED as Zoe related the story of the centennial that might not be.

At first he wanted to laugh. After all, the fact that Hiho, Ohio, a little town in the middle of nowhere was ninety-nine, not one hundred, wasn't much of a story. But as she went on and explained the ramifications a centennial mix-up could have on the college's endowment—an endowment they'd already borrowed against—he began to see the issue in a different light.

"That's what I was talking to Rob about last night."

Mace didn't want to reflect on the fact that he felt a surge of relief that she was out with Mr. Weak-Chin because of a story, and not because she was dating him.

"And what did…" He almost said *Mr. Weak-Chin,* but thought better of it. Zoe might misinterpret the comment and think it had something to do with jealousy, rather than a simple bit of brutally honest insight.

Instead, he said, "…the lawyer have to say?"

"Rob's basically playing the ostrich, burying

his head in the sand. He doesn't want to know. Doesn't want to have to hold off awarding the endowments until next year."

"But despite the fact he asked you to let it drop, you're going to investigate?"

"How can I just let it go? You might not think much about the *Herald,* though it's only a small weekly community paper, I've tried to make it the best paper it can possibly be. I'm a reporter. This is a story. Reporting it is what I do."

"So where do we start?"

She thumped one of the big bound volumes of back issues on the table.

"I pulled out some of the oldest *Heralds.* Let's go see what they were writing about back then."

Mace's admiration of Zoe grew as the morning hours melted away in a haze of dusty old volumes of the *Herald.* She was intense in her perusal of the old papers.

He knew he wasn't nearly as focused. He kept stealing glances at her. She didn't even notice, but he noticed a lot of things. He noticed that she chewed on her lip when she was concentrating.

It was cute.

Endearing even.

And thinking any woman was cute and endearing was enough to make him want to gag. Mace forced himself to get back to the task at hand and forget all about lip-chewing, cute, endearing Zoe Wallace.

After all, he was only in town a few more days.

Then he noticed that she twisted her hair on occasion. Just an absentminded little gesture. It made him want to reach out and simply touch her hair and see if it was as soft as it looked.

The urge was so strong that he folded his hands on his lap and tried to concentrate on the paper in front of him.

Nothing could come of this…attraction he felt for her. He had to remember that.

"…Listen to this," she said with a laugh. "Mrs. Rose Caruthers hosted a tea today for the ladies of the Seventh Avenue Church."

She looked up, and he noted there was a smudge of dirt on her nose.

"They list her complete menu," she said. "Not exactly news, is it?"

Mace had an overwhelming desire to wipe the dirty smudge off for her. To take his finger and lightly trail it down the outline.

He firmly kept his hand in his lap. No way was he rubbing Zoe's dirty nose.

After yesterday's kiss, he planned to keep as far away from her physically as he could.

If a chaste little peck on the lips could leave him fantasizing about more…well, it was best not to take any chances. After all, he was out of here first thing Monday morning.

He was so anxious to get back to Erie he planned to be up at the crack of dawn and hit the road so he...

Mace lost track of what he was thinking as he stared at Zoe. She did look cute, dirty nose, laughing over old menus.

"You know, I just had a great idea," she said, as she flipped through the book. "What do you think about a new column? Each issue of the *Herald,* I could go back and find an old story, such as Mrs. Rose's tea menu and print it. I bet readers would love the look at our history."

She went on, rambling about the new column, about possible ideas about...

He lost track of what she was saying. He was simply lost in her. She was, without a doubt, captivating.

If a dirt smudge made him want to caress her, then this excitement made him want...just made him want her.

And that didn't make sense.

They were opposites.

He loved the big city, he longed to advance his career, he was working toward bigger and better things.

Out of nowhere came Zoe's question.

What about happiness?

Why couldn't he shake that one small passing comment?

Of course he wanted happiness. But unlike Zoe, he didn't think a one-horse, Podunk town was the magic elixir to all his frustration.

No, leaving WMAC was.

No more *nice news*.

Hard-hitting, meaningful stories, that's what he needed.

No, he had nothing in common with Zoe.

And that was that.

"Are you hungry?" he asked, needing to get out of this intimate isolation. Out in the real world he'd be more able to keep his thoughts on business. They had a story to chase down and they couldn't do that if they stayed hidden in this office, together…alone.

"Sure," she said. "I don't think there's anything in the paper itself."

"Let's give it a break. We'll get some food, then we'll walk out to the fairgrounds and I'll take some footage. We'll come back to the search later."

"Sounds great."

It was a relief to get out of the office. They started walking down Main Street toward the restaurant.

"Tell me about this history thing you do," Zoe said as they walked.

Mace told her about *Erie Chronicles,* about the stories he'd covered, about how satisfying he found the work.

Satisfying.

Even as he said the word to her, he realized that he did find the *Chronicles* fulfilling. That it was his favorite part of the job.

That one tiny facet of what he did made the rest of the job bearable.

What did that mean?

Steph had told him to spend this time figuring out what he wanted.

What did the *Chronicles* have to do with it?

"Mace?" Zoe said.

"Yes?"

"You just passed Pete's." She pointed to the window.

"Oh." The woman had him totally bemused. Why?

As the day passed he wasn't any closer to an answer. It was as if he was walking through a haze and everything was a bit of a blur. They ate, walked out to the fairgrounds. He got a bunch of footage of the town with Zoe narrating. Rather than do a voice-over, he wondered if she'd consider being featured in the documentary part.

He wondered a lot about Zoe.

He should be wondering about the story, about the centennial-that-possibly-wasn't.

But mainly, as the day progressed, he found himself wondering what it would be like to kiss her again.

What it would be like to hold her.

What it would be like to...

"Geesh, Mace. Stay with me here, okay?"

"What?" He gave himself a physical, as well as a mental, shake.

"You keep drifting off," Zoe said.

"I never drift," he said quickly, probably too quickly. "I'm just thinking about the centennial and Bertram's accusation."

"Me, too. I can't get it off my mind. Even when I was meeting with those vendors, I was thinking about it."

"What if we grab a pizza and head back to your office? There has to be something more than a tea-party menu in those old papers."

"There's a lot about the incorporation, about the celebration when the town was official, but there's nothing the following year about messed-up paper-work."

"But maybe no one wanted it known," he said. "Just like no one wants it known now."

"Maybe."

"Do you have any other records...not the papers, but other notes?" Mace asked.

"Yes. The paper has always been owned by pack rats. You can't believe the number of old boxes in the basement, all filled with old files. I keep two dehumidifiers running full time so that they don't rot. I keep swearing I'm going to go through them all, but have never had the time.''

''So what do you say we make time tonight? Pizza and a treasure hunt?''

Zoe smiled and the sight hit Mace right in the gut.

''You're on,'' she said.

Off, not on.

He had to turn *off* all these wild fantasies about Zoe Wallace. Fantasies that were moving beyond kissing.

He had to turn them off hard and fast.

Hard and fast.

Wrong thing to tell himself, as it brought even more vivid pictures into his head.

He needed to think about something else. Something safe.

Food.

He was going to think about food, not about everything he'd like to do with Zoe. ''So what do you like on your pizza?'' he asked. Ah, now there was a safe subject. Pizza. You couldn't turn that into some hot mental image.

''Everything,'' Zoe replied, oblivious to his raging fantasies. ''I'd like everything.''

Mace groaned, knowing he'd like everything, too.

5

ZOE YAWNED for the fifteenth time.

She knew it was the fifteenth time because she was counting.

Even worse than that, she was sitting here thinking about yawning, in hopes she would yawn, because if she yawned it indicated she was bored, and if she was bored she couldn't possibly be interested in Mace.

But, as logical as the plan sounded, it wasn't working.

The man was driving her nuts in countless different ways. He worked with a drive that rivaled her own, something she was unaccustomed to. He had a killer smile and a great sense of humor that made her laugh one minute...the next he was annoying her so much she'd find herself gritting her teeth.

But mostly, despite the fact she didn't want to, he was driving her nuts because she wanted him.

Oh, not in a soul mate sort of way—she hadn't known him long enough for that—but rather in a carnal, strip-off-his-clothes-and-have-her-way-with-him sort of way.

She had to get away from him before she acted on her desire.

"Mace, maybe it's about time to go to bed."

She realized what she'd said and hastily added, "I mean, head home. Not that you have a home here. You don't. Your home is in Erie. But…well, what I mean is why don't you head back to Aunt Aggie's and I'll head back to my house and then we can both go to our own individual beds and get back to this tomorrow because I've done about all I can do tonight. Why, I've yawned fifteen times and—"

She yawned again just to prove she could. "See, I felt that sixteenth one coming on, and there it was. Anyone would have to agree that sixteen yawns indicate that you're tired, too tired for—"

"Zoe?" Mace said, interrupting her.

Zoe wasn't going to inform him that interrupting was poor form, but it was and she noted it with satisfaction. Just one more reason why she should not be attracted to Mace—he was rude. Rudeness annoyed her.

And at this point she welcomed the fact that there was something else to be annoyed about.

"Yes?" she asked.

"You know you tend to rattle on about absolutely nothing when you're nervous. The question I have to ask myself is, *why is Zoe nervous?*"

"I can't imagine where you got that idea because I'm not nervous." The denial sounded weak even to her own ears.

It must have sounded just as weak to Mace's ears as well because he quirked an eyebrow at her. She found the whole crooked eyebrow thing sexy, so she glanced at his ears, since ears were rarely sexy, but darned if Mace's weren't just as hot as the rest of him seemed to be.

She'd never thought about ears being attractive, but his were. Small, close to his head. They'd be fun to nibble on.

Oh, no, she was thinking about nibbling on Mace's ears?

Quick, she tried to force another yawn, but couldn't quite manage it.

She realized Mace was talking, and forced herself to ignore his cute ears and listen to what he was saying. "...you definitely are nervous and the question is, why?"

"I'm tired. Not nervous. If you knew me better, you'd recognize the difference, but we've only known each other a couple of days, so of course you don't know me well enough to tell. So if I rattle on a bit—which I'm not admitting I do—but if I do, then it's only because I'm tired. Why, I've yawned fifteen times...oh, it's sixteen now, isn't it? Why, that demonstrates being tired, not nervous.''

There. She told him. She was so unaffected by his presence, that not only was she yawning, but she was counting those yawns.

''I don't think being tired is why you're rattling.'' He moved closer, just a fraction of an inch, but still, it was closer and closer wasn't what she wanted to be with Mace right now.

Okay, maybe closer was what she wanted, but it was what she should avoid.

''Then what possible reason would I have for yawning if it wasn't because I was tired?'' She wished she could back away and put more distance between them, but she was up against the arm of the couch and had nowhere to move to.

''I wasn't talking about the yawning. I was talking about the way you're jabbering on and on about nothing. I think it's because you're nervous, and I think you're nervous because you're thinking what I'm thinking.'' He moved another fraction of an inch closer.

''And what are you thinking? Because I don't have a clue. Actually, I have a hard time figuring out what any man thinks. Maybe it's because their brains are wired differently than females. And females are ever so much more logical than males because of that wiring difference. And—''

''Take a breath, Zoe,'' he paused and added,

"And move a little closer. Meet me in the middle and we'll see if we can figure out why you're nervous."

Zoe wasn't moving even one more inch closer to Mace. She wanted distance from him. She cursed herself for buying such a small sofa. She should have bought something bigger for the office.

Podunk.

Podunk.

Podunk.

She chanted his insulting description silently, hoping to get annoyed all over again with his big-city-superior attitude, but instead, she found herself sliding a tiny bit closer to him.

She was sure the slight movement was just the way the couch tilted, because she didn't want to want to be closer to Mace.

"A little closer," he prompted.

"What if I don't want to come closer?" she asked, hoping he'd say something really stupid and irritating so that moving closer to him would be the last thing she'd want to do, rather than the thing she yearned to do.

"You do," he said.

Do? Just what did she do? She'd lost track of the conversation and how on earth was she going to get irritated if she was losing track?

"My brain," he continued, "might be wired

differently than yours, but I think you're thinking the same thing I am and if you move closer I'd like to do what we're both thinking about.''

Oh, they were going to do what they'd both been thinking about. Not that she wanted to do that. And she was pulling out a level and shimming the couch tomorrow so it wasn't so darned crooked. Why she was pretty sure she'd shifted a little closer because of the darned tilt.

"What do you think I'm thinking?" she practically croaked because she couldn't remember what she was thinking again. Mace must be practicing voodoo and wiping her thoughts out of her brain moments after she thought them.

Oh, no. She'd felt it for sure that time. She'd scootched a tiny bit closer. Before she could move away, Mace pulled her toward him, eliminating the remaining space.

"I think you're thinking this," he said, his breath brushing softly against her cheek because she was that close. Too close.

Suddenly he was even closer, his lips pressing to hers.

It was a kiss. It was only a kiss.

She kept the words in her head, hoping to make herself believe it…but she didn't.

Podunk-chanting didn't help either.

Maybe nothing was helping because the tender touch of his lips to hers was a total different species than *just a kiss*. It was Christmas and the Fourth of July all wrapped up in one—surprising and explosive.

It went on and on, until she forgot everything else but the feel of his lips on hers.

She forgot that Mace was leaving in a few days, that he thought her paper was Podunk, that her couch tilted, that he wanted bigger and better while all she wanted was happy.

The last part was easy to forget, because while they kissed, her body molded along his, she was indeed happy.

Content.

Excited.

When the kiss ended, she couldn't have said how long it had lasted. Maybe just seconds. Maybe minutes. Maybe a piece of eternity.

All she knew was it hadn't been long enough.

"That wasn't what I expected," Mace muttered.

"You said the same thing about my house," she felt the need to point out, hoping to annoy herself again, but she didn't feel annoyed, she felt surprisingly unannoyed.

"I seem to say that a lot about you, Zoe." He stroked her hair. Just a small casual gesture, but even that was something to be treasured.

"Maybe that's your problem, Mace," she said.

"What do you mean?"

"You go into things with a preconceived notion. You thought I'd have an Aunt Bea-ish house. I didn't. You thought there couldn't be a story here in Hiho. There is. And you thought...I don't know what you thought about kissing me."

"Thinking about kissing you is all I've been able to think of for quite some time. Last night, when you were with that lawyer, I was crazy with thinking you might kiss him."

"Kiss Rob? Ew."

Robert Pawley was the vanilla pudding of mankind.

Now there was nothing wrong with vanilla pudding, if a person liked that sort of thing. But Zoe was pretty sure she preferred...what would she call Mace? He wasn't a dessert at all.

He was barbecued wings.

Not just plain old barbecued wings. No. The killer variety that some restaurants served. Hot, spicy and just a bit dangerous to the brave souls who gave them a try.

"And how do you feel about kissing me?" he asked.

"I'll admit 'ew' isn't the first word that comes to mind," she said.

"What word is?"

She wasn't sure he'd appreciate being compared to wings—barbecued or otherwise—so she settled for saying, "Confused. I don't normally... I mean, we've only known each other for such a short time, and I don't…'' She sighed. ''Let's put it this way, *it's not what I expected.*''

He smiled, obviously understanding the joke, recognizing his own words being thrown back in his face.

''Well, now that we both know what to expect when we kiss, what do you say we do it again?'' he asked.

''Mace, I don't know if we should.''

''Zoe, you said I should concentrate on being happy, well, kissing you is about as close to being happy as I've been in a long time. I'd like to try it again and see if maybe I can get even happier.''

She was moving toward him, knowing that smart or not, she was going to say yes.

But before she could get that one small word out and plant her lips on Mace's, she heard, *''Psst.''*

MACE TURNED, knowing who he'd find standing in the doorway. ''Mr. Barky. Can we help you?''

Zoe scooted back across the couch to her own corner and looked like a girl whose father had just come in and caught her necking with a boyfriend.

''Bertram,'' she said, her voice a little higher than normal, ''how did you get in here? I know I locked the door.''

''I still have a key.'' He held a keyring aloft, jiggling it for effect. ''Remember?''

Zoe gave a quiet little groan that Mace was pretty sure Bertram missed.

When she didn't say anything, he said, "So what can we do for you?"

"I came to see Zoe." There was a bit of antagonism in the man's voice.

More than a bit, as a matter of fact.

Mace didn't need to be a scholar on human nature in order to recognize that Mr. Barky wasn't pleased with the idea of him kissing Zoe.

If he was honest, Mace would have to admit, he wasn't so sure he was pleased either.

Not that he didn't enjoy kissing Zoe. He did.

A lot.

But kissing Zoe made him want to try other things...things that would be even more complicated. He was leaving first thing Monday morning and, despite what Zoe might think—and she did seem to be prone to thinking the worst of him— he wasn't in the habit of casual relations with a woman.

As a matter of fact, it wasn't that he wasn't in the habit of—he didn't have casual relationships, period.

"Well, I'm right here, Bertram. What can I do for you?"

"I see that. You're here late at night, with a practical stranger."

"Yes, she is," Mace said, with forced ease.

"And I'm not quite a stranger anymore, am I Zoe?"

She didn't answer, but Mace didn't really expect her to. She did however blush, which wasn't what he expected at all.

He felt a tiny bit smug about that hint of pink in her cheeks. He knew that the blush meant that she knew that they were more than just strangers. Exactly how you'd describe their relationship, he wasn't sure, but *more than strangers* was at the very least accurate.

He smiled and continued, "We were looking for your evidence, Mr. Barky, but we haven't found anything."

"I don't think you'll find it in old newspapers. I've been over them with a fine-tooth comb. You'll notice there are issues missing from the archives. Maybe they got to them. But maybe they haven't got to the old files."

"I wonder who this *they* is," Mace muttered.

"Bertram," Zoe said, "We already realized that we weren't going to find anything in the archives and we're going to go through the old files tomorrow."

"And yet, you're both still here, sitting on the couch. Just what were you doing, eh?" He studied them both with a practiced stare.

Zoe's cheeks turned an even brighter shade of

red, but she said, "Bertram, I don't think that's any of your business."

"I think you're wrong, missy." Bertram waggled a finger in her face.

"Missy?" Zoe said, annoyance evident in her tone. "Now, see here, I'm an adult and I'm quite able to decide who I want to spend time with and—"

Bertram interrupted her. "I don't think so."

"Pardon me? I must have heard you wrong because I thought you said—"

"I don't think so," he repeated, interrupting her. "You wouldn't be the first woman to be taken in by a pretty face. And I'm afraid that's all this man is."

"Hey," Mace protested.

He was more than a pretty face. He was a reporter. An undervalued one perhaps, but a good one.

"Sorry. You seem like a nice enough guy, but you're not for our Zoe."

"Why do you say that?"

It wasn't as if Mace pictured himself settling down forever with Zoe Wallace, but it grated being dismissed out of hand like that.

"You've got the big-city itch all about you," Bertram said.

"What?"

"It's a restlessness. A need for the type of fast-paced world you'll never find here in Hiho."

Mace heard Zoe mutter, *"Bigger and better."*

"How would you know? You don't know a thing about me."

Neither did Zoe, for that matter. Oh, she knew the feel of his lips pressed against hers now, but she didn't know him, despite her attempts to psychoanalyze him. And suddenly it struck him that he wanted her to know. He wanted to share things with her and he wasn't sure why.

"You'd be surprised," Bertram said. "I could tell you all sorts of autobiographical information. What college you attended—that first little station you worked for in New York after graduation—when you started working for WMAC. I could probably even guess at how frustrated you are with the current direction the station is taking with its news program. I suspect you're thinking about a move, but I can guarantee you're not thinking of moving in Hiho's direction. And since that's the case, if you and Zoe start something, she'll end up hurt."

"How could you know all that?" Mace asked.

"I was a reporter…and it's not something you retire from. It's in your blood. An itch you can never quite shake. I see something new, my first instinct is to explore it. I checked you out, Mace. You're a fine reporter. And I was very impressed with your *Erie Chronicles,* but you're not for Zoe.''

''Bertram, you've been a good friend,'' Zoe said, ''but that doesn't give you the right—''

''Zoe, now, your aunt—God rest her soul—was my best friend. It was always Zoe-this and Zoe-that. I knew you long before you took over the paper. And she'd have my hide if I didn't look out for you. So, like it or not, I'll say what you don't want to hear, don't mess with him,'' he jerked his head toward Mace. ''You'll wind up hurt when he leaves.''

''But—''

''And leaving is about the only thing you can count on from him,'' the old man said to Zoe.

''Bertram, I don't think you came to discuss me and Mace, did you?''

''No. I came to see if I could help, but since you don't want to see the truth about the town or the man, I guess it's time for me to go.'' He started toward the front door.

''Bertram, wait.''

He turned. ''What?''

''Walk me home, okay?''

''Zoe?'' Mace asked. Now what was she thinking? ''You don't have to go.''

''Mace, Bertram's right. He's right about it being my duty as a reporter to find out the truth about Hiho's beginning and he's right about you and me.

You'll be leaving when the Centennial Celebration is over, looking for bigger and better. Me? I've found happiness in Hiho and I'm content with that. I'm pretty sure that even if being with you temporarily makes me even happier, in the long run, it will hurt me.''

"You don't know that.''

"But I do. Been there, done that, learned my lesson. I'll see you tomorrow bright and early for work…nothing else. Lock up when you leave, okay?''

Mace watched Bertram shepherd Zoe out the door.

It was probably for the best.

As much as he wanted Zoe, he had to admit that the odds were that he would indeed hurt her. After all, though he was looking to make a move from WMAC to something new, like Bertram said, he didn't think Hiho was the location he'd be moving to.

He looked around the office. Zoe had mentioned boxes of old files in the basement. He might as well go have a look because the chances of him getting any sleep tonight were slim to nil.

HOURS LATER, countless boxes opened, searched then closed, he found…nothing. He had the last box on his lap, with some of the oldest papers he'd found to date.

He pulled out a file but his eyes got heavy and he decided to just close them a moment before he took a look.

A moment turned into hours. There was light outside the high basement window when he finally woke up from a dream...a dream starring Zoe Wallace, co-starring him.

Coffee.

He needed coffee to wake up and remove any lingering taste of Zoe from his mind.

He decided to take the file with him and go through it over at Pete's.

Zoe had been right when she said the small restaurant with the simple name would soon feel like home.

He'd settled into a booth and was leafing through the papers, coffee in hand, when a voice— a decidedly female voice—said, "What a morning. You wouldn't believe it. That darned new sheriff gave me another ticket already. The man starts his rounds early just so he can ruin my morning. And speaking of mornings, you're up mighty early for a city slicker."

"Clover." Mace said. He felt a stab of guilt over how he'd treated her on their *date*. "About the other night—"

"Don't worry about it," she said, brushing away his apologies as she took the seat opposite him. "Sometimes the spark is there, sometimes it's not. So what are you doing?"

"Looking through old files from the *Herald*."

"What for?"

Mace wasn't sure if she'd heard about the centennial that might not be, and he refused to start rumors, so he settled for saying, "Just looking for any information on the town and its beginnings. I'm not only covering the centennial, but looking for information on Hiram for a short documentary series I do."

"If you want insights into the town's origins, I might be able to help."

"How?"

"There's always been a Clover in the family since the first Clover founded the college." She paused and added, "I know that's not going to help you. But the fact that the women in my family are notorious for keeping journals just might. Big, long, extensive journals. And it just so happens I have a number of them that the first Clover wrote."

"Really? Do you think I could see them?"

She smiled. "I think that could be arranged. After you're done eating, stop over at The General Store. I'll have them for you."

"Thanks so much." He leaned across the table and kissed her lightly on her cheek. "And thanks for understanding about the other night."

He was glad Clover understood him, because he certainly didn't understand himself. All he knew was that since the moment he saw Zoe Wallace and her bad makeover, she was all he could think about.

"Hey, I don't know if there's anything in them that will help. I don't think I've looked at them since I was in my teens."

"Well, I appreciate it no matter what they turn up."

6

_____

ZOE BREEZED INTO Pete's Eats later that morning, firm in her resolve.

She was not kissing Mace again.

As a matter of fact, she felt a bit ashamed that she'd let last night's kiss bother her to the extent that it had. Why, she'd practically run away afterward. You'd think she was a silly schoolgirl afraid of her first infatuation.

Infatuation.

It was a good word. It brought to mind something transitory, something that was just a passing fancy.

That's what Mace was—a passing fancy.

Oh, he was attractive enough, but he was just passing through, looking for something she wasn't sure he'd ever find. When someone was counting on *more* to make them feel fulfilled, it rarely ended well. There didn't tend to be enough *more* to ever satisfy anyone.

She'd learned that the hard way.

She felt a wave of sadness that he wasn't looking for happy. Mace Mason was a man who should be happy.

She cleared her thoughts again.

His happiness wasn't her concern.

Her own was. And she was going to be happy not kissing Mace Mason if it killed her.

Pasting a smile on her face, she called, "Hey, Pete."

"Hey, Zoe."

"Have you seen Mace?"

"Sure. Me and half the town," he snickered. "He was in here a bit ago, kissing Clover and making plans to meet up with her."

"Kissing Clover?" she repeated, not because she cared. Why, he was a legal, free adult and could kiss whoever he wanted to.

"Sure. The two of them there, bold as brass and he kissed her."

Podunk.

Podunk.

Podunk, Zoe chanted, just to remind herself that Mace was an annoying small-town-biased man. Why she didn't care even the tiniest little bit who he kissed....

She realized that she was lying to herself.

The fink.

He kissed her last night, and this morning he was kissing Clover.

Oh, he'd shown his true colors. And more

power to him. Maybe he'd given up on bigger and better, and simply decided to concentrate on sheer quantity.

"He said he was heading over to Clover's when he finished his breakfast."

"Well, that's great. If he's with Clover I don't have to worry about him. I've got a thousand and one things to take care of today before the dinner."

Just great.

She didn't care who Mace Mason was kissing.

As long as it wasn't her.

Because she definitely didn't want to be kissing him again. As a matter of fact, she wasn't going to see him any more than she absolutely had to. Not because she was hurt that he'd kissed Clover, but because she was busy. Too busy to put up with his shenanigans.

She was rather proud of the fact that she was true to her word and managed to avoid Mace all day.

Not that it was very hard.

She didn't see hide nor hair of him, so avoiding him was actually downright easy.

He was probably kissing Clover right now.

And she hardly even minded when she thought about it. Not that she thought about it all that much. Why she'd managed to go as long as ten minutes once without thinking of Mace at all. On one of those rare occasions when she had thought of him, she realized she didn't even like him. Kissing him last night had been the result of a sleep-deprived system. She did a lot of crazy things when she was tired.

Why, in college, after cramming for finals, she was so sleep deprived that she went to a karaoke bar and sang "Feelings."

"Feelings!"

Only the truly judgment-impaired would sing "Feelings" to a crowded bar...or kiss Mace Mason.

As a matter of fact, she was glad he'd been absent all day. She'd got a ton of work done. She had just enough time to go home and get ready for the big dinner tonight at the college.

Tomorrow the festival started and she'd be run ragged until it ended with the fireworks on Sunday.

Talk about sleep deprived.

She'd better make it a point to stay away from karaoke machines and Mace Mason. That way, even if she did have a sleep-deprived, judgment-impaired moment, she wouldn't have to worry about making a fool of herself by singing...or kissing.

Yeah, that was for the best.

She let herself into her house and waited for the

wave of ease that generally swept over her when she entered.

The only wave she got was a wave of annoyance when she realized her flowers were wilted and she hadn't thought to pick up another bunch.

She took the vase into the kitchen and tossed the flowers into the garbage. As she walked back through the living room it looked cold without the normal splash of color that lent the decor its drama and focal point.

Cold and almost clinical.

She didn't like it.

Even her house felt off-kilter since Mace arrived.

Thank goodness he was leaving Monday morning.

She'd just stepped out of the shower when she heard the doorbell. Wrapping her bathrobe around her, she padded barefoot to answer it.

She peeked through the peephole and her heart gave a small leap when she saw Mace.

She willed her heart back into its normal position.

Darn. He'd found her. So much for her avoiding abilities.

He knocked again. Through the peephole, his nose looked rather bulbous and distorted, but even the distortion couldn't disguise his impatience.

He knocked louder. "Zoe, I know you're in

there. I saw your neighbor, the older lady with the garden. She said you'd just got home.''

In New York she could come and go at will and no one ever noticed, but here, everyone knew everything. That was the one big downfall to small-town life. Not that she'd admit there was anything negative about small-town living to Mace.

''Yes?'' she called through the door.

''Are you ready?'' he called back.

''Ready for what?'' *More kissing?* she wanted to ask, but didn't. Because she wasn't. And wouldn't be. Ever.

''Ready for the party.''

Of course, he wasn't talking about kissing. He was kissing Clover now.

''Oh, the party.'' She looked down at her bathrobe and clutched it a little tighter. ''No, I'm not. I figured you'd be going with Clover.''

''Now why would you—'' he stopped, and said, ''Zoe, it's ridiculous talking through the door. Are you going to let me in?''

''I just got out of the shower.''

Her robe was thin. Why hadn't she noticed that before now? No way was she letting Mace in when the only thing that covered her was a threadbare bathrobe.

''So, unlock the door and I'll wait out here and count to twenty before I come in.''

''I wasn't expecting you.''

"I don't see why. We'd talked about going together."

"But…" She couldn't think of an argument for not opening the door.

"Are you going to let me in?" he called. She looked through the peephole one more time and studied his big, flaring nose. She'd remember the way it looked and any thoughts of kissing Mace would evaporate instantly. Why it would work better than chanting *Podunk*, which hadn't worked well at all.

"Yes." She fumbled with the locks. "Count to fifty before you open it."

"Okay."

Zoe rushed back to the bathroom. She closed and locked the door and rushed through dressing, uneasy, knowing Mace was somewhere lurking in her house.

Lurking.

Yeah. Thinking of Mace lurking was good.

It sounded ominous. Sinister even.

And that was better than kissable.

She toweled her hair and hurried through drying it. A light touch of makeup and she was done.

She remembered when she lived in New York, the idea of getting dressed to go out in under an hour would have appalled her, getting ready in under ten minutes would have totally mystified her.

But she looked in the mirror and was pleased with the effect.

She enjoyed the feeling because she was sure it wouldn't last. She had to deal with Mace, and dealing with Mace never left her feeling pleased.

Aggravated.

Annoyed.

Antsy.

Those were just the *A*s. She could probably go through the entire alphabet describing how Mace made her feel and never use the word *pleased*.

"Now, about the party," she started to say when she walked in the room.

Mace turned and let out a long whistle. "You look good."

"Uh, thanks. You look all right as well."

That was the biggest understatement she'd ever made. *All right* didn't even begin to cover how Mace looked in his suit. He looked like eye-candy.

A boy-toy she'd love to play with.

Not that she was playing with Mace.

No, but he was toying with her.

Her and Clover.

Remembering about him kissing Clover made her feel better.

"About the party—" she started to say, but Mace interrupted her.

"Where are the flowers?" he asked.

"What?"

"Last time, you had flowers on the table. They really stood out because of all the white, which is probably the only reason I noticed them. Noticing flowers isn't something I normally do. Or decor. I'm not the kind of guy that notices things like that, but you couldn't miss how white this room is, so of course, that made me notice the flowers. Where are they?"

"Well, thank you for clearing up your manly disinterest in interior design and flowers."

"So, where are they?" he pressed.

"I didn't have time to get any. I've been busy trying to run a business and get everything ready for tomorrow."

"And is it?" he asked.

"Is what?"

Zoe was lost. Normally she could follow a conversation no matter how many zigs or zags it took, but Mace was zigging way too much and looked way too good in his suit, which made her mind zag in uncomfortable directions.

"Is everything ready for tomorrow?" he asked.

"As ready as I can make it."

"Good. Then let's go." He started toward the door.

"About that, like I said, I figured you'd be going with Clover and made plans accordingly. You don't have to feel obligated to take me."

"Obligated? Is that how you think I feel?"

"Sure. You're dating Clover, kissing her in public, so of course you'd rather take her."

Darn. She wished she could take back that last part of her sentence—the kissing Clover part. She had planned on not mentioning the kissing Clover part to show him she didn't care, because of course, she didn't care.

"Kissing her? I never…" he hesitated and then started laughing. "Oh, that little peck on the cheek I gave her this morning? Is that what you're referring to?"

"I'm not referring to anything, I'm just saying, you're welcome to take her to the party tonight. I can manage myself."

"What if I told you that it was just a friendly little kiss. She'd gave me a new lead. The kiss—no, not kiss—the peck was just a thanks."

"If that's how you thank women for giving you information, what do you do when someone gives you something really important?"

"You know what, Zoe, you sound a bit—" he paused, and looked as if he was searching for the right word, then smiled as he continued "—jealous. Yes, jealous would be the word I'd use to describe how you're acting."

"Jealous?" Zoe scoffed. A loud, barky sort of scoffing sound. "Me, jealous? Of what? You?"

"Of me kissing Clover."

"You've got to be kidding."

"Are you sure you're not upset about thinking that I've been kissing another woman?"

"Positive. There are things I'm absolutely positive of. I'm positive that the moon orbits the earth, just as the earth orbits the sun. I'm certain that I don't like brussels sprouts or liver. And I'm certain that there's no way I could ever be jealous of you kissing anyone."

There she'd told him.

Of course, maybe she felt the slightest twinge of something in the pit of her stomach every time she thought about Mace and Clover together. So it was a good thing for her that she didn't think of them often.

Hardly at all.

Why, the picture of Clover clinging to Mace, locked in his embrace rarely flitted through her mind.

"Well, if you're sure," he said, sounding skeptical.

"Totally sure. Why if I was any surer, I could…" She couldn't think of a single thing to say. What a stupid comment. She wasn't someone who was prone to stupid comments and the fact that she was making them now was just one more sin to pin on Mace.

"Well, since you're that sure, I won't worry about it. Let's go."

"Go where?" she asked, confused again.

"To the party."

She shrugged her shoulders, just to remind herself of his annoying shoulder-shrugging habit. "Whatever."

"Ah, don't be so enthusiastic, Zoe. You're embarrassing me."

"You think you're funny," she said, hoping she added just the right inflection to let him know she didn't think he was.

"I know I am."

She couldn't think of any brilliant retort, so she said, "So did you find anything?"

"Switching gears again," Mace said with a *tsk*.

The *tsk* was almost as annoying as his shoulder-shrugging.

She wished he'd *tsk* her again. But instead, he asked, "Find anything about what?"

"About Hiho's true centennial date."

"I still have some more research. But I don't want to talk about it tonight."

He was hiding something. She was reporter enough to recognize the evasion.

"If you found something and are holding out on me..." she left the threat hanging, hoping it sounded ominous.

"Zoe, there's nothing I'd hold out on you. As a matter of fact, you're welcome to hold everything I have." He wiggled his eyebrows suggestively, a huge grin pasted on his very handsome face.

She stood up straight and looked him right in the eyes. "I don't think so."

Looking in his eyes was a mistake. She hadn't reckoned on how dreamy they were. Dreamy and captivating.

Darn.

"Your loss," he said with a grin and a shrug.

He whistled as she closed up the house and they headed out the door without another word.

His car was parked in her driveway. "I know you're fond of walking, but I thought we'd ride tonight."

"I normally just walk because it's faster than worrying about parking spaces when you're only going a couple of blocks. But I do own a car and have been known to ride in one."

"Glad to hear it."

Zoe might not mind riding in cars, but she didn't want to ride in Mace's. She stood there, wondering how to get out of it without him starting on his you-want-me refrain again.

"Are you getting in?" he asked.

"I was just thinking that it might be better if I took my car. That way if I'm ready to go and you're still having a good time, you don't have to worry about me and vice versa."

"That's not what you're thinking. You're thinking that if I meet up with Clover I'll be free to leave with her.''

He was wrong, but she let it slide and gave a noncommittal shrug.

''What do I have to say to get it through your thick skull that I'm not interested in Clover Addison?'' He moved away from the car and toward her.

''Nothing,'' she said, taking a step away, keeping a nice bit of distance between them. ''I mean, my skull's not thick and it doesn't matter if you're interested in her.''

''I think it does.'' His voice was low and silky.

Zoe swallowed hard. ''Are we back to that jealous thing again?''

''Yes.''

''No.''

''No?'' he asked.

''No, I'm not jealous. And you don't have to convince me that you and Clover aren't an item because it doesn't matter.''

''I think it does and I think I do.''

''Forget it.''

''Come here.'' He didn't wait for her to move toward him. For a big man he moved fast. He closed the space that separated them in the blink of an eye.

Zoe knew what was coming. She could have turned away. Could have run screaming in the other direction. But instead she waited, wanting him to kiss her.

She'd thought last night's kiss was powerful, but this one...

It was the sucker punch of kisses.

Last night's kiss, which she'd thought was so hot, was in reality vanilla pudding and tonight's kiss was the barbecued wings.

"Wow," he muttered when he finally broke it off.

He broke it off because Zoe couldn't have, just like she couldn't run from the kiss.

The truth was, she was addicted to Mace Mason's kisses.

But that didn't mean she liked him.

And it certainly didn't mean she was jealous.

She brushed off her skirt and tried to adopt a blasé look as she said, "Let's go."

It might have worked except her voice was breathy, as if she'd just run a marathon instead of having kissed a man.

Darn.

This was going to be the longest party ever.

MACE HAD MET half of Hiho's population, he was sure.

He'd met the librarian, Katy Sloane, who'd given up her reign as Miss Hiho. He'd met Brandi, the runner-up who was now the reigning Miss

Hiho. He'd met Joel Carter and his boss, Big Bert. He'd met the mayor, a cute will-o-the-wisp woman named Victoria Robertson. She was petite and extremely beautiful, but he'd hardly given her a second look.

That was Zoe's fault.

He should be ogling the cute little mayor.

Or even kissing Clover.

Not just some peck on the cheek, but a full-out kiss.

Clover was a beautiful lady. Beautiful and not nearly as complicated as little Miss Don't-Kiss-Me, I'm-Not-Jealous Zoe Wallace.

She was jealous. He was sure of it.

Well, pretty sure.

She'd been thinking about him and Clover all day and it was driving her nuts.

Good.

Turnabout was fair play. She'd been driving him nuts since he left last night.

This whole town was driving him nuts.

He thought of the journal he'd found that afternoon.

That first Clover had a wonderful, candid writing style and had recorded a frank portrayal of her town. It had given him insights into Hiram Hump which would make portraying the three-dimensional man ever so much easier.

There had also been a lot about Hiram's wife, Hortense.

Clover wrote about tutoring Hortense. The woman could read, but complained that the words seemed to move around right in front of her eyes.

Mace suspected that today she would be diagnosed with dyslexia. But back then…well, Clover had written that Hiram referred to his wife as *addlepated*. Clover had noted that he'd always said it with a smile of affection.

Affection.

That was the word she'd used to describe the Humps' relationship. And that affection was what led Hiram to come to Clover after he'd discovered that there had been a mix-up in the paperwork to incorporate the town.

Clover had fixed it and the town had been official in February of 1904. Not May of 1903.

Bertram was right. Hiho wasn't a hundred.

It was ninety-nine.

Mace looked at the crowd.

He spotted Aunt Aggie and Pete.

There was Clover, talking to the mayor.

And Zoe.

There she was talking to the infamous Mrs. Pete, the woman who injected such terror into Bertram and Pete's hearts, and could cook with the skill of an angel.

If he let this information out, he'd hurt all of them. The college would lose its endowment until next year. An endowment it had already borrowed against. He wasn't sure if they could put off payments that long. What would that kind of financial hardship do to the small, private college? And if something happened to the college, what would happen to the town?

Mace knew he couldn't sit on the information, as much as he wanted to protect Hiho and its residents.

Despite himself, he'd begun to like them all.

"Ah, you're that reporter boy that's been mooning over Zoe."

"Pardon?" Mace saw a small, older lady standing at his side. He knew he'd met her, but he couldn't quite place her.

"Cora. Cora MacIntosh."

He nodded. "Ah, yes, the pie-judging scandal."

"Are you mocking me, boy?" There was more than a hint of reprimand in her voice.

"No, ma'am, of course I'm not."

"I realize a small-town pie competition might not seem like all that important to you, but my sister and I take great pride in our cooking."

"I'm sure you do. Truly, I wasn't making fun of you."

He remembered when he'd talked to Steph right after he'd heard about the toothless judge. He had been making fun of the MacIntosh sisters' concerns.

He felt a wave of shame.

"See to it that you don't." She waggled her finger in a way that made Mace wonder if she'd been a teacher once upon a time.

"Now, about your attraction to our Zoe," she continued.

"What?"

"You heard me. Everyone's noticed and is talking about it."

"Everyone in this town is out of their everlovin' minds if they think there's anything between me and Zoe." Even to his own ears his denial sounded less than forceful.

"Really? Well, let's see, there's the fact you two spent the night together—"

"In her office working. It was as platonic as can be." Well, practically platonic. One kiss didn't unplatonic it.

As if she'd read his mind, Cora said, "I don't call kissing platonic. And you did in fact kiss Zoe before you came here."

"How on earth do you know that?" It had only been, what, a half hour? How on earth did this woman know?

"Well, Lani Standish lives across the street from Zoe. She's been Zoe's aunt's neighbor for years…you did know that Zoe's house belonged to her aunt, right? Not that Zoe left it as a memorial to Betty. Zoe made it her own, though I don't know what she was thinking when she made that room all white. Why, imagine when she has children one day what they'll do to a white room. And it's sort of cold.''

Mace wasn't about to argue that rather than cold the room was inviting, although the absence of flowers today bothered him. Zoe had said she was busy, but somehow he wasn't buying that explanation.

The bright splash of color in the room had spoken of hidden passion. Its absence made him wonder if Zoe was trying to hide her sensuality. And if so, was she hiding it from him or from herself?

''...and so Lani told Bertram, who said that you'd spent last night at Zoe's, so kissing made sense, even if it didn't make any of us happy. And that's when I decided it was my duty to tell you to be careful. If you hurt our Zoe we'll hunt you down.''

''Ah, just who is the *we* that will be hunting me?'' Mace asked, not overly intimidated by the woman. As a matter of fact, he was touched that she was looking after Zoe.

From the sounds of it, half the town was looking after Zoe.

Mace tried to think of anyone in his life who would defend him with such vehemence, but he couldn't think of anyone. Oh, he was friendly with his colleagues and had a waving relationship with his neighbors, but there wasn't the connection that this small community seemed to have.

Mace knew the blame was his. He was so focused on his work that he rarely took time to concentrate on the people who surrounded him. Maybe that's why people were telling Stephanie he was terse. Maybe he was.

"Ma'am, I assure you that I don't intend to hurt Zoe."

"And you know what they say about good intentions paving the road to hell, don't you?"

"I—"

"Mace, there you are. I want you to meet Rob Pawley," Zoe said, rushing in to save the day.

Mace waited to see if Cora was going to warn Zoe as well. But the older lady simply smiled and said, "Zoe, I was just getting to know your Mr. Mason."

"He's not my anything," Zoe replied quickly. Too quickly.

Cora shot Mace a look that said, *let's keep it that way,* and then started talking to Zoe.

Mace turned to the weak-chinned Rob Pawley. "I had hoped to have a chance to talk to you tonight. I understand you're in charge of the Pawley endowment."

"Yes. And I understand you're digging into this whole alleged centennial mix-up. Don't."

"I'm a reporter," Mace said. "Digging is what

I do. And even if I don't like what I find, I have to report it.''

''Even if what you find is going to hurt a lot of people. The whole community?'' Rob Pawley asked, echoing Mace's own concerns.

''So you believe that the town doesn't really turn one hundred until next year?'' Mace asked.

''I'm not saying that,'' the weak-chinned man said hastily. ''I've seen no tangible proof, just a lot of accusations.''

Mace could show him written documentation, but he didn't say so, instead he said, ''Is it possible for me to see the actual paperwork for the endowment?''

''See it?'' Pawley echoed.

''The paperwork.''

''The original document is old and fragile,'' he said slowly.

''A copy is fine. I just want to read it for myself.''

Mace could see that Pawley wasn't pleased with the request, but the man gave him a curt nod. ''Come to my office Monday and I'll get you a copy.''

''I leave town on Monday.'' With the way news circulated in this town, Mace was sure the man knew that. Heck, he probably had heard about the whole kissing-Zoe thing as well. ''Is there any chance you could get it for me tomorrow?" Mace asked.

"I don't normally have office hours on Saturdays." Pawley sighed. "But I have to go in and do a few things, so I guess I could. Why don't you stop by about eight, if that's not too early."

"No, that's fine."

Someone across the room called Pawley. He turned and said, "I'll see you in the morning then, Mr. Mason."

Mace wasn't sure why he wanted to see the document. But when he did a job he tried to be complete and the endowments for the college and library were the crux of the entire matter. If it wasn't for the endowments, the fact that the Centennial Celebration was a year off wouldn't matter.

But it did matter.

It mattered to the college.

It mattered a lot to the whole town.

It mattered to Zoe.

And because of that, it mattered to Mace.

7

_____

"I'M SO GLAD that's over," Zoe said as they pulled in her driveway three hours later.

"You didn't enjoy yourself?" Mace asked.

"It was a bit too formal for my taste." Zoe didn't want to add that she'd spent the better part of the evening watching Mace, sure that he'd gravitate to Clover.

But strangely enough, other than a brief greeting the two hardly spoke. And they certainly hadn't kissed.

She had to stop thinking about Mace and kissing...whether she was thinking about him kissing Clover, or kissing her.

She might not like the thought, but she certainly liked the kisses, even though she wasn't sure she liked Mace.

Oh, he'd seemed like a nice guy, at first. After all, he hadn't laughed at her disastrous makeover.

But then there was the whole *Podunk* thing.

And the fact that he was driven to succeed with no thought at all about happiness.

Plus, just for good measure, there was the stone-hard fact that he was leaving Monday.

Yes, she certainly should keep her distance from Mace.

And yet, when he turned off the car and walked her to the door, rather than bolting in the house and shutting the door in his face, she heard herself ask, "Would you like to come in for a drink?"

"No," was his flat response.

"Oh." Maybe she'd been mistaken, thinking that Mace was as attracted to her as she was to him. She opened the door and started inside.

"But," Mace said, gently holding her shoulder, "I'd like to come in and pick up where we left off earlier."

"And where was that?"

"I'd show you, but your neighbor, Loni Something—"

"Lani?" Zoe asked, not sure what he was talking about.

What had the snoopy old lady done now? It wasn't that she didn't like Lani, but the woman knew everything that happened on the block... knew it, and publicized it with an efficiency that rivaled the paper's.

"Seems she likes watching out her window, and reporting our kisses to the whole town."

"Oh, no." She should have known better than to do anything in her front yard that she didn't want the entire town hearing about.

"Oh, yes. I've been warned to keep my distance or else I'm to be a target for a town-wide manhunt."

"Who said that?"

Zoe loved Hiho, loved being part of a community that looked after its own, but there was a difference between looking after and butting in.

"It doesn't matter. Part of me agrees with them. I should just walk away and forget how attracted I am to you." He stepped closer.

Zoe could smell whatever aftershave he used. Hot and spicy. The thought made her think of barbecued wings and she couldn't help but smile. "And the other part?"

"Wants to follow you into the house and pick up where we left off earlier."

"This is probably a mistake," she said, knowing that that was a vast understatement, "but I think I agree with that second part."

"You do?" He sounded as surprised at her confession as she felt.

"Yes. I don't know why. You make me crazy. I think you've got your priorities all wrong and I know you'll be leaving Monday. And yet none of that matters." She opened the door. "I want you to come in."

They both entered the house and Zoe shut the door with a bang. Closing them away from Lani's prying eyes.

Closing the door on her doubts.

"And now…" She stepped into his arms and it felt like coming home. Worries slipped away. Thought as well. All that was left was feeling. A feeling of rightness. Of something more than that…

His lips lowered and met her anxious ones.

The sweet kiss went on forever.

And ever.

Sweetness gave way to need…more than need, urgency.

Zoe was the one who broke off the kiss. She ran her fingers through his hair, toying with it. "I need to tell you that I don't…I mean, we've only known each other such a short time and during that time you've annoyed me as often as you've delighted me. This…whatever it is, well, it's different than anything I've ever felt. I know you're leaving and I know this can't last, but none of that alters the fact that I want you. Want you more than I've ever wanted anyone."

"I can't make you any promises," Mace said softly.

"I know. That's why I'm not asking for any. I just want…"

Zoe made her living with words, using them to explain things. But this once, words failed her. She couldn't explain this to Mace, mainly because she couldn't explain the powerful feelings she had toward him to herself.

So she abandoned words and simply took his hand, leading him toward her bedroom.

"Are you sure?" he asked.

"Shh," she said.

She opened the door and drew him inside, closing it behind them.

MACE LOOKED AT ZOE. Studying her, trying to memorize the sight of her.

She was so different than any other woman he'd ever met. If asked, he couldn't have explained the difference. But she made him question himself, made him want to be more than he was, made him feel as if anything were possible.

This moment that seemed so impossible was proof of that. He reached out and stroked her hair. Black. True black, not that blackish brown. It might overpower some women's looks, but Zoe's sky-blue eyes and warm smile acted as a perfect foil for her hair.

She was beautiful.

Stunningly, breathtakingly beautiful.

Not just on the outside, but inside.

Her love for her community, her care of it, was just the surface of her kindness.

He remembered the first time he saw her, big hair, bobbling eyelash. She'd gotten the makeover, knowing what she was in for, because she couldn't bear to hurt someone's feelings.

A quick mind, a tender heart.

Yes, Zoe Wallace was beautiful.

"I don't want to hurt you," he said aloud, voicing his fears.

"I want you, Mace. If you left me now, that would hurt."

She took his hand and drew him toward the bed.

He finally took his eyes off her long enough to glance around the room.

After seeing her decorating taste in the living room, he would have thought this room would be ultramodern and chic as well. Instead, it was soft...romantic even. Pastel blue walls, sheer fabrics. Her bed was huge and had a canopy of some gauzy stuff.

She sat down on it and pulled him next to her.

A soft flannel comforter covered the bed.

Taking in the detail with a reporter's eye gave way to taking the woman with a man's passion— a passion that surprised him with its sheer force.

Zoe sat next to him, hesitating a moment, then she moved closer and kissed him again, untucking his shirt as her lips parted, inviting more.

Zoe had surprised him again. He'd expected her to be timid, to let him take the lead. He realized he shouldn't assume anything about Zoe Wallace. Every time he did, she bewildered him yet again.

He started to unbutton his shirt, but her hands stopped him.

"Let me, please," she asked. Her proper and polite request seemed incongruous with her intense exploration of his body. She unbuttoned the shirt and her lips skimmed his skin, touching and tasting as if he was a gigantic treat she wanted to savor.

She pulled the shirt off his shoulder and tossed it to the floor. She eased him back on the comforter and continued to remove clothes until he was fully naked and she was still quite clothed.

"I don't know if this is quite fair," he said.

"Oh, it's not," Zoe assured him without stopping her exploration. "I've found that keeping an upper hand with you is wise."

"I—"

"You're not going to start a fight now, are you, Mace?"

She sighed and before he could get out another word she said, "Probably. Fighting with me seems to be your favorite pastime. So, in an effort to stave off any complaints of unfairness, I guess I'll just have to strip."

He sat up at that proclamation. "I could help," he offered.

"No. You just stay put. It will only take a minute."

She stood on the bed, right above him, a huge

grin on her face as she did this provocative little shimmy, pulling the dress over her head with excruciating slowness.

Inch by inch, she eased it up and over her head, then threw it over her shoulder onto the floor.

''More?'' she asked, a siren's smile on her face saying she knew exactly what she was doing to him.

Mace gulped convulsively and couldn't seem to force words past the constriction in his throat, so he simply nodded.

Zoe laughed then, a sound of pure joy and power.

She slid her hands behind her back and unhooked her bra, easing it slowly down, revealing herself to him.

She shimmied out of her panties and they joined the rest of their clothes on the floor.

She stood naked and completely uninhibited before him.

''There. Now, it's all even. You're naked and I'm naked, and...'' she knelt by him, a knowing smile on her face. ''And I can get back to the study I was making.''

''Study?''

''Oh, yes. I've always been very studious. I like to uncover all the facts about any particular subject I'm interested in.''

''And what are you interested in now?''

"You. And you're making a fascinating subject." She was once again exploring his body with her lips and her hands—hands that moved lower and stopped. "You know how I said bigger isn't always better?" she asked, looking up at him, laughter in her eyes. "Well, maybe—just maybe—sometimes it is."

She burst out laughing, and Mace couldn't help but join her.

"And here I was about to admit that sometimes happy is the most important thing. You know what would make me happy?"

Still smiling her eyes met his. "What?"

"This." He rolled, taking her with him, and switching their positions so that he was on top, pinning her lush body beneath him. "I want you," he whispered, the laughter in his voice replaced by desire. "I want you now."

"What are you waiting for?" she said.

"Just one thing." He leaned over the bed and fumbled for his pant's pocket. "I wasn't planning on this, but I wanted to be safe if—"

"Shh," Zoe said, taking the foil packet from his hands and turning the act of being responsible and safe into something sensuous, as she slid the condom in place with a soft deliberate slowness.

Mace had reached his limits. He rolled her onto her back and sank into her delicious warmth, merging their two bodies into one.

His entire world narrowed and focused until all there was in it was this woman, this moment, this joining. He couldn't get enough, couldn't get close enough, couldn't bear to withdraw the merest inch. Needing to bury himself as deeply as he could in Zoe.

"Mace," she whispered. Just that, just his name. But in that single syllable he heard her need, her desire climbing to its pinnacle and as he pushed into her warmth deeper than ever before he heard just the smallest exhale of breath, a small gasp as her entire body tightened in its completion.

That was all it took for Mace to explode. The intensity of the orgasm robbed him of every thought except Zoe. Her image wrapped itself around his brain, just as she had wrapped herself around his body.

He sank onto her too exhausted to move.

Zoe's eyes met his and she smiled, a small intimate smile and whispered, "Yes, sometimes bigger is better."

He chuckled. "And sometimes happy is."

He kissed her. Despite their lovemaking, there was still desire in the kiss, but more than that, there was a tenderness Mace had never felt for any woman.

A tenderness and something else…something more. He wasn't sure what that something was and his brain was too fogged with what they'd just done to puzzle it out.

He'd figure it out in the morning.

Zoe woke and lay perfectly still for a moment, replaying the night before.

She wasn't a total innocent, but what she'd done with Mace was completely out of her scope of experience.

She thought of her little striptease and felt her cheeks warm. She'd never been so brazen with anyone before, but with Mace she'd been totally uninhibited. She'd wanted to see every inch of him, and had no compunction about showing him every inch of herself.

She remembered joking with him about the whole bigger-happier thing and chuckled. She'd never joked with a man during intimacy.

There seemed to be a lot of firsts around Mace. He annoyed her more than any man she'd ever met...and conversely, he delighted her more than any man she'd ever met.

She rolled, ready to let him delight her again, and realized the bed was empty.

Her heart sank and she felt cold.

He'd left.

After their amazing night he'd left without even a goodbye.

She flopped back on her pillow, then realized

there was a faint rumbling noise coming from outside her bedroom. A noise that wasn't a normal house noise.

He was still here.

Her heart sped up and she smiled as she climbed out of bed and tossed on her robe. She ran into the bathroom and took the quickest shower in the history of showers. She wanted to be with Mace, wanted to bring him back to her bedroom and have her way with him again.

Then she remembered the Centennial Celebration.

Darn.

Well, maybe tonight when it was over, he'd come back to her house with her.

She wrapped a robe around herself, not wanting to wait to dress to see him again. To reassure herself that he was indeed still here.

He was in the living room, looking out the window, a cell phone to his ear. "...yes, I got it, but I was busy.... You were right, there is a story here. A newsworthy story even.... It has to do with a centennial that wasn't.... No, I'm not ready to do a spot on it. I still have a few facts to get straight.... Yes... The History Channel?"

Mace was silent for a long time, listening to whatever whoever was saying.

Zoe hugged her robe tighter.

Aunt Betty used to say you never heard anything good when you eavesdropped.

That might seem like an odd sentiment for a reporter to have, but Aunt Betty wasn't the type of reporter to get her stories on the sly. She was upfront and honest in all her dealings.

Unlike Mace—the ratfink—Mason.

He was going to run with the centennial that wasn't story.

Had he found some proof?

Probably. Zoe doubted he'd print the story if he hadn't.

He was going to lose the college and library their endowments and, in so doing, hurt the community that she loved.

But Zoe could have forgiven that. Mace was a reporter after all, and reporting was his job.

But he'd held out on her.

She was sure he had proof...proof he hadn't shared.

She thought they were closer than that.

Oh, she didn't expect words of undying love, but even before last night, even when they fought, she'd thought they'd had a connection. A friendship even.

She'd trusted him.

Back in her New York days she would have known better than to trust another reporter with a big story. New York had been a dog-eat-dog, watch-your-back-at-all-times sort of atmosphere.

But here in Hiho, she'd learned to let down her guard.

That was her mistake.

Letting down her guard with Mace both professionally, and more importantly, personally.

The creep had double-crossed her.

"...What's to think about?" he said. "My future... Yes, I realize it's an opportunity of a lifetime, but I need to be sure it would be a lifetime I could live with, that I could be happy with.... Yes. Monday morning. Bye. And Steph? Thanks."

He flipped his cell phone closed.

Zoe stepped into the living room.

Mace smiled. "Good morning."

He took a few steps toward her, but Zoe countered his every step with one of her own, keeping distance between them.

"Don't good morning me, you fink."

He stopped in his tracks. "Zoe, after last night, I thought I'd warrant at least a good morning before we started fighting again. What did I do this time?"

"You have something about the centennial, something you didn't share."

He raked his fingers through his hair, and Zoe could almost feel the texture of it, feel the urge to plunge her own fingers into it, to tangle them up with his, to...

No.

She was done lusting after Mace—the ratfink—Mason.

He nodded. "You're right. I should have shared that I want to fix whatever you're annoyed with, and take you back to bed and—"

Zoe interrupted. "Don't play games with me, Mason. You have some proof about the centennial."

"Yes, I do," he said with a slight frown. "I was going to tell you."

"When? After the story was headlined on your show?" Zoe couldn't believe she'd been taken in, that she'd fallen for Mace Mason's good-looking facade and hadn't seen past it to the ratfink underneath.

"I—"

She interrupted, not being in the mood for excuses. "Or better yet, were you going to wait until Rob was presenting the endowment checks to Leonard Stanley and Katy Sloane, then drop your bombshell? Ah, that would make for a good sense of the dramatic. Why, you could even get it on tape, I imagine. It would make for a good news segment. More news than the non-news stuff you said you hated reporting."

"Zoe, do you really think I'd do that?"

He sounded...hurt.

But Zoe wasn't going to be taken in again. She wasn't going to believe his act this time, nor was she going to believe the small tug coming from somewhere in the vicinity of her heart—a small tug that whispered Mace wasn't a fink. He was special.

Ha!

A special sort of fink, that's what he was.

"Listening to you made me realize I don't know you at all," Zoe said. "I thought I did. I thought I could trust this feeling I had for you, even though I only met you at the beginning of the week. I thought maybe that at-first-sight stuff was right."

"Love at first sight?" he murmured.

"I didn't say that *L* word. If I'd used an *L* word at all it would have been lust at first sight. Maybe even friendship, but not love."

"So, do you go to bed with everyone you lust after?" he asked.

"Of course not," Zoe said.

He stepped closer, but this time she didn't move backwards, she held her ground.

"How about friends?" Mace asked. "Do you sleep with all your friends?"

"Don't be ridiculous and insulting. I told you that I don't normally do things like this."

"Then why me?"

That was the question. Why him? Something

different than just friendship, than just lust whispered again, but she pushed the thought away. No matter what it was, she was done with Mace Mason.

"I don't know," she said. "But the point is, I didn't know you the way I thought I did. You're a fink. You used me."

"I used you?" he asked. There was a soft, dangerous quality to his tone that she'd never heard before.

"Yes. You used me to get the story. I didn't expect you to sit on the story if you found proof, but I told you about the situation assuming we'd share not only the looking for answers, but the finding of them. Once upon a time I would have known better."

"Zoe." His voice was sharp with censure.

Zoe felt a spurt of guilt, as if she was the one who'd done something wrong. But she knew she wasn't. The one who'd done wrong was ratfink Mace Mason.

"Get out, Mace. It's time for you to go. I have to get ready for the parade and the festival."

"Do you want to know what I'm going to do with the information?"

"No," she said. "You wanted the story so bad, it's yours. You run with it. And when you're done, I hope you run home to Erie and forget all about

Hiho and about me, because I plan to do my best to forget about you."

"Zoe, I—"

She interrupted him. "Goodbye, Mace. Thanks for reminding me why I moved here. I'd almost forgotten what it was like before I came to Hiho, the looking over my shoulder, not truly trusting anyone. You go get your bigger and better life, and I'll stay here and settle for happy."

"I—"

"I don't have time for this. Goodbye, Mace."

She turned and walked away from him, walked away from the man she hadn't just lusted over, hadn't just felt friendship for.

Zoe was afraid she'd finally figured out just what it was she felt for Mace. She was very much afraid that she'd done the unthinkable...that she'd fallen for Mace in an uncharacteristically love-at-first-sight fashion.

But if she could fall in love with someone so fast, certainly she could fall out of love just as easily.

She fervently hoped so.

Zoe Wallace shut the bedroom door, not wanting to hear the man she thought she loved leave.

8

MACE HAD HIS CAR, so he did something rather unheard of in Hiho...he drove. He drove to Rob Pawley's office. It was only a few blocks from Zoe's. But then, there wasn't much in Hiho that was far from Zoe's.

Right now he felt a lot farther than ten blocks away from her.

And he didn't like it.

He really had planned to tell her about his find in Clover's journal. But last night his mind wasn't on the town's centennial that wasn't.

It was on Zoe. And only on Zoe.

Not just a casual thinking of her, of what it would be like with her, but a total focused, forget-everything-else sort of way.

Her crack about not knowing him hurt.

Although, he'd be the first to admit that his immediate connection to her was...well, it wasn't like him. Not at all. He wasn't one to trust someone wholeheartedly even after years of knowing them.

He was a reporter. He dealt in facts, not feelings.

And yet, with Zoe there was an immediate spark even the first time he saw her with that horrendous makeover and falling eyelash.

Zoe was a beautiful woman, with an astounding capacity for caring…she showed it in the way she dealt with everyone from old *psst*ing reporters, to runaway bulls, to pie-judging concerned old ladies. But more than that, she challenged him. She stood right up to him and argued her points.

This time she was wrong. He truly had intended to tell her what he'd found.

But she'd been right to make him question exactly what he wanted in his career. She'd been right about bigger not always being better.

She was right about being happy.

And being with Zoe made him happy.

So, how was he going to fix…all this?

He mentally made a list.

Fix the centennial-that-wasn't scandal so no one was hurt and he could retain his journalistic integrity.

Fix his career.

And last, but certainly not least, fix things with Zoe, because he suspected he'd never be happy without her. And he'd discovered that she was right when she said that was what mattered.

He pulled up in front of Rob Pawley's, anxious to start solving all the problems he suddenly had.

Rob handed over a copy of the endowment, obviously not thrilled to be doing so. He, like everyone else in town, didn't want to know the truth. But the truth was out there. And if Mace could find it, someone else could, too. So all that was left was to deal with it.

Speaking of dealing with it...it was time for the parade and he still had a story to cover.

He pulled up a few blocks from the parade route, grabbed his camera from the trunk, along with a tripod, and made his way to the grandstand.

Zoe was sitting up there with a bunch of people. Mace knew he'd met a few of them last night at the party, but after a while their names all ran together.

There was the mayor, a tiny thing, but a real in-charge sort of lady.

Mace made his obligatory greetings to the crowd as he set up his camera.

Well, he greeted everyone but Zoe, who made it a point of moving out of greeting range. He moved forward, she faded back. He moved toward the back of the crowd, she headed for the side.

How on earth was he going to convince the woman he wasn't a...what had she called him? A fink.

Yeah. That hurt.

Zoe started announcing the parade. "And leading our parade in style, this year, is Joel Carter. Joel is the great-great-grandson of our founder, Hiram Hump. Let's give a warm Hiho greeting to Joel."

The crowd clapped wildly.

"And here's Cloverleaf College's marching band with the school mascot, Bessie."

Mace let the tape roll, capturing the parade on film. But try as he might, he couldn't pay attention to the parade. He kept glancing back at the woman announcing.

The woman he'd spent the most amazing night of his life with.

The woman who thought he was a fink.

As Bessie walked right in front of Mace, a bull blundered out onto the parade route from behind the grandstand.

"Jed," Mace muttered.

No one in the crowd was doing anything, not even Zoe, the fearless cowgirl.

Mace sensed a chance to force Zoe to acknowledge him, to look at him. He grabbed a cable that he hadn't needed, but had inadvertently brought for the camera, and fashioned it into a crude lasso, jumped off the grandstand and headed toward the big bull.

The closer he got, the bigger it looked.

Bigger than it had looked when Zoe lassoed it.

Bigger than even Paul Bunyan's Babe.

The thing was a monster.

"Hey, Jed," he crooned, as he approached, lasso ready to go. "Hey, boy."

Mace threw the lasso over the beast's head, reminding himself that Zoe had said the bull was as gentle as a lamb.

As the lasso slid over the bull's neck, Mace suddenly registered that the crowd was quiet.

Not just quiet, they were silent.

But the bull wasn't.

It was snorting.

And it didn't look the least bit lamblike.

As a matter of fact, it looked annoyed.

Very, very annoyed.

It shook its giant head, then snorted as it charged, right at Mace.

"Mace, it's not Jed," Zoe cried, breaking the silence.

"Oh, no," Mace cried, as he ran, a bull hot on his heels.

The crowd scattered.

Pandemonium ensued.

But the bull-who-wasn't-lamblike-Jed ignored everything and everyone except Mace.

Mace headed back away from the crowd, toward the back of the town square, knowing that a non-Jed-ish bull could really hurt someone.

He dodged behind trees, keeping one step ahead of the brute.

He ran around a park picnic table. It was big enough to keep the bull from reaching him, and yet small enough that the bull couldn't cut the corners as tight as Mace could, which gave Mace the advantage.

The cord flapped around, uselessly behind the brute.

Suddenly, Mace had an idea.

He sprinted around the table, coming up behind the bull, and grabbed the long cord.

A huge plug that attached the cord to the camera flapped at the end of the line.

As the bull rounded the table, trying to catch Mace, Mace wedged the cord into the space between the picnic table slats.

The bull charged.

The line went taut.

The plug wedged tightly in between the slats and the noose at the end of it pulled tight around the bull's neck—tight enough to stop the beast who was surprised by the weight of the table.

Mace ran out of harm's way.

The crowd started clapping wildly.

Mace looked around. He'd forgotten anyone else was there.

Suddenly Zoe was at his side. She slugged him

in the arm. "That was a stupid thing to do, Mace Mason."

"Hey, what did you do that for?" He rubbed the spot she'd hit.

"You scared about a decade of life out of me. What were you thinking, chasing after that bull?"

"I thought it was Jed," he muttered, suddenly feeling foolish. He'd wanted to impress Zoe, like some schoolboy doing wheelies on his bike to impress the girls on the playground.

"It wasn't Jed," she assured him.

"I realized that when the beast decided it would be fun to gore me to death."

"If it was Jed, don't you think someone from Hiho would have grabbed it? And didn't you notice that while Jed is a warm cinnamon color, this beast is quite black?"

"No. I just saw a bull heading toward Bessie and thought, *Jed,*" he muttered, feeling even more foolish.

"You didn't think and that's why I slugged you. I'm so mad I could slug you again." She raised her hand, looking as if she indeed might slug his shoulder again, but instead she reached out and simply laid it on his arm. "You could have been killed."

"Would you have cared?" he asked softly.

"Of course I'd have cared. If the bull had gored you I would…it would have ruined the festival."

Mace thought maybe, just maybe she'd been about to say she'd be upset.

She turned away from him and hollered, "Come on, everyone. Let's get back to the parade so we can get this festival started."

She motioned to a group of men and said, "Fellas, take care of that beast, okay?"

There was a chorus of "sure things" and "you bets" from the group.

"And what about me?" Mace asked.

"You…you just stay out of harm's way and finish your story."

"Can I see you tonight?" Before she could protest that she'd be too busy, he added, "After the festival?"

"It's a free country. You can see whoever you want."

"The only one I want to see is you. Please, Zoe, let me explain things."

She sighed. Not a happy girly, *I'm going to see the man I care about* sort of sigh, but a put-upon, *why me?* sort of one.

Mace didn't care what kind of sigh it was as long as she said yes she'd see him and let him explain.

"Zoe?" he prompted.

"Fine. Ten o'clock. I'll meet you at the fairground's entrance."

"I'll be there."

"TOM WALTERS, you put those teeth in."

Zoe had a headache that industrial-strength aspirin couldn't begin to touch. Runaway bulls, vendors who didn't show up and finally a pie-judging, toothless man....

And Mace, a quiet thought whispered.

No matter how many other annoying problems dropped in her lap, Mace Mason was the spike pounding in the center of her brain.

"But Zoe, I hate those teeth. They hurt. And I don't need no teeth to taste. I taste just fine without them."

"Zoe," Cora MacIntosh said. No, *said* was a generous description. Whined was closer to the truth. "Zoe, you said you'd take care of this. You know he's going to be biased to the cream pies if he's gumming his pie. Gumming nuts doesn't work."

"Speaking of nuts," Tom grumbled.

Zoe was at her wits' end. "Tom, either put them in, or I'll have to find another judge."

"Then find yourself another judge," he said as he walked away.

"Great, just great," Zoe mumbled, looking over her shoulder as she watched her pie judge walk away.

She spied Mace, a couple tents away, camera raised. He was shooting the crowd. He turned, the camera lens was focused directly on her.

Zoe snapped her head back around so all he could see was her back. She resisted the urge to make a universally known gesture, not because she worried about offending Mace, but because she knew he was perverse enough to leave it in his piece.

"Zoe, now what? The pie judging was supposed to begin at two. Where are you going to find another unbiased, well-toothed man?" Ida asked.

Cora nodded. "Someone who can handle nuts."

Nuts.

That's how Zoe felt.

"What seems to be the problem?" Mace said from behind her.

Slowly, Zoe turned around and came face-to-face with the spike in her brain.

"Nothing you need worry about," she said.

"But maybe I can help."

"Sure you can, by leaving. Don't you have a story to research?"

"I'm researching even as we speak."

"Good for you." Oh, what a horribly lame retort. Mace Mason had reduced her to the level of a five-year-old. "Now, if you'll excuse us, we have things to see to."

"What sort of things?" Mace asked, obviously not taking her not-so-subtle hints and leaving.

"Well, that Tom—"

"The one with the false teeth?" Mace asked.

"Yes," Cora said. "The false teeth he refuses to wear for the pie-judging contest."

Ida nodded. "Zoe told him to wear them or don't judge."

"And he's not judging?" Mace asked.

Zoe nodded and regretted the movement as it aggravated her headache. She must have winced because Mace looked all concerned and asked, "Are you okay?"

"Just a bit of a tension headache," she admitted. "Just the stress of the festival. I took some aspirin and I'm sure it won't last long."

"Would it help your tension level if I volunteered to judge the pie contest."

"You'd do that?" she asked, feeling surprised that he'd pitch in and help.

"Sure. It'll be a piece of…pie."

"I believe the phrase is piece of cake…." Ida stopped short and laughed. "Oh. You were being funny."

"Not very funny," Zoe muttered, though the two older ladies weren't minding her grumbling. They were practically fawning over Mace.

What was it with this man and women? First Clover, now the MacIntosh sisters. Pretty soon he'd have the entire town's female population bowing at his feet.

The entire town…except her.

Oh, she might have been slightly infatuated with

him, before she found out he was a ratfink, but now that she knew the truth, she didn't feel the least bit of anything for him.

Nothing.

She watched him work his way through the pies. And finally pronounce Ida and Cora's pie the winner.

Zoe might have suspected a bias on his part toward the two if she hadn't had their pie before…it deserved to win.

When the crowd in the tent thinned out, Zoe saw Mace was talking to Clover.

Probably setting up a date with her.

The two walked toward her.

"Thank you for the help, Mace," Zoe said, wishing she didn't sound so stiff, that she could sound as unaffected as she wished she was.

"No problem," he said with that killer grin of his.

A grin that made her forget where she was momentarily, despite all her good intentions.

"Well, you two go have a good time. I've got to get to the bandstand and make sure that it's all set up for the Larry Morris Trio."

"How's your headache?" Mace asked.

She stopped, surprised that he remembered. "Fine."

"Are you sure?"

"Sure I'm sure. Don't worry about it. It's not your problem."

He sighed a put-upon, this-woman-is-driving-me-crazy sort of sigh.

Zoe was glad she was driving him insane, because turnabout was fair play.

He gave a curt nod and started for the door.

"Zoe, if you're not feeling well, maybe I could help," Clover offered.

"No, really. I'm fine." She smiled at Clover, not wanting her friend to think Zoe minded that she'd been talking to Mace, probably planning another date.

"If you're sure," Clover said.

"Positive."

With obvious reluctance, Clover followed Mace toward the tent flap.

Mace stopped. "Hey, Zoe, don't forget, ten o'clock."

She'd hoped he would forget, but obviously he hadn't. "Fine," she said.

She breathed a sigh of relief as he left with Clover.

How rude, setting a date with one woman when he was out with another.

Men were pigs.

Zoe was glad she had a few peaceful Mace-free hours before she had to meet him.

It was a meeting she wasn't looking forward to. Not at all.

MACE LEFT the festival around dinnertime. He let himself into the *Herald*'s office and finally had a chance to study everything he'd accumulated about Hiho's Centennial problems.

He started with the journals Clover had lent him, copying the pertinent sections.

Then he pulled out the copies of the endowment Rob Pawley had given him earlier.

He read through the old document, which was actually short and to the point. The endowment instructions were in a codicil to Pawley's will, instructing that money be set aside and should be awarded to the college and the library upon the town's centennial.

Mace read the document over a number of times, rubbing his temple, wondering if headaches were contagious, because if they were, Zoe had infected him with hers.

He set the paper down and leaned back on the couch, closing his eyes, hoping if he rested them a few minutes, he could will the headache away.

He must have dozed, because he awoke with a start and an idea. A great idea. A brilliant idea.

He reread the codicil.

He had it!

He knew how to fix the centennial thing.

At least he thought he did. He'd have to make some calls and double check his facts, but he was pretty sure he had a way out.

He glanced at his watch.

It was ten-thirty.

Darn.

He was late. Zoe was already upset with him and he didn't think standing her up was going to improve her mood.

He bet she wasn't waiting for him—Zoe wasn't a wait-around kind of gal—but just in case, he'd drive by the fairgrounds before heading to her house.

Once he got to her house…well, he was pretty sure how to fix the centennial mess, but he'd have to wait and see if he could figure out just what to do with Zoe Wallace.

9

ZOE WASN'T WAITING for him at the fairgrounds.

Mace really hadn't expected she would be there.

So he turned around and headed the few blocks to her house. He was nervous. Acid-eating-away-at-the-lining-of-his-stomach kind of nervous.

He arrived and knocked at her door.

No answer.

She was going to be difficult.

He smiled at the thought. He liked that Zoe could be difficult, that she kept him on his toes, challenging him at every turn.

He liked the way she laughed.

The way she smiled.

The way she made love to him.

Thinking of making love to Zoe left him wanting to get into her house.

He thumped loudly on the door.

"Zoe, I know you're in there. If you don't open the door I'm going to start to sing. Yes, I'll serenade you, right out here on your porch. Can you imagine the rumors that Loni lady will spread then?"

Still no answer.

He cleared his throat and started, *"Zoe, my lo...ove..."*

The door flew open. "Shh," Zoe told him.

"Are you going to let me in?" he asked with a grin he hoped was endearing.

But Zoe wasn't so easily won over. She glared at him. "No."

He cleared his voice again. *"Zoe, my lo...ove..."*

She grabbed his arm and pulled him into the house, slamming the door behind him.

Mace grinned. "See, I knew you couldn't keep your hands off me."

"What do you want, Mace?"

"I'm sorry I was late," he said, taking a step toward her.

She backed away. "It doesn't matter."

"Yes it does." He took another small step. "I stood you up and I'm sorry. I was working and then fell asleep. You see, I didn't get much sleep last night and was tired."

She blushed. "Well, then you better head to Aunt Aggie's and get some sleep tonight."

She hadn't countered his step with one of her own and Mace felt heartened at the small point. Right now, he'd take whatever he could get.

"I should head to Aunt Aggie's, but I'm not. We've got an awful lot to talk about."

"We don't have anything to talk about." She

seemed to notice he was closer because she took that step keeping distance between them.

"I'm relieved you think we haven't anything we need to talk about, because I don't want to talk right now."

"You don't?" She took a step backward making the distance between them even wider.

"No." Not willing to have anything separating him from Zoe, he closed the gap.

"If you don't want to talk, why are you here?"

"Because I've been dreaming of doing this all day...." He pulled her into his arms, amazed at how right she felt there. She was a perfect fit.

"Do you know how rare this is?" he murmured as he brushed his lips against her neck.

Zoe stood stiff, not fighting, not pulling away, but not exactly melting into his embrace either.

"Rare? You mean that reporters come to town and accost women?"

"No, this...this thing we have between us. I've dated a lot of women before and I've never felt anything nearly this powerful. It's more than a connection, more than the fact we're both reporters. It's something deeper."

Mace suspected he knew just what it was, but from the look on Zoe's face, she wasn't ready to hear it.

"I want us to be together tonight," he simply said.

"Mace, this can't work. I don't know if I can trust you. You held out information on me."

"Not intentionally. I have so much to tell you, and I'm willing to tell you everything you want to know, but I'd like to wait long enough for me to do this...."

No longer willing to wait, he kissed her. For a moment, he thought he'd blown it, but the moment passed and Zoe joined in the kiss, an equal partner.

Finally, she pulled away and said, "I do want those answers, and I'm willing to wait a while longer for them. But I'm not willing to wait for other things."

"Like what?" he asked.

"Something bigger and better comes to mind." She shot him a smile, letting him know that she forgave him, that she knew he wasn't holding out on her.

She believed him.

He gently touched her cheek, awash with something more than desire.

Whether she admitted it or not, they did have something between them, something big, something better than anything he'd ever experienced.

Something that made him very, very happy.

Zoe looked at the man sleeping by her side.

She hadn't got those answers, but it really didn't matter. She trusted Mace.

It was absurd.

She'd been in a big city long enough to know that trusting another reporter was career suicide, but it wasn't Mace the reporter she trusted.

It was Mace the man.

This man she trusted.

A dark strand of hair tumbled down on his forehead and Zoe gently brushed it back. She wondered how someone she'd known for such a short time could have come to mean so much to her.

How much did he mean?

She knew the answer and was afraid that knowing it was going to make her hurt even more when he left.

Even more was the operative phrase, because she knew she'd miss him as soon as he'd gone.

It was Sunday. Their last day together.

Oh, maybe he'd call a few times. Maybe even make the trip down to Hiho from Erie, or whatever bigger and better place he ended up in.

But it wouldn't last.

Long-distance relationships never did.

And he hadn't even said he wanted a relationship.

She sighed. She just couldn't unravel the knot she'd gotten herself in.

"What was that sigh for?" Mace asked, his voice husky with sleep.

"Nothing," she said, not willing to voice her concerns and doubts. "Just the sigh of a well-pleasured lady."

"Well-pleasured?" he asked, grinning.

"Don't get too conceited there, Mace. For I believe you were a well-pleasured man and you haven't had the good graces to sigh even once this morning."

"If my lady wants a sigh, she'll have one." He drew in a long, exaggerated breath and let it out with excruciating slowness. "There. And I must tell you, that the sigh was only the slightest indication of how truly well-pleasured I was."

He reached over and gently touched her hair. That small gesture was enough to make Zoe want to purr her contentment.

"And though I'd like to see if we could be that well-pleasured again this morning, I'm afraid we don't have time. I'm waiting for a call and have a few things to take care of before this evening's closing ceremonies."

"And we still have to talk," she said.

"Yes, we do."

"Maybe, after the talking and the busy work we have in front of us today we could have one more night before you go?" She worked at keeping her pain at the thought of his leaving out of her voice. She even managed to force a smile.

Mace gave her an odd look that Zoe couldn't even begin to interpret. "After the fireworks tonight, you've got a date."

She let out her breath. She hadn't realized she'd been holding it while she waited for his response. "Good."

"I should probably head over to the bed and breakfast for a quick shower and a change of clothes."

Zoe realized how deeply she didn't want him to leave, which made her force an even bigger smile than she'd intended. "That's good."

"I'll meet you back here and bring some of Aunt Aggie's muffins. We can grab a bite while I catch you up on all I've discovered."

She nodded but Mace didn't see her. He was already pulling on his clothes.

He was in an awful hurry to leave.

She had to play it cool, had to convince him that she was okay with him leaving now, and leaving permanently tomorrow morning. That she wasn't emotionally involved in their relationship.

Which meant, she had to do the best acting she'd ever done, because truth be told, she was more than a little emotionally involved with Mace.

She'd quite gone and lost her heart to him.

She must have been in the shower when the phone rang because the answering machine light was blinking when she got out.

She pushed the message button.

"Zoe, I'm sorry to stand you up again," Mace's voice said over the machine. "I promise to explain everything to you later and you'll know why I couldn't come back this morning. Trust me, okay? I know we haven't known each other long, in terms of days, but Zoe, I feel like I've known you forever. Please, just trust me. I'm trying to see that everything works all right for both of us."

Trust him?

Could she afford to?

He was leaving tomorrow and taking her heart with him. It didn't make any sense, but there you go...love never made sense. Look at Bessie and Jed.

As much as she wanted to see Mace, to know what was going on, she decided to do as he asked and simply trust him.

SOMEHOW Zoe made it through the longest day of her life. The festival had a few glitches that kept her running, but on the whole, things went smoothly enough, she thought with a satisfied feeling settling over her. She stood on the grandstand, looking at the people milling all over the fairground.

"*Psst.*"

Bertram.

Just what she didn't need.

"*Psst,* Zoe."

She turned and found him hiding in the shadowed area at the side of the stand.

Feeling like a woman on her way to her executioner, Zoe walked over to him.

"Yes?"

"What did you find?"

"Mace found something. He was going to tell me, but got called away on business."

"You mean, you two had the entire night together and he couldn't find time to share his discovery with you?"

Zoe knew she was blushing as she thought about all they did manage to share last night. "Bertram, that's really none of your business."

"Well, if you feel that way, I'm betting you think it's not anyone in town's business, which is a shame because this town tends to make everyone's business their business. They're all buzzin' about you and your new beau."

"He's not my beau," she said.

She couldn't let the town know how much it was going to hurt her when Mace left. If they were sympathetic, she'd simply drown.

"He's not your beau?" Mace said.

She turned and resisted—barely resisted—flinging herself into his arms. Instead, she smiled and hoped he could see how glad she was to see him. "Hey, you're back."

"Sorry to stand you up again."

"So what did you find, boy?" Bertram asked.

"I'll tell you all everything later. Right now, I want to talk to Zoe."

"Zoe, Zoe," Pete cried, then he spotted his uncle. "Uncle Bertram, what are you up to?"

"It's okay, boy," Bertram said with a smug look on his face. "They know."

"They know what?" Pete asked slowly.

"They know that Hiho isn't a hundred until next year. Mace here has proof."

Pete sighed. "And I suppose it's too much to hope that you're not going to run with the story."

Mace looked as if he was going to say something but Zoe jumped in first. "Pete, this isn't the type of thing we can keep quiet. The council tried when they took Bertram's proof. But Mace has found more. It's likely that, given enough time and searching, even more evidence will surface. We've got to come clean."

"What about the college?" Pete asked. "Cloverleaf has already borrowed against that money."

"I know and..." Zoe turned to Mace.

"Do you trust me?" he asked her, watching her with a strange intensity.

"Yes."

If she could fall in love with a man in a week, she certainly knew him well enough to trust him.

Mace turned to Pete and Bertram. "It will all turn out right. It's almost time for the closing ceremonies. Rob Pawley is supposed to present the checks then and you'll see, it will be fine."

"But, but," Pete sputtered.

"What are you up to, boy?" Bertram asked.

Mace grinned his self-assured little grin that set Zoe's heart beating proudly.

"It's good, if I do say so myself," he said.

"But—"

"If you'll excuse me, I have to talk to Zoe." He led her away, behind the grandstand.

"Before I say anything, I have to do this...." He kissed her hard and long, as if they'd been away from each other for months, rather than just most of a day.

"Wow," Zoe murmured. "I missed you, too."

"Did you?" he asked, that weird intensity there in his gaze again.

"Yes."

"Zoe, do you believe in fate?"

She shook her head. "No. I've always thought fate was an excuse, something to blame when things didn't work out the way you plan."

"Then how about love at first sight? Do you believe it can happen? You said lust at first sight, but do you believe there can be more than that?"

"I never did before," she answered slowly.

"Before?" he repeated.

"Mace, this last week has taught me about one thing I believe in absolutely...something I never knew existed before this week."

"What's that?" he asked.

"You." She reached out and traced her forefinger down his jawline, marveling at how beautiful he was. "I believe in you, Mace."

"Zoe." His voice was a hoarse whisper.

"It's okay," she said. "You don't have to tell me what you found, or what you've got planned. As a reporter I should demand to know, I should be chomping at the bit. But Mace, I believe in you like no one I've ever met before. I trust you."

"But I want to tell you—"

"Zoe," Vicky, the town's mayor, called. "It's time."

"Listen, Mace, I trust that whatever you do is what you feel you have to do."

"Before you go," he said. "I have one thing that can't wait."

"What?"

"I love you."

10

"WH-WH-WHAT?" Zoe sputtered.

Mace grinned. It wasn't quite the reaction he'd expected, but then, when had Zoe ever done what he expected?

"I asked about love at first sight and fate because I think that's what this assignment was… fate. And that first time I saw you with that horrendous makeover and that little dangling eyelash, I think I fell in love with you."

"But, it's been less than a week. That doesn't make sense."

"I don't think time really matters when it comes to the heart. A very wise woman once told me that love's like that, that sometimes there's just nothing you can do to stop it. It will break through any obstacle…even time itself."

He saw that she recognized her own words, the ones she'd used right after she'd lassoed Jed.

He reached out and caressed her cheek. "I've dated plenty of women before, a few a lot longer than a week, and not one has ever made me feel like you do."

"But—"

"I'm not asking you to say the words back, I'm just asking for a chance, for time to make you see that you love me, too."

"How much time will you give me?" she asked.

"As much as you need." Although Mace knew each minute of not knowing would kill him.

"Well, now, it could take a bit of time." Zoe glanced at her watch.

"Like I said—"

"Zoe," Vicky yelled.

"Mace, I've got to go. The closing ceremony is about to start and I have to be there."

"Go. We'll talk after."

She started running toward the grandstand, then stopped and turned around. "About how much time I need. I had enough before you finished speaking. I love you, too." She turned around and fled.

Mace watched the woman he loved head onto the stage, surprised to hear those sweet words so soon. He figured it would take a lot longer...at least until after the festival.

But that was Zoe, always surprising him.

He smiled. Well, she had a few surprises of her own ahead of her.

"...AND NOW, I'd like to introduce—not that he needs an introduction—Rob Pawley."

Rob came out on stage carrying two huge checks. He walked up to the microphone and said, "Citizens of Hiho. It's come to my attention that we have a slight problem. You see, although we've always been told that the town was founded in May of 1903, it has been discovered that due to a clerical error, the town wasn't actually officially a town until February 1904."

A murmur ruffled through the crowd.

Zoe saw Cloverleaf's President Stanley and Katy Sloane both wince and she felt horrible for them. The library could probably limp by another year, but the college was counting on that money, having already borrowed against it.

Rob held up his hand. "Let me read to you the actual wording of the endowment. '…the endowments to be presented to the Hiho Public Library and Cloverleaf College when the community celebrates its centennial.' As I said, there is now proof that this year is not our centennial."

The crowd was muttering now. Loudly.

People were obviously upset.

Zoe sympathized. She was upset as well, but she didn't blame Mace. He'd done what he needed to do, what any good journalist would do—he'd told the story.

"But," Rob was saying, "Hiho's newest resident, Mace Mason, a documentary filmmaker for the History Channel, pointed out that the Pawley endowment was to be awarded when the town *cel-*

ebrated its centennial. And thanks to our own Zoe Wallace, I think this festival counts as one of the best celebrations I've ever seen. What do you think?''

The crowd roared its approval.

Zoe registered the fact that the endowments were saved, but she was more focused on what else Rob had said. *Newest resident? History Channel?*

Zoe scanned the crowd, searching for Mace as Rob presented the endowment checks to Katy Sloane from the library and Cloverleaf's president, Leonard J. Stanley.

Where was he?

''*Psst,* Zoe,'' Bertram said, from offstage.

''You heard?'' she said, still looking for Mace.

''Yeah. He's a smart one, that boy is. But it's not about that. There are a few of the college students over behind the stables and it looks like they're up to something. I've been a reporter too many years not to know when something's up and something's definitely up with those boys. They're—''

''Zoe, will you come here, please?'' Rob asked, beckoning her to the microphone.

''I'll check it out as soon as I'm done here,'' she stage-whispered as she rose and walked to the microphone.

Vicky was back at the microphone. ''Zoe, on behalf of the entire community, I want to thank you for the wonderful job you did coordinating this festival.''

''Thank you, Mayor Robertson. It was my pleasure.''

She turned to go back to her seat, but Vicky said, ''Before you go, there's one more thing....''

Zoe turned back and walked to the mike. Mace came out of the far wing and walked up to the microphone.

''I just want to thank everyone for all their help this week as I worked on my piece about Hiho for WMAC news in Erie. I'm sorry to report it's the last piece I'll be doing for WMAC because I've turned in my resignation.''

''Mace?'' Zoe whispered.

Rob's comment about Mace being Hiho's newest citizen sank in. Her heart felt as if it were going to beat out of her chest.

''You see, someone I care about told me that I'd been chasing a fool's dream. I thought that I wanted bigger and better things in my career, but I've found this person was right...happy is what matters the most. So, I've taken a position doing a documentary series on obscure figures in history for the History Channel. The new position allows me a great deal of freedom in choosing where I live, and I choose...''

He paused and smiled at Zoe.

''I choose Hiho, Ohio. At least I do if Zoe will agree to consider marrying me.''

The crowd screamed so loudly that Zoe wasn't sure Mace could even hear her as she flung herself into his arms and whispered, "Yes."

But his whoop of happiness told her he had.

They left the microphone and Vicky stepped back up. "And now, to close out this Centennial-that-wasn't Celebration, let me present the Cloverleaf marching band and our fireworks."

Explosions of light lit the sky, as the band played Hiho's town song. In the back of her mind, Zoe realized that it sounded much better without the words.

But that was way in the back of her mind.

In the forefront was a sense of wonder and awe that she was being held by the man she loved…a man who loved her back.

A man who'd learned that happiness mattered.

"Zoe," Bertram hollered, no *psst* at all this time, just a horrendous sense of urgency. "Those boys—"

Suddenly there was a huge bang overhead from a much closer distance than the fireworks.

Much, much closer.

A fine dust sprinkled down on the crowd and suddenly…

Zoe itched everywhere she had bare skin. She wasn't the only one. Everyone in her vicinity was scratching.

The firework display continued, but the band had stopped and was scratching as well.

"—those boys shot off itching powder in some homemade rockets," Bertram finished. "I got Sheriff Smith, but it was too late."

Zoe groaned as she scratched.

Mace laughed.

"You know, I thought a small town would be boring, but with mysterious centennials-that-aren't, runaway bulls and itching powder...well, let's just say it's a bit more exciting than I anticipated." He grabbed her and pulled her into his arms. "And with the woman I love in it, it's the most exciting place on earth."

"I love you, too," Zoe said, mid-scratch. "But I think we better get home and shower this stuff off."

"And then?"

"And then we'll talk about fate, about love at first sight...about us."

"Sounds just about right to me," Mace said.

The following week's Hiho Herald's *front-page headline read,* THE CENTENNIAL THAT WASN'T. *The two other headlines proclaimed,* FORMER ERIE REPORTER FINDS A SOLUTION *and, finally,* LOCAL PAPER OWNER, ZOE WALLACE, IS ITCHING TO TIE THE KNOT WITH HISTORY CHANNEL'S NEWEST DOCUMENTARY PRODUCER, MACE MASON.

Epilogue

"*HIHO, OHIO, a quiet, lovely town. Hiho, Ohio, where no one wears a frown…*" the chorus sang. Thankfully the crowd's applause drowned out the last few bars of the song, saving Zoe's ears.

She stepped forward on the stage of the college's new theater and stared out at the audience and smiled.

"Welcome to Hiho, Ohio's *Second Annual* Centennial Celebration," she said into the microphone. The crowd once again applauded wildly.

It was bigger than last year's crowd. The whole centennial-that-wasn't story that Mace put together for WMAC had been picked up on a national level.

Six months later, his documentary on Hiram Hump had aired on the History Channel. His documentary series, *Hazy History,* was doing well. He'd leave town for a week or two at a time, but he always came back home.

Home to Hiho.

Home to Zoe.

"And now, let me introduce our mayor."

Zoe stepped back as Vicky took center stage and started speaking.

Two arms wrapped around her and Zoe leaned into her husband's chest, his hands resting on her slightly rounded stomach.

"How are you feeling?" he whispered in her ear, his breath tickling against her neck.

She turned and smiled at Mace, "Fine. We're both fine. You don't have to worry."

"Ah, but worry is what we husbands do best."

"Mace, do you remember what you asked me here last year?"

"What?"

"You asked if I believed in fate and in love at first sight."

Those words were etched in her mind as some of the sweetest she'd ever heard. How on earth had she got so lucky?

She thought she was happy when she left New York and settled in Hiho, but how she felt then couldn't even begin to compare to the amount of happiness she felt now. It was bone-deep and so strong it occasionally took her breath away with its intensity.

"When I asked you, you said no you didn't believe in love at first sight or in fate."

"I said no I didn't believe in them...but I believed in you. I still do. So go knock them dead." She kissed his cheek even as Vicky said, "And now, I'd like to introduce Hiho's resident historian, Mace Mason."

He stepped up to the microphone. "A year ago, I came to Hiho to do a small piece on its centennial and a short documentary on Hiram Hump for my station, WMAC. And here I am, a year later, a resident of Hiho and about to unveil my newest installment for *Hazy History* called, 'Hiho, Ohio, and the Centennial-That-Wasn't.'"

He stepped back and the theater darkened as the screen lit up and Mace's voice narrated, "Someone once told me that bigger wasn't necessarily better, that happy was. Here in a lazy little town in central Ohio, happy seems to be the name of the game...."

Mace came back to Zoe and sat next to her.

And at that moment, during Hiho, Ohio's Second Annual Centennial Celebration, Zoe Wallace Mason sat next to her husband, her hand resting on her unborn child and knew that happy didn't even begin to describe her life.

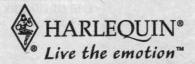